Dancing to Memories

Joanne Brand

First Edition 2015
Copyright © 2015 Joanne Brand

All right reserved
ISBN: 13-978-1511691536
ISBN: 10-1511691530

ACKNOWLEDGEMENTS

I give a special thanks to my soft editing friends Cathy Tomczak, Mary Jo Duckworth and Pat Quinlan. I so appreciate their help with suggestions and corrections in working through my manuscript page by page. My brother, Jim Morris, and my nephew, Kevin Morris, gave some suggestions and information. I thank my niece, Geralyn Lockstein, for her information on the Lee/Morris family history.

Deep appreciation must be given to my Heather Gardens Writers Club friends for helping me in the long process of critiquing and for their suggestions.

Thanks to my children, Tina, Greg and Susan for giving me encouragement. A special thanks to Tina for designing my cover, to Greg for his help with the photographs and to Susan's constant support.

I attribute some of my research to *History of South Dakota Fourth Edition, Revised* by Herbert S. Schell and South Dakota State Historical Society Press, Pierre. I gained knowledge from the novel *The Bones of Plenty*, by Lois Phillips Hudson, about North Dakota in the Great Depression, and the book, *Land Circle, Writings collected from the Land*, by Linda Hasselstrom, a woman rancher in South Dakota. I highly recommend both books. These, and other books, helped me with history, the people of the land, ranching and farming. Of course, I am so grateful for the Internet's vast resources on history, especially the Great Depression era, the economy, the government and South Dakota history.

I am also very grateful to my God for giving me the inspiration to write this story!

INTRODUCTION

Grace, a young teacher, had many a beau, yet preferred the one that owned a new 1925 automobile. Suddenly her life was threatened. She ended up in the Black Hills of South Dakota fighting for her life, lost and lonely.

Jack 's childhood ended when he became an orphan and his life changed for the worse. Later he became a wandering cowboy searching for peace. By the 1930's he landed in the Black Hills of South Dakota.

Grace's faith, Jack's searching and the Great Depression did not prepare them for what was to come. Their love was all they had to carry them through this life.

Joanne Brand wrote this as a possible concept of her parents' lives. She researched history for validity of her characterizations and the timeframe. She had very little information about her father since her mother did not talk about him or display any of his meager possessions or pictures. Nor did her mother talk about their life's trials. However, she did write a brief description of her family's ancestry. She only gave a fragment of information about herself and her husband.

A few years ago, the author received some items of her father's that her mother had hidden away. Brand started to piece a fraction of his life together as well as what may have been her mother's life. The rest was up to her imagination of how her parents' personalities, emotions and lives might have been.

Brand decided to write what may have been a resemblance of their lives. Family lore helped in portraying characters in this story. Their deep love is real, yet imagined.

The author's other books may be seen on her website or with Amazon.com.

View the Brand's website: **joannebrand-author.com**

Dance as if no one's watching,
sing as if no one's listening,
and live everyday as if it were your last.

An Irish saying

CHAPTER 1

1925 - NEVER TO RETURN

Whispering, Grace Lee asked, "Will I ever see you again, Mama and Papa, or is this my death sentence?"

She waved goodbye to her parents standing on the platform as the train signaled it ready to depart Yankton, South Dakota depot. Trying to smile and hold back tears, she waved goodbye.

On the edge of her seat with her face turned to the window, she saw her mother standing straight, more rigid and thinner than usual with lips pursed tight showing deeper worry lines. Grace looked to her father in his pinstriped overalls covering his expanding middle. He kept one arm tight around Mama, the other hand sat under his bib while he pursed his mouth as the train began to pull away.

Grace covered her mouth with a handkerchief. She and three others like her sat separated from other passengers and looked down at the floorboards as passengers walked by. Travelers had various reactions when they saw the four companions. Some looked at them with curiosity or sadness while others gave a "humph" and quickly put their handkerchiefs to their faces in an effort to avoid breathing the same air.

Faith was all Grace had to hang onto. Her shackles, though not of iron, felt like a life sentence. Taking a second look when the whistle shrieked signaling departure, she hoped to see her beau standing on the side and waving goodbye. Her searching eyes did not find his tall lean form with a shock of dark wavy hair parted in the middle. She slumped. Why didn't he come and at least wave or write a note telling her he'd be there when she returned—if she returned?

She and Hobart had been courting for almost six months and had good times with their friends at dances, picnics or parties. She knew she had strong feelings inside telling her it might be love and she knew he did too. He told her he wanted to be financially sound before making a commitment. She liked that, only why wasn't Hobart at the depot?

When the train pulled out of the station, Grace gave her parents a final wave, not holding back her emotions any longer. Settled back in her seat, wiping tears away, she wanted to know why this had to happen. She had just begun her second year of teaching elementary students at Kimball, not far from her family home. Then she acquired a fever and exhaustion persisted along with a hardy and steady cough. "Just a lingering cold," she told herself. Finally, a week after school began, exhaustion reigned and her cough grew too severe. She made an appointment with the town doctor. "I think I have tuberculosis," she told him certain of his diagnosis.

After a thorough checkup the doctor told her, "You're right, Miss Lee. You have tuberculosis. You must be admitted to the hospital immediately." Within hours, 25 year-old Grace lay in a hospital bed—quarantined. The prognosis for TB was dismal; only the strong might conquer that dreaded bacteria since there was no medicine to fight it.

A nurse in her white gown and starched cap attended Grace in the hospital. Shortly after she arrived, the nurse told her, "You know, Miss Lee, people do survive. I think you are one of them." Her smile couldn't be seen behind the mask covering her mouth and nose, but her eyes showed care. That reinforced Grace's determination to fight. She had to believe in herself.

In a few days, the hospital scheduled a transfer to a tuberculosis sanitarium at Sanator, near Custer, South Dakota in the Black Hills. Sanator was not a regular town, just buildings to treat tuberculosis patients. Grace learned that it was approximately 400 miles from her home and family.

She told another patient, "My parents don't have money to go back and forth on a train. Besides, they have the rest of the family to care for and my father's sawmill to run. Now he also has my sanitarium bills to pay. How am I ever going to pay him back?"

Six of her eight siblings still lived at home, plus two of her grandparents and a dear uncle. Her brother, Charlie, was only five years old and Grace would dearly miss watching her baby brother grow physically and intellectually.

There didn't seem to be a choice except for her father to pay her medical bills. Sanitariums were expensive, anywhere from $5.00 to $10.00 per week in the Midwest. That huge cost would be a burden to Grace's family even if the state paid part, yet she knew they would not abandon her. Tuberculosis facilities were not plentiful and usually no more than one in a wide area, which often covered more than one state. At least she would still be in South Dakota. Some other states charged even higher rates.

Grace thought back to 1918 when she came down with the Spanish flu, a world pandemic that killed an estimated fifty million souls worldwide. Her mother and Uncle Steve never contracted the flu, but felt overwhelmed in tending to the suffering family 24 hours a day. Recovery was slow and all survived. Now family and friends needed to pray once again for her recovery from TB even though many were afraid a funeral might be imminent. This dreaded disease brought death to many too often.

Sanator sat at a high altitude in the Black Hills. The air was less humid than along the Missouri River in the lower southeastern part of the state where she had lived all her life.

It didn't take long to learn that patients at the sanitarium lay in beds separated according to a class designation. The patients not expected to live were in one class, separated from the others and monitored hourly. The ones who possibly could survive were in another class. Those who seemed to be on the recovery end sat separated as well and had moderate exercise. All had healthy food and the diets included a reduced animal protein regimen because animal meat seemed to be suspect for curtailing recovery, according to the latest studies.

Patient beds sat out on the large white painted wood verandas year round, so patients could breathe continual fresh dry air. Activity was minimal. The night air filled with muffled coughs as patients tried not to disturb others, or some became loud bursts gasping for air and wheezing. Each tried to ignore others as they struggled to sleep in between their own coughing.

At the time of Grace's diagnosis of tuberculosis, she heard about possible cures. Some doctors practiced the method of collapsing the lung. She asked a nurse about this.

"They thought maybe by allowing the lung to collapse, rest and then inflate again, TB could possibly be cured. It didn't seem to have much success." The nurse shrugged her shoulders. "We don't do that here.

Grace was glad of that. The pain of a collapsed lung would be unbearable. The best care seemed to be clean, dry air, rest and good nourishment—if there was a cure. Whenever she spoke, the coughing seemed to interrupt each sentence. Reading tired her and sleeping seemed to fill a large portion of each day. She was exhausted. When awake, she began to enjoy the view of the Black Hills from her bed, breathing the fresh air. Wild animals scurried around and deer busied themselves searching for food.

On warm sunny days, Grace sat up in her bed on the porch enjoying the warmth while watching birds flit back and forth singing staccato songs competing with her coughs. As she struggled to breathe, she thought that it was probably what miners endured after inhaling the black dust from the mines. The Homestake Gold Mine in Lead, or coalmines swallowed up many men, eventually ruining their lungs. Many of the men working underground looked as if they could never erase the black soot under their fingernails. A picture of a miner surfaced and she knew she could never marry one. He'd die too soon.

Her mind shifted to ranching and farms whenever she saw a tractor plowing a field far off in the distance. She wondered if cowboys ever had trouble breathing after inhaling the pollen or dust swirling behind a cattle drive. At least they were out on the range often breathing the fresh air. They would come home sweaty and dirty smelling like an animal or worse. Maybe that would be tolerable if the cowboy washed up good.

She had seen some handsome cowboys that could sweep a girl off her feet. Even she flirted with one back in Springfield. He was so attractive and his dancing was like walking on air with his arms around her. Could she ever marry a cowboy? She didn't think so.

Next, her mind retreated to Hobart again. Now he was more like it—a business man with a good future and he wouldn't bring home mine dust, dirt or barnyard smells. With a husband like that, she would have a nice home and she'd be a good wife and mother. Oh, she so wanted to have a family.

Grace wrote to her beau often and told him about similar things she told her family, only in his letters, she added details about the depressing sanitarium life. Too often, someone in a nearby bed breathed their last and nurses quickly moved the deceased out of view. It was deeply depressing. She hoped she hadn't upset Hobart with her descriptions, yet needed to tell how she was affected by the dismal atmosphere. She had to tell someone and tell about her fears, but she couldn't tell her family. She didn't know if she would survive TB or be carried out to the morgue someday.

Letters from Hobart were short and didn't comment on her fears. He didn't tell much of what he and their friends were doing. Did he go on picnics with them? Did they go to the dances at the park pavilion? Who did he dance with? Hobart seemed to make the letters too generic, yet always signed them, *Yours, Hobart*. Why didn't he tell her more of what he was doing? Maybe, like her brothers, he just wasn't much of a correspondent.

Winter arrived before all the gold and burnt orange leaves had fallen. The cold and straw-colored landscape provided a drab picture for the patients. Homemade quilts with squares of many colors, or plain wool blankets kept the patients from freezing. Patterns of reds, blues, yellows or grey piled high on top of each bed. All that peeked out from the mound was the nose of each patient. The winter passed so slowly and many grumbled or moaned, wanting sun and hot days again.

Letter writing was hard when Grace viewed the dreary days and she felt so worn out with coughing. Loneliness and despair creeped into her mind almost every day. Short one-page notes were the best she could do with her mental and physical condition at such a low. How could she write cheerful letters when she felt life was cruel?

Her view only included the fields covered in white or muddy puddles when the snow melted. Birch trees showed bare grey skeletons turning upward as if asking for their covering again. The dull-green Scotch pines stood tall and the Spruce seemed to reveal a grey-blue on the upper side of the needles, all patiently waiting for spring. The patients were also waiting just as eagerly for the cold season to pass.

Finally, the winter slowly died and spring unfolded with new growth. The valley and the hills budded into new green sprouts; tiny blossoms of wildflowers peeked through and began to display a variety of colors.

On March 3, 1926 Grace celebrated her 26th birthday without family, friends or any fanfare. But spring soon began to surface anyway and brought color and maybe a little hope.

Is this my last year on earth, or will I be cured?

CHAPTER 2

1925 - SURVIVING

Jack Morris sat tall in his saddle as he searched for the lost heifer on a fast warming-up morning. His squinting blue eyes squinted against the sun as he scanned the rolling Nebraska prairie splattered with tall native grass and wild weeds probably fighting for the moisture buried beneath them. Off in the distance he saw antelopes bounding up and down looking like they were on an avocado colored ocean vaulting with buttery waves.

He shifted in his saddle to scan another direction, and listened closely to the distant bawling. Jack nudged his horse and trotted closer to a shallow ravine looking into the earth's downward slope.

"There she is. Damned anyway, she's got stuck in a bog. We'll have to pull her out. Okay, Sparky, let's go get her," he spoke to his mount while patting his horse's neck. The heifer looked worn out and she stood like a statue afraid of sinking farther into the mud. Her round brown eyes showed her fear and begging.

"At least she's not a big un."

After a hardy struggle by man, horse and heifer, he finally gave the last pull on his rope along with Sparky backing up. His boots dug into the damp earth as he leaned in to tug and ended up with mud and grass stains up and down his one side. The heifer landed on the grassy slope ready to get away. Jack held tight to the rope until he could get it off her neck.

"Okay, you troublemaker, go find your friends and tell them to stay away from here." He tried to dust off with little luck since the mud was still damp. "Damn, now I'll be a muddy caked mess until I get back to the ranch."

Back on the saddle, he prodded his mount to catch up with the herd, following the stray. He removed his Stetson and waved to the other riders letting them know all was fine. He swiped his sweaty forehead on the back of his shirtsleeve and ran his fingers through his damp strawberry blond hair hoping to loosen the waves to allow some coolness before putting his hat back on. Then he settled down to his usual pace, relaxed in his saddle and in his own thoughts. That rope around the heifer reminded him of his youth and the feel of a rope around his wrists. He shuttered and soothed his wrists while saying under his breath, "I'd still like to kill that bastard if I saw him again!"

After two days in the saddle rounding up the cattle for sale, the men reached the stockyard and herded the cattle to the pens. By the time the last gate closed, the men were ready for a quick wash up and head to town to find some women and maybe somebody to sell them some moonshine; it always seemed to be available.

One of the hands mumbled, "It'd make it a lot easier to relax and enjoy life if the government just made liquor legal again."

Another laughed. "Where's that place you talked about, Sam, where you can get moonshine and a woman?" They knew, though, since they frequented the place before when in town.

The boss gave each his pay and scowled telling them not to give the ranch a bad name in town. "If I end up in jail, you can just head on down to the next town."

The cowboys nodded with a grin, knowing he was serious. "We won't get into trouble." As they drove out, they whooped and yelled, "Ladies, here we come."

Jack's eagerness was not as high as the younger ones now that he was in his mid-thirties and had done his share of partying. When they arrived at the establishment, they found a large room containing chairs, small tables and space for a few dancers on the well-worn wood flooring. A piano sat in the corner near the bar. When the cowhands arrived, the piano player fingered the keys for long stretches before taking a break.

Dancing was something Jack loved and he found a petite looking woman, not made up like a store mannequin, for his partner. They enjoyed each other's company while he bought drinks and jammed money into the pianist's jar sitting on top of the piano. After a few hours, Jack's age told him he wasn't as full of energy as the younger men and it was time to leave. Besides, the place was getting rowdy since another group of ranch hands arrived, and he could do without a brawl over women. When there weren't enough women for all the men, it always seemed to create trouble, especially when moonshine was added to the mix.

He decided to splurge and stay at the hotel for the night and go back to the ranch in the morning. The others would be spending the night somewhere, possibly in jail or at a woman's quarters. When Jack walked into the hotel, he noticed the polished furniture and lye smell lingering from the scrubbed wood floor.

A short slender man with a wild mustache and receding grey hair greeted him from the hotel shiny cherry wood counter. He gave a disdainful look when he saw the cowboy attire and dusty boots.

"Can I help you?" he asked as he pushed his spectacles up on his nose.

"Got a room for tonight?" Jack asked. He held his hat in one hand and his other rested on the counter while he leaned in.

"I doubt that we do. Are you sure you don't want to check the hotel down the street?" The clerk's nose had lifted higher and his eyebrows rose. His attitude showed that he considered Jack was one of the rowdy cowhands from the Double YZ ranch, or maybe the Slash AW, or some other. There were enough cowhands around that area.

"I've got the money, mister," Jack replied and stood taller. "I can sure use a long hot bath and a good night's sleep." He pulled out his roll of bills just far enough from his pocket to give the clerk a peek and maybe a nudge to find a room.

"Well, I'll see." There was a long pause as he checked the book. "I have one in the back above the kitchen. I'm sure you would find it satisfactory."

"How about one that faces the street?" Jack gritted his teeth. He could see that the town wasn't busy with travelers and sure more than one room would be available.

The flustered man pushed his glasses up again and checked some more records. He breathed deeply and it assured him that this persistent cowboy had not been drinking heavily.

"Is it just for you, or will you have someone joining you?"

9

"Just me and I've had a long day so I will be going to bed early tonight. I won't be having one of *those* women, if you're wondering."

Once again, the clerk looked and almost ate his lips. The cowboy standing on the other side of the counter didn't look like he'd be trouble.

"Oh, we do have a room just above the office here. I think that will do."

After they settled the price, Jack registered and walked up the steps covered in deep red and black checkered carpet. When he found the room and entered, he immediately surveyed the luxury of the surroundings compared to the bunkhouses he had lived in while working for ranchers in the past. At least now, he rented a room in a house with his friends back in Arlington and he had a good mattress. He no longer shared a bunkhouse with the cowhand and drove the short distance to the ranch. He plopped on the thick mattress and leaned back. The pillows were plush and he felt each just for the pleasure. Then he got up and began filling the tub with hot water. What a treat to sink in, lean back against the tub and have the warm water soothe his muscles! It had been far too long since he had a good long hot bath and never in a fancy white enamel tub that sat on copper claw feet. He soothed his muscles until the water turned cold.

"Now, that was worth it," he said as he got dressed and fell back onto the bed. His head sunk in the thick pillow, "I feel great. I'll wake up clean and bright-eyed and bushy tailed while the boys will hardly be able to raise their aching head."

His mind automatically shifted back in time and thought about sleeping on his pallet at that damnable house beginning when he was only ten years old. The past plagued him and he tossed and turned, slowly clearing his mind of those days.

Other thoughts then meandered to the couple he rented a room from, Bill and Mildred Ramser, back in Arlington, Nebraska. He just lucked out finding them when he was looking for a place to stay. They were a good husband and wife team, loving each other regardless of what came along. She was a great cook, nothing fancy, just meat and potatoes, only with great flavors. The best was her desserts, which she excelled in and just the sweet aroma made a man's mouth water. He felt she treated him like her brother and he liked that.

He thought of all the women he had known, especially when he was in his twenties. The girls in Nevada, Montana and Wyoming were eager to leave home and marry. The rodeos always attracted the girls who loved to flirt with the cowboys. They tried to flatter Jack by telling him how much they liked his roping tricks. He had his fun back then, but never found a girl he wanted to marry—yet.

For some reason, none of those females had what he was looking for. There was one who suited him back when he was in the Army. His romance with Sarah never developed because suddenly she disappeared and he never knew what happened to her.

Why couldn't he find a good woman? She could be right beside him in his plush hotel bed. He felt he was getting on in years now that he turned thirty-six and pretty soon it would be too late. Forty years old was not that far away. Any woman he could get interested in had to be at least thirty or older and love him, like Sarah did.

Jack wondered if there were any women left near his age who weren't already married. He was foot-loose and fancy-free, yet not happy. Would he ever find the one for him. He guessed he'd just keep searching.

Damn!

CHAPTER 3

1926 -SPRING WARMTH

Grace felt that spring always gave some hope for new life beginning. She hoped this would be the season to be cured and released from the sanitarium. A letter home was as cheerful as the sunny day.

May 25, 1926
Sanator, South Dakota

Dear Mom and Dad,

I am sitting here enjoying the warm sun while I view the hills. I wish you should see them. The spruce trees are so tall and veil the earth under their branches as they climb up the mountainside, so different from the cottonwoods at home. No wonder they call this the Black Hills. Of course, there also are birch, and Cottonwoods along streams. In the valley below us, the wild flowers are blooming with cornflowers, wild roses, blue asters, and more. They are all over the fields and in front of our porch. The yellow dandelion blossoms brighten the fields in between the tall grass. The meadowlarks are always ready to snatch a worm in the field, and then swoop up high and head to their nest, probably to feed their newborn. Deer are always around, with their heads down eating the greenery. Oh! I saw an eagle the other day soaring high above. He was so beautiful. The sun and fresh air seem to give me added strength now and I know I will soon be well. I feel your prayers helping me also.

You take care of yourselves, and say hello to everyone for me. I have a book to finish reading. The recently published novel is "The Great Gatsby" by F. Scott Fitzgerald about this new Jazz Age and already acclaimed as his best so far. It tells what city life is like. At least you do not have to worry about me acting like an irresponsible woman!

I miss all of you very much. Keep praying for me.
Your loving daughter,
Grace

Before tuberculosis, she had just begun to get the feeling of the Roaring Twenties and the jazz music that blossomed. She and her friends attended dances and saw a few girls from out of town called Flappers with their short fringed-bottom skirts, beaded hair bands and feathers, strands of beads around the neck flopping side to side—all attire considered improper by her and her friends. Grace's landlady would never have allowed her out the door of the boarding house if she dressed like that, let alone acted that way. Besides, she would report Grace to her parents and the school board.

She thought about the summer of '25, before her life changed, she and her friends were getting into the spirit of jazz that enveloped the country. She did not master the Charleston before she got TB. The Prohibition Act on January 17, 1920 was a setback—no more alcohol, unless a man knew where to get bootleg. They still had fun dancing and laughing and the boys took their breaks out to their automobile for maybe a quick nip.

Now in the sanitarium, Grace sorely missed the dances, her beau, and laughter with friends! Would she ever be able to do that again?

She read all the newspapers that came to Sanator. One paper said there were 30,000 to 100,000 speakeasies alone in New York City. Their locations were hard for the law to find and shut down. Chicago probably rivaled that city in numbers of speakeasies. She shook her head and had to smile. Government was struggling to control the situation, to no avail.

It would have been fun to get into a speakeasy and see all that excitement! Would Hobart ever have taken her to one? She would probably never know now.

The sanitarium staff set up a radio so that the patients could hear the news, music and other programs. It helped to keep their minds off their condition. Even with all the people around her and the sound of the radio, Grace felt so lonely without her family and friends nearby. Often tears couldn't be stopped.

Hobart's letters were getting shorter and came less often. He wrote about his business and about the weather. He never included many comments about a social life or their friends. Gradually his letters became sporadic and often just a hastily written note.

He hadn't written her a letter in over a month now and it wasn't even a year since she left. How could he forget her already, or was he just busy with work? They had gone out to dinners, picnics, dances alone or with friends. She thought he was serious, so why hadn't he written?

Finally, a letter arrived. Grace sat on her bed and opened it eagerly, hoping to hear how he missed her. She read it slowly trying to keep the tears from flowing.

July 3, 1926

Dear Grace,

I will be honest, I don't think you will be coming back here. You must understand that I need to move on with my life. Please don't think that I want to hurt you; I am just facing reality. We had a lot of fun together and I will always remember those good times.

However, lately I have been seeing another woman and I decided that I can't continue our long distant friendship. I'm sorry, but I will not be writing again.

I do wish you the best, Grace, and a healthy, happy future.

Hobart

Grace was devastated even though she suspected this might be why she hadn't heard from him. At first, her anger boiled up while she asked herself how he could possibly treat her that way. Why couldn't he see she didn't get TB on purpose and she had planned to go back to him. Later she began to rationalize.

Maybe he wasn't the one for her, especially if he wouldn't wait for her. Other thoughts crept into her head, as well.

Now I have no one when I get out of here. No one! I so hoped to have him waiting for me.

Oh, how she hated TB. It took her life from her and now it took Hobart away too. There was no one now.

She lost Hobart and all hope for love. Tears came easily every day. Depression set in and she seemed to lose the health previously gained. Letters to her family were shorter. She wasn't sure life was worth fighting for anymore. No man was going to want her now.

Some mornings Grace didn't feel like she wanted to face another gloomy day. Why did she have to? Far too often, another patient lost the battle to live. Spirits spiraled downward when the pallet fully covered with a sheet was taken away.

Misery sat heavily on top of her and she couldn't open her eyes to a bright day promising hope. Grace just wanted to curl up and let go of life—doomed and probably never able to find a job or have a family even if she did get out of this blasted place.

Why am I even living?

CHAPTER 4

1926-WASHINGTON COUNTY, NEBRASKA

Jack liked his room that he rented from Bill and Mildred Ramser. They had three children, so his rent helped them. The two men became good friends and Mildred always teased Jack about finding a woman. When hunting season arrived, the two never failed to bag an antelope. The prairie seemed to blossom with animals. Being a good marksman, Jack dropped the antelope with one shot.

One evening as the men sat on the porch smoking, they discussed going to the Black Hills to hunt for deer.

They quickly made their decision: Black Hills it was for hunting that year. They left with the horse trailer hitched up to Bill's old pickup, with two horses and their gear. The arrived near Custer, in the Black Hills, and found a nice quiet spot to park and set up their camp amid a cluster of birch and pines. They tethered the horses with enough room for them to munch on the surrounding tall grass. After they tied everything down and food placed in dangling bags high on a tree branch, they saddled the horses.

Each took their mount in opposite directions around a herd of deer in a meadow they had spotted. Both men shot almost simultaneously, bagging their bucks with one shot.

"I can't believe this," Bill shouted. "Here on the first night, we both bagged a buck."

Jack nodded. "Now we have to get these monsters back down to camp. You help me lift mine up on my horse and I'll do the same for you."

After accomplishing that task, they felt saddle sore from climbing the hills, and foot sore from leading the horses down a steep trail. Back at camp, they hung the bucks, gutted and cleaned them. Then they cut the meat in quarters, the saw the block of ice they brought with them was half melted, but enough remained to keep the meat cool while they headed back. They'd stop and get more ice as they drove the highways home. They had enough meat to last the whole winter.

Jack muttered as he rubbed his sore toes, "My feet are killing me. These boots sure aren't for hiking and I'll bet I got plenty of blisters." Even though he was tired and ached, he liked the Black Hills. A feeling of belonging seemed to creep in and he wondered what it was that pulled him to those hills?

The next morning they hauled the two bucks, the saddles and other equipment into the bed of the truck. Then they coaxed the two horses into the trailer and gave them a pat on the rear as they closed the gate.

They arrived home with big smiles. "Got you some meat, Millie," Bill yelled as they walked through the kitchen door, tired but happy. After a piece of pie and coffee, they unpacked the truck.

She replied, "You cure it and then we can all help cutting it into smaller pieces." She was not one to do all the work, but glad to have the meat. "Some meat would go to the local butcher to store in his cooler until they needed it. "I'll make some sausage too. Deer sausage has its own sweet taste the way I fix it."

Jack knew that Mildred usually stayed out of the way when the two men talked business and politics. Listening was enough for her and their disagreements did not affect her. Sometimes, though, she might yell through the window, "That's enough boys," and they obeyed. Her attention to Jack was more like a sister, one that he never had. She remembered his birthday and they celebrated with cake. Mildred did not have a brother and maybe that was why she adopted him as her own sibling.

Recently, a friend died when a bull gored him. The man didn't have a will and no one knew of any relatives. That got Jack thinking and he discussed what to do with his money and belongings. He didn't have much, but enough that he wondered what would happen if he died suddenly. The government would get it if no one was named as a beneficiary and he wasn't wild about that.

While sitting on the porch. Bill looked up at the passing clouds for a moment and puffed on his rolled cigarette. The discussed the friend. Jack told Bill that he didn't have any relatives who he could leave his money to.

"Think where you would like your money to go if something should happen," Bill said after taking another long drag off his cigarette.

Silence filled the warm evening as they sat on the porch watching the sun fade into a deep violet blending into deep blue. The field grasses were swaying to their own tune while the men enjoyed the cool breeze. Jack thought of mountains and about a home that he remembered up to the age of ten years old near Okanagan in Washington. As a child, he sat on that little porch stoop many times playing with his dog, chipmunks or squirrels, pretending he was a mountain man. He pondered things in his mind, such as what his mother might have been like. He waited for his father to return from trapping or logging and learn more. He would give anything to have that again and didn't understand why it had to be taken away from him.

After a few minutes, Jack changed his thoughts, then raised his hand and with a quick snap of his fingers, he said, "I know what I want to do. You two are the closest thing I have to a family. If something happens to me, what if I give my money and belongings to Mildred?" He looked at his friend with questioning eyes and pinched lips.

Bill's head jerked up and he looked to see if this was a serious question. "What do you mean, not to me?" he joked and tried to look like he'd been punched.

After laughing, Jack knew what to say. "Well, I can trust her with my money, but not you, my friend. You'd be out there buying some damnable contraption that wouldn't do any good for anyone." More laughter followed.

When the few details were on paper later, he signed his handwritten Last Will and Testament bequeathing all he had to Mildred on August 28, 1922. He never thought he'd have much, at least he knew he'd never be rich. Maybe even a little bit would help her if she needed something.

On weekends, Jack usually went to dances at the town Pavilion. The bands were just local men, but they were good with fiddles, banjos, and pianos. Bands always included at least one good lead voice. They knew what people liked and played the popular songs as well as old-time favorites.

Jack never lacked a dance partner even though he would not attempt the Charleston. Not only was he handsome with a pleasant physique, a worldly appearance, but light on his feet. He appeared to enjoy each partner. His acquaintance with one young woman advanced and every time there was a dance, the two stepped to the music all through the night. She was from the nearby town and came with some friends.

"Sometime you come home with me, okay?" Her indication gave Jack a rise in anticipation. It wasn't long and they planned a night for him to come to her home. She told him that she lived alone.

The nights continued until Jack found himself in the hospital.

"Why the hell didn't she tell me she was married?" he bellowed through swollen lips.

Bill sat by the hospital bed trying to keep a smile from surfacing. "Well, my friend, did you ever ask her? I heard she probably was. Now that you found out the hard way, I'd say stay away from her. That husband of hers did a nasty job on you."

Jack felt like a team of horses had trampled him. He thought his head would explode even though held tight by a bandage wrapped around a nasty cut. Two black and blue puffy eyes made it hard to see well, so he kept blinking to try to clear his vision. Three ribs were broken, yet his bruised chest felt like all ribs were jabbing into him.

"That son-of. . . ," he stopped, thinking a nurse might hear. "He didn't even give me a chance to tell him I didn't know she was married and I was sorry. He just started pounding me. I was down before I knew it."

Bill couldn't hold back anymore. "Well, I'll betcha it won't happen again, will it?" His laughter echoed through the room.

"It's not funny! You damned bet it won't happen again. I'm going to stay away from women now. Damned women anyway!"

Several weeks passed before Jack felt up to par. Even then, he kept an eye out for the irate husband in case the man wanted to finish the job by killing him.

Jack was glad he had signed a will. If he hadn't survived, at least Mildred would have had something. Not much else, but maybe a hundred might help her. He tried to find a comfortable spot on the bed.

Damn!

CHAPTER 5

1926 - HIDDEN MEANINGS

Gold and rust hues tumbled to their burial ground as the fall winds dried out the landscape. Trees stood naked when winter blew in snowy and bitter cold. Patients managed to stay wrapped in layers most of the day and another blanket or quilt added at night. Grace, like all patients, slept most of the time curled up under the mound covering her and thinking winter would never end. Her depression was lessening even though the icy air wouldn't. Her body felt stronger and her mind had begun to think past her loss of Hobart. Maybe there was hope—somehow.

Eventually winter dwindled and dribbled into spring with warm sun and the daylight hours lengthened. Robins chipped their arrival while perched on branches that were beginning to bud with new greenery. Various wild flowers in the fields began to poke their noses upward. The spring days brought out smiles and more energy among the patients. Grace slowly walked the length of the porch, inhaling the scent of growth with the new season.

She wasn't cured, however her letters home sounded more cheery. Should she write Hobart? She decided a definite *no* on that thought. He dropped her and she would not belittle herself to beg him to come back to her. Loneliness plagued her.

The latest letter to arrive from her friend back home gave her hope of hearing something about Hobart.

July 8, 1926
Kimball, So. Dak.

Dear Grace,

The July sun has brought hot, humid days here. I am having a hard time keeping my new starched dress from wilting. I bought it two weeks ago at the new boutique. You would like that store. I hope that you have lovely days without horrible perspiring. Is it actually drier there? I could stand some dryness right now so my dress would not look like a dripping washcloth.

We had the usual July 4th parade. The school band had extra drummers this year and everyone kept in step. The park was full with games and fun along with picnics, band music and dancing. At night, the fireworks lit the sky with the bursts of white, red, blue and gold—what a great way to finish the celebration. Maybe next year you will be here with us. Did you have a July 4th celebration there?

Tommy and I have been seeing each other regularly. I think he is getting serious. I am! I must get busy and write others. Take care of yourself. Do keep writing. Be assured the gang is praying for you. We miss you.

Love,
Millie

There was not one word about Hobart. Even though Grace liked to hear what was happening with her friend, she knew some of the events were missing and her shoulders sunk. Millie was able to go to a shop and buy a new dress while that was not an option for Grace. She longed to have a new dress, even handmade. Of course, it wouldn't make any difference at the sanitarium. She couldn't go into town to show off new apparel. She couldn't impress Hobart with a new outfit. Reading Millie's letter, the statement *Maybe next year you will be here with us*, hurt deeply. She couldn't go back and she didn't have any friends in the Black Hills. How could she enjoy a July 4th celebration anywhere next year?

She couldn't even have a new dress, couldn't enjoy any festivities and didn't have a beau. Was Hobart there with the other woman? What was he doing? Did he marry that woman? All those questions were running through her mind.

She knew she needed to stop thinking of him and yet there was no one else for her. Millie's letter sat on her nightstand and then she curled up in her bed pulling a blanket over her head. She tried to hide her crying and silently asked, "Will I ever get out of here?" Then she had another question. "If I get out of here, will any man ever want me?"

Time crept forward revealing she had been at the sanitarium almost a year. Her color was better and the cough had lessened. Maybe, just maybe, she would get out of this hated prison one of these days soon. Yes, she hated the sanitarium even though she knew it was helping her. She detested it because bed after bed revealed suffering. And she lost her beau because of this disease. There was little to brighten a patient's morale. She desperately needed smiles, friends and fun!

She needed to write Mom and Dad again. She had to be cheerful.

July 9, 1926
Sanator

Dear Mom and Dad,

Today is beautiful here. I hope it is nice there. How is the garden? The berries along the streams must be bountiful. Did you make any jellies or jams, or did you, Dad, use them for your medicinal drink?

Dad, I wonder how your sawmill business is doing. I hope you have enough help and are not overworking.

I don't think I wrote you that we had a July 4th celebration here. Custer had the school band parade in the field off our porch. My, they certainly did great, even though I saw a couple youngsters that turned the wrong way or got out of step. It didn't matter and we enjoyed it anyway. Our dinner was chicken, potato salad, fresh vegetables, and we finished with apple pie and vanilla ice cream. I enjoyed the day.

I'll close for now. As I said, I am getting better and I am looking much better, if I must say so. Your prayers have done that. Thank you and keep those prayers up. I also pray for you.

Love,
Grace

She didn't tell the truth about everything. Many patients were too sick or exhausted to applaud the band and many were too sick to eat much at all. Broth always helped the cough, though. Writing that she was getting better was the truth. They didn't need to worry about her.

Mom wrote short notes often between all her family duties. Her handwriting was legible, but not as neat as her daughter's penmanship. Grace didn't mind. Mom's father made her quit school when she was only ten years old. He dropped her off on a street in town, told her to get a job and he would collect her pay every week. Grace admired her mother for what she had accomplished in her life, learning with her children who all went, or were going, to school except little Charlie. Mom and Dad decided that all their offspring were going to get a good education and not have to quit and go to work.

Time seemed to move forward so God-awful slow for Grace. There was progress, though, and optimism brought more energy. Hope and faith were strong healers and she accepted both with open arms even though she felt so lonely knowing she had no family when she was able to leave the sanitarium.

More weeks and months passed. Some of her friends were gradually sending fewer and fewer letters or just notes. She knew she would never reconnect with most and began to slow her letters as well.

When Grace got out of the sanitarium, she would have to make new friends. Would anyone want her as a friend, or court her anymore? She resigned herself to the fact that she was probably going to be a spinster and never have a family.

What will happen with me? How will I survive?

CHAPTER 6

WOMEN and MOVING ON

Once again, it was time for the Washington County Fair in Arlington. Jack's boss always provided cattle and horses used for the event. The ranch hands, including Jack, delivered the animals and took care of them during the fair. This provided each with a pass for the activities.

The food booths always had delicious assortments to tantalize the nose and stomach and desserts disappeared quickly. The children's corner kept Jack smiling while he kept watch over the cattle in that section. He liked to see happy, exploring children.

In a quiet moment, his mind blocked out the present, and he was back in the cabin he shared with his father. He saw all the fun he had in the mountains trying to befriend the squirrels, chipmunks, birds, and deer. Once he even tried to coax a wolf to come to him. He quickly realized that was a bad idea when the wolf growled menacingly, ready to pounce. He jumped inside the cabin, slamming the door just as the beast sprang. Why couldn't his dad have lived? They had it good even though his mum wasn't there with them. Why did his dad get killed? He was only ten years old when that happened. He muttered, "Damn it anyway!"

Jack thought back to when he got a helper's ticket for the Missouri Centennial Exposition and State Fair at Sedalia, Missouri because he helped his boss bring the cattle. Work at the Fair wasn't difficult; he didn't consider it as hard as wrestling a calf in the dirt and mud during the branding season, or helping with birthing.

While in Missouri, an uncomfortable feeling crept into his mind. Sedalia wasn't too far from where he landed at ten years old. He'd recognize that S.O.B. if he came to the Fair. After Jack was done with that man, he'd have been arrested. Once again, he muttered under his breath, "Goddamn him anyway. He probably wouldn't get enough gumption to come here, so he might be lucky and not run into me. After five years under him and his whip, I hope he is rotting in hell." He paused and rolled a cigarette. "Wonder what ever happened to his son. Lester hated the ol' man as much as I did."

He shook himself back to reality. Then he saw a little boy approaching and Jack started to coax a young bull up to the fence so the little boy could pet it. Several nudges succeeded and the child got to pet the wide-eyed calf. "Oh, he's so soft! I want one, Mama."

She laughed and so did Jack. He took over, "Well there, young man, that young calf is cute now, but see that bull over there?" He pointed to the pen with the adult cattle. "Well, that's what this little guy will grow up to be."

The little boy's eyes widened in astonishment when he saw the horns and how big the bull was. He squeezed his mother's hand tight as he took a step backward.

The mother smiled and nodded a thank you to Jack. "Now, that is a huge dangerous looking animal. I don't think we want a calf that's going to grow that big, do we Billy?"

"No! Let's go Mama." He pulled her away leaning outward as he pulled on her arm.

She gave Jack a smile and nodded as her son led her off.

Jack was still smiling after they left. He loved kids and he would like some of his own. He wanted a woman like that mother who is caring and teaching.

Later his mind wandered again as he looked over each older man while talking about farming or ranching.

Several times, he asked if anyone knew Drake. One shrunken old timer looked up quick and said, "Yeah, I knew of him.

You know that no-good-for-nothing?" and rubbed his fingers over his mustache smoothing out the curled ends.

"Is he still around?" Jack's heart began to beat faster and pounding his chest. He saw the man's face turn into a question mark as if wondering who Jack might be. Then he dropped his eyebrows and spoke.

"He died from alcohol poisoning a couple years ago. That was an agonizing slow death, let me tell ya." He took a long drag on his cigar. "He suffered bad before dying. I hear he ran off his boys back several years ago."

There was the question in the man's eyes again and Jack assumed the man wanted him to say he was one of the boys at that house back then. He squinted and frowned, not answering the unasked question.

Instead, he said, "I hope he suffered all the pains of hell! What happened to his wife?"

"Oh, she up and burned the house down . . . left with just a trunk. Have no idea where she went. Most of the town's men knew she went through hell with him."

"Yup, she sure did. Thanks for the information." He gave no explanation, but walked away with his jaw jutted out and his eyes revealing rage.

Jack thought that Drake got what he deserved. He just wished he could have gotten to the S.O.B. first. Somehow, he couldn't help but feel good about his dying that way. Then it dawned on him that he'd lost his box with the only possessions he had of his father. He left it at Drake's and always meant to go back for it. He wouldn't have been afraid of that devil anymore when he was in his twenties. Why didn't he go get it? Now he had nothing of his father or his mother. That hit him hard, like a blow to his stomach.

Arlington, like all towns, celebrated Veterans Day. Jack, a veteran of the Great War, was a member of the American Legion. All the vets were proud of their service and felt they had a kinship with others who served.

On July 4 celebrations, the American Legion invited him and all vets to join in the parade. Jack donned his uniform, still fitting perfectly, and joined the others as they marched down the street in step. He was proud of his service even though he never did get to go overseas and fight. He was ready for whatever the Army wanted, but he wished he could have gone to Europe and killed some enemies.

All the veterans liked to hear the applause as they marched by with their backs straight, heads proudly held high. Patriotism was high and people waved flags while some young women ran out to kiss some of the vets as they passed. Jack certainly didn't mind that. A school marching band always provided percussion and patriotic music. At night, the fireworks produced whoops and claps. July 4 never failed to give Jack a good attitude and hopes for a brighter future.

Jack received his free ticket and two children's tickets for the Washington County Fair again. The woman he had been courting for a several weeks had two children. As a widow, she needed to work and couldn't attend the fair. Still, he wanted her children to see the fair and in between his duties, he could show them around.

"Thanks, Jack," she smiled as she and her two children met him at the gate.

"No sweat. We'll have fun." He smiled and tried to kiss her only to have her turn her head and his lips landed on her cheek. "What's that for?"

"Oh, you know—people are looking," she replied and squeezed his shoulder before stepping back with a smile. "See you later," and she spun around quickly walking away. Her long unbuttoned tan coat flew to the sides as she hurried off trying to keep her balance in her high heels in the dusty, uneven dirt path.

Jack gave a quizzical look when she left and then turned to the ten and twelve year olds. He liked both and felt he could be a father to them. The older one was a boy and the younger one a girl who didn't mind getting dirty like her brother.

When the Fair closed down for the night, Jack walked the two weary children home. Their mother didn't invite him in. The exchange was unexpected and short as she blocked the entrance with one hand on the doorframe and the other on the half-opened door.

"Thanks for taking the kids today." The children burst through and headed for the kitchen to search for sweets.

"Okay, then. I'll see you tomorrow," he said, still not sure what the problem was.

She shook her head, "No, Jack. I can't see you anymore. I am going to marry Barry. He owns the grocery store and I've worked there a long time; we've been close. Now he's serious and wants to get married. He'll give my children a good life." She paused, then added, "I'm sorry."

In shock, his mouth flew open and immediately shut while staring at her. In a second, he spoke. "Why the hell then did you let me get so close to your kids? I love them. You just played me." His anger rose as well as his voice.

"I'm sorry. This proposal just happened today. I didn't know he was that serious. I didn't mean to hurt you, Jack."

"Well you sure as hell did a good job." Jack spun around and stomped down the street muttering. "Damn, damn, damn. I can't seem to get a woman to stick with me. What's wrong? I don't think I'm that bad. Just one good one is all I ask!" He kicked dirt and swore all the way home.

By 1926, Jack was getting restless again. He'd been there for a few years and had never settled in a location for very long. He was searching for something, but it wasn't here. There were no ties to keep him in one spot so he figured he'd just move on. "I think I might head to the Black Hills. I hear the gold mines are looking for miners and they pay good. I heard they may pay around ten dollars a week." Jack told Bill one evening as they sat on the porch smoking. "I don't know if that's true, but I'd like to see that much each week." They looked out over the fields about ready for harvest.

"Well, maybe we'll join you. I'm ready to go somewhere else." Life was changing and not for the good. He saw jobs disappearing. The gold industry was going strong.

With a nod, Jack added, "We can go together and see if we can get some money in the bank. I'd like to get a new auto sometime."

"I'll talk to Mildred and see what she says. She usually goes along with whatever."

In the next few days, they agreed to head for Lead, in the Black Hills. Bill had his own auto and they'd go as a caravan of two.

Jack gave his boss notice. He'd miss ranching even though he thought maybe if he got more money, he would have better luck with women. As he drove away, he decided he needed to follow a new path. He'd been on his own since he was fifteen and here he was almost thirty-eight and still didn't know what he was looking for—besides a wife. He wondered if the Black Hills would be the answer.

On their way, Jack told the Ramsers that he was going to take a side road and visit an old friend. They agreed to meet in Lead.

The Pine Ridge Reservation came into view and Jack felt at peace. He'd renew his friendship with Benjamin Black Elk. As a teenager, when they first met, Ben's father, Black Elk, took him under his wing. That was the only time that he felt he *belonged* since his own father died. Now everything looked different, yet the same. He drove to Ben's home, parked and walked up to the door.

29

Ben opened and smiled broadly at his old friend. "What's up with you, Jack? You look good, but I don't see no woman with you. You don't want one?" Ben grinned as he looked at the empty auto.

"Haven't found a good one yet," he grinned and wished he had a wife and a batch of young ones in his car.

The two had a long conversation over coffee in Ben's home. His wife poured their coffee, sat the pot on a pad in the middle of the table and quietly left the room. Jack learned more about the gold mines. Then the conversation changed and they caught up on old memories and the two laughed over some of the things they did as teens.

When it was time to leave, the two men shook hands and said their goodbyes. Jack waved as he spun out the drive with dirt and dust flying high behind him.

The climb through the hills took longer than driving the same distance through the prairieland. Sometimes Jack worried if his auto would overheat before he got to the top of a hill. He made it each time with a sigh of relief, and the worry lines disappeared for the moment. When he rolled into Lead, he found the Homestake Gold Mine and immediately signed up for work with instructions to begin the next day at the Wasp #1 mine. He never had problems getting work and he didn't again this time. He felt good.

Soon Jack found his friends at a café and they exchanged information about the town. The Ramsers said they found a home to rent with a high price, only a little less than the other rentals available. "We have to fix it up a bit. My pay better cover next month's rent."

Bill raised his fork and pointed at his friend. "Say, how about staying with us again? We've a big attic and part was made into a separate room. You can stay there. With our three kids, you might be able to get a bit of peace and quiet up there." They all laughed remembering how boisterous the three children could be.

"That would be great. I'm not picky as long as I can eat your wife's cooking." Jack enjoyed the idea of staying with his almost-adopted family again.

The next day Bill and Jack walked to the mine and began work. Neither was happy about being underground, but the pay was good. The economy seemed to be slowing in the Midwest and they wanted to build up some reserve for a just-in-case time that might come. Wherever they went, the talk seemed to be about the economy.

That night the two came home with soot covering them from head to toe. Mildred, in her full big apron, tried to dust them off on the porch before they came into the house. They washed up and put on clean clothes before supper was ready.

Mildred said, "Well, I can see I'll have extra washings. You can't wear those clothes again until they are cleaned."

After supper, Jack took a walk around the town. When he returned, he told Bill and Mildred, "Well, I found another miner out checking the town, Auggie Lehmannn. He told me his wife took in washing if I ever needed her. He's at the Cutting Mine. He said his wife would sure like to meet you, Mildred. She has three boys and they drive her crazy at times."

Mildred smiled and nodded. She would be glad to meet another miner's wife. Maybe she'd learn how to get all that dirt out of the clothes.

By week's end, the two families met and got along well. They all would be friends. The women met while the men worked. Mildred told her about a few of Jack's past loves that didn't work out.

"Also, Bill told me that Jack had a tough life." She filled her new friend in with the little details she knew. "He'd make a good husband and father. He's great with my kids."

Both women began to be on the lookout for a nice eligible woman for Jack. When they would find one, circumstances changed their views and they'd shake their heads *no* as they continued their search. Bill knew Jack best and he also nixed one after the other.

Jack had a hard time adjusting to mine work, being below ground. He missed the open space. When he returned to his new home at night, supper was ready and he devoured the meal, but still had room for her apple dumplings.

Lying on the bed in his new room, Jack began to relax. He looked out at the hills turning a deep blue-black on the hillside.

He hoped this was a good move, leaving Nebraska. The money was good, but he felt penned in down below the ground. When he got enough money, he'd leave and work a ranch again. He sure missed his horse on the ranch back in Nebraska. He really missed the animal and pasture smells; it sure was sweeter than that stink underground. Maybe he shouldn't have come to South Dakota even for better pay.

Damn!

CHAPTER 7

1926 - WE'RE COMING!

"Miss Lee, you have to live in a drier climate the rest of your life," the doctor emphasized. "You cannot live near the Missouri again because the tuberculosis mycobacterium thrives on humidity. If you are infected again, it would be fatal." He paused to make sure she was paying attention and then stressed, "You should never marry, Miss Lee. You should never have children because you will not survive to see them grow up, go to school, or see them marry. You will never live to see grandchildren. Try to make a comfortable life for yourself." He was honest, still the words stung deeper than a swarm of bees.

That statement given to Grace was devastating and confirmed what she already suspected. That warning ruined her dreams of having her own family. Even harder to manage, was the thought of writing her folks that coming home was not an option. She would wait until she was closer to a release time before she told them. She would only tell her parents about needing to be at a higher and dryer altitude. The rest of the doctor's warnings didn't need to be their concern. Deep down, she was hurting beyond anything she ever felt before, even worse than the loss of Hobart. She felt so alone and no one to comfort her.

Grace wondered how she was going to live in the Black Hills. How would she find a job? Would a school hire her as a teacher if they knew she had TB? What was she going to do?

She felt hopeless. Asking God would not bring the answer even though she needed to know what God planned for her. When released, she would walk out into the world with nothing, no family, not even a friend—no one who would care about her. She was only 26 years old and felt her life was over.

Where will I go? What will I do? God, help me please

When Grace wrote letters to her family, she could honestly tell them that she was getting better, if nothing else. Time passed much too slowly with each tick of the clock on the wall counting the minutes, hours, days and then months. She just wanted each day to end quickly.

Even as depressed as she was, Grace made remarkable progress. The doctor finally told her to prepare for dismissal by winter or early in 1927. He would continue monitoring until her release. "You are making great strides and you are one of the lucky ones. You're going to survive, Miss Lee," he smiled.

She wrote home telling them her discharge might be soon, but she was not coming home.

July 20, 1926

Dear Family,

> *I have great news! The doctor says I'm getting close to being released. It won't be long now and I'll be completely cured.*
>
> *When I'm released, I will stay here in the Black Hills. I can't return to the humidity back home to Tripp, Yankton, or anywhere close to the Missouri where the TB germs thrive. I intend to keep that nasty little bacterium away from me! Besides, the Black Hills are not like having to live in a desert or the North Pole. I like it here.*
>
> *When I'm released, I can room free at a home until I secure a job. There is a network here of local people who offer help. They must be angels! The room will include my meals and so you won't have to pay anything, Dad. Isn't that great? I'm sure the meals won't be as good as yours, Mom, but at least I will be well fed.*
>
> *I am so looking forward to working again. Of course, I'll miss you all, but I will be fine. I'm so happy to be close to getting out of here! I will let you know when later.*

Your grateful daughter,
Grace

Her mind drifted when she folded her letter. She straightened her shoulders, determined that she would be fine, just so lonely. She wiped her tears away before they fell on her stationery. After sealing her letter, her jaw jutted out with lips pursed, trying to reassure herself. She would start a new life and make new friends. She could do it and all would be fine. Just get in the right mindset.

A letter arrived within the week from her mother. She read that her father was devastated when he heard she would not be able to come home. Mom wrote that he bellowed through the house, "Well, we can't have that! We're family. We're moving to the Black Hills. Some men have wanted to buy me out for a long time. Now is the time. We're moving there and Grace will come home to us!"

The letter continued telling that the family was moving to the Black Hills. Grace was to live with them in their new home when she left the sanitarium. She ended her letter with, "Dad says to tell you that we are on our way, we are coming. I will be so happy to see you again."

Grace couldn't believe the news. Overwhelmed by the sacrifice her parents were making, she broke down in tears. How could she ever repay them? How blessed she felt to leave the sanitarium and go home to her family!

The next week she received another letter from Nellie. Fred and Bob, Grace's brothers, took life as it came and would adjust. Little Charlie thought it would be a great adventure. Laura didn't like leaving her friends behind, but didn't have a vote in the decision. Nellie wrote she decided to go to nursing school at the hospital in Rapid City, so she would be close.

Grace learned that the all-cash sale transaction of her father's sawmill was not as much as he'd hoped, but was a fair sale. He always said, "No one ever got hurt on the corners of a fair deal." He took a quick trip to the Black Hills and found what he was looking for near the little town of Whitewood. The property contained a large two-story home, barn and some outbuildings, sitting close to Crook Mountain.

Her dad didn't believe in debt and was a good horse trader, usually receiving enough to make a fair deal. The land had plenty of room for his sawmill business and he could serve towns in the area with lumber. Within five days he was back home and started the process of relocating.

Grace's last letter from the southeastern corner of the state explained what the family did after the sale. The hard part came with packing and moving. Her father kept the 1922 Ford Motor truck he used for lumber. It had wood racks on the sides and they loaded his equipment and much of the furniture in it. They squeezed in kitchen items, blankets and clothing between nooks and crannies of the furniture. The men anchored a canvas tarp over the top and sides in case of rain. Charlie rode in the truck with Dad and Mom. Bob drove their Ford Model T C Cab, which was just that—a cab for driver and passenger with a small bed attached in back. It bulged with tools, household items, bedding and clothing and was then canvas-covered. Nellie was his passenger. Fred drove his 1923 Triumphant automobile with a sedan top attached and Laura rode with him. The back seat and trunk area bulged with more items.

On the departure day, Grace read that the family climbed into the vehicles and took their last look at their home as they drove down the dirt road to a new beginning.

Nellie wrote a long letter to Grace after they arrived at their new home by Whitewood.

September 5, 1926
Whitewood, SD

Dear Sis,

We finally got here! Our trip was quite the experience. We looked like a circus parade with our three vehicles overflowing with our belongings. We bounced along the roads with enough distance between us to settle some of the dust from the one in front. Every few miles we switched places. The lead vehicle driver waved his hand out the window motioning for the next auto to pull in front—time for the switch. The last auto then moved in second place and the one leaving the front took up the rear. This went on until each had a turn in front and didn't have to eat dust and dirt all the way. Finally, we traveled on oiled roads and breathed easier—no more dust and dirt invading my nostrils!

Since each auto was overloaded, we couldn't attain the speed we wanted. Each time there was an incline Dad's truck slowed and chugged along, often decreasing the speed to ten or fifteen miles per hour. The other two autos kept the same pace so we could remain together.

We arrived at Chamberlain by dusk, parked between some large cottonwoods near a field for the night and camped out. We were back on the road by dawn the next day and arrived that evening at a little town called Kadoka. The sky was turning the horizon into beautiful pinkish streaks amidst the clouds as the sun lowered into the horizon. Dad said we deserved a break and he'd rent something for the night.

Our caravan pulled into the drive where several little cottages sat near the home of the property owner. Dad paid for two and we were quite pleased with the accommodations.

Dawn came too soon with early light invading through the curtains. We ate and then cleaned each bungalow thoroughly. By eight, we were loaded up and returned to the highway heading west, still about 130 to 150 miles away from our new home.

When we drove into Sturgis, we stopped for supper at a café— our first time to eat in a café or restaurant! We didn't arrive at our new home until darkness was setting in, We sure gave a sigh of relief. The two-story house stood tall and the grey clapboard siding hadn't seen paint in years. A long porch sat in front. It is very similar to our old home.

We unloaded and assembled the beds, table, chairs and of, course, the food and cooking supplies. That was enough for the night. We crawled into our beds and in a flash the house was full of sighs and snoring.

I must go help Mom with the cooking. She said that she'd write soon.

Love,
Nellie

Grace read and reread the letter. This was her first letter from Whitewood, which she hoped would soon be her new home with her family.

What a trip her family had—all because of her. She pictured some automobiles speeding past the slow caravan waving and honking their horns. Travelers were trying to find work or had found it, and were moving their families to new locations. She read about people moving east to work in the automobile industry or manufacturing and chemical companies. Others were heading west to find work in California with the up-and-coming motion picture industry. The economy was bustling in the early 1920's and many new banks had opened. Now the bustling changed to a slower pace in some areas.

When her family headed to the Black Hills, the future had turned uncertain for everyone in the country. Grace prayed that her father's new business would be good and he would continue to prosper.

Please Dear Lord, cure me and let me go home soon.

CHAPTER 8

1927 – LEAD

Jack felt that life was rolling along with work, sleep and not much else. He was too tired and depressed by the end of the day to go to a bar with some of the men after leaving the mine. His attitude was becoming gloomy just like the air in the tunnels. He hated mining.

While trying to sleep, his thoughts often turned to the open prairie shining with tall native grasses and fields of wheat, rye, alfalfa or corn. He dreamed of being back on a horse and herding cattle again. He also thought of finding a small cabin in the hills that would bring back some of the joy he once had when his father was still alive. He could almost smell the forest aroma.

While turning over once again, he wondered why he ever quit being a ranch hand. What got into him? Was it only because he wanted change and to earn more money? Being a miner wasn't worth the money for him! Mining seemed like a soot-filled abyss while ranching was more like a sunny, free heaven. What was he thinking when he decided to go to work in the mine!

He, the Ramsers and the Lehmanns relaxed on most Sundays. The women took turns cooking, but helped with cleanup. The group discussed the town, mines, local and national governments, gossip, and anything else that came to mind.

Mildred teased Jack. "When are you going to find a good woman and bring her to meet us? You know I have to approve. Go to some of the dances at the hall. Find someone!"

He shook his head and laughed. "Lay off, woman," He playfully frowned at her. "I'll pick the one I want, not who you come up with," he teased. "I'm not going to any dances. I prefer staying away and staying healthy."

Bill gave a hardy laugh. "I wonder why?" He knew exactly why.

Jack was not about to end up with another married woman and have a husband come at him like in Nebraska. There weren't many single women around his age anyway. Divorced or widowed women usually refused to marry again, or they wanted someone who could give them a secure future.

"I'm fine by myself," Jack muttered and wanted to change the subject. "What have you heard about the ranching and farming lately?"

"From what I hear and read, farmers have plowed up more land to plant wheat and corn because the price is so good," Bill stated after he took another drag on his cigarette. "And, the stock investors are buying up the surplus so they can make big money when they sell."

After a nod, Jack looked off in the distance. "Why plow up the native grasses if there's so much surplus?"

"Don't ask me. I don't keep up on that stuff. New York City can do what they want and I'll do what I want." Bill replied with a laugh.

Neither paid that much attention to investors and only wanted to earn as much money as they could and as soon as they could. Jack thought he might have enough money saved in a few more months to buy a better auto. He couldn't afford a new one, but needed a good one, better than what he had. His old one was going to quit altogether on him one day.

Even though he was underground all day, he could see that the economy was changing in the above ground world. He also saw that the climate was getting drier and even winter didn't bring as much snow to Lead. Old timers didn't mind and appreciated not having to shovel or plow as much, but they suspected drought was coming. The Ramsers and Lehmanns were glad they didn't have to climb up on their roof and shovel off several feet of the solid packed white.

Jack got a hunting license and used his Sundays to climb the hills looking for a big buck. At least he only had to start climbing the hills from the Ramser house. That was easier than before when he and Bill came from Nebraska.

Without much snow, he had a hard time following deer tracks. His instinct told him where to look and by noon, he found a herd stomping and chomping on the little grass that remained around birch tree trunks. The smell of deer and dust from the hooves filled his senses. With his eyes squinted, he looked closer and found a trophy buck. He whispered to himself, "My God, look at his rack! Can I get him before he decides to move?"

He sneaked a little closer while trying not to make a sound. Cautiously, he inched up trying to avoid crunching sticks, leaves, or stumbling and making a racket. When he felt he was in the right position, he raised his rifle to his shoulder and sighted in. Almost afraid he'd miss, Jack stalled. He looked at the tan white-tailed beauty and hated to ruin its life, but he wanted that kill. He pulled the trigger and down went the buck. The other deer bolted to the trees.

When he got over to the buck, he knew the one shot did the trick. Without thinking, he blurted out, "Damn! He's a big beast. How am I going to get him back to the house?" He stood staring at the lifeless animal then answered his own question. "Okay, okay. I know what I gotta do."

He heaved the animal up around his shoulders, grabbed the legs on each side, holding the hooves, and began to ease his way down the hill leaning because of the weight. He thanked God that he was hauling his load downhill while he wondered if the trophy's weight was going to give him a hernia or break his back. Yet he didn't want to give up. Determination to make it down to the house straightened his back

After struggling downhill, stopping to catch his breath and then starting out again, Jack finally got to the house. When he dropped the buck, Bill saw him and ran out. "Damn! You got a big one. Wish I'd gone with you. Where'd you find him?"

Jack told him, gave the complete story of how he downed the buck.

"Yeah, but look at the meat we have for the rest of the winter. It will sure be sweet and tender since you downed him with one shot and he didn't run. I still got three more pictures on the camera. Let's take them of this beauty."

"Okay," Jack answered with a smile.

Days passed while they waited for the pictures and speculated if it could go in the newspaper so Jack could brag. The week passed with both men working and Mildred washing overalls and shirts. She had a new wringer-washer. All she had to do was take the wet clothes while they dripped back into the tub and push them into the wringer. No more turning the wringer by hand to drop the clothes into the rinse tub and start over. She didn't mind laundry duties as much as she used to.

Once the film was developed, they viewed the photos and thought Jack looked pleased—which he was. Mildred purchased a small frame for his snapshot and he kept it on the stand by his bed.

When 1928 rolled in, the country was not in good economic health. Neither was Jack in good mental health. He felt like he had soot in his nose and throat. On Sundays while others were in church, he enjoyed the fresh air, especially as winter was dwindling. He took long hikes and watched the birds hovering over newborns, squirrels and chipmunks searching for fresh food and even deer finding new growth to munch. The ground was beginning to show tiny buds of green pushing through the dirt while wildflowers were already blossoming in their yellows, blues and reds.

"God, I love spring!" He said to the Ramser's dog that followed him everywhere. "I got to get back above ground." He knelt down and scratched the russet and white-colored mutt's neck while viewing the scene. The response was more tail wagging and he seemed as content as Jack felt.

"I got to start thinking about a different job. Maybe I'll spend next weekend searching."

Then it was Monday, and he was back in the tunnels. Jack did his work well, but the dust affected him more both physically and mentally. Maybe it was his attitude that made it seem worse. He hated his life right then.

"Bill I, think I'm going to see if there's any ranch work around here. I like the Black Hills, but I hate mining. You lucked out by moving up and ending up with a supervisor's job. That works better for you doesn't it?" Jack wished he had gotten a job like that. Maybe then, he could stand the work, bet even at that, he doubted it.

"You bet it's better. I'm sorry you haven't gotten a break, Jack. If you want a ranch job, you best be starting to look. I hear the Midwest is getting into trouble. Maybe here it won't be so bad, in the hills." Bill paused and lit his cigarette. "We will miss you, but if something comes up that is better for you, I wish you well."

Jack started his search while continuing to stay with the Homestake Mine. Every day off, he drove around and asked at ranches if they needed a hand, with no luck. At least he got out in the country and breathed the fresh air deeply.

The golden leaves fringed in burnt orange and the straw-colored fields told him that it was too late to find ranch work for the year. Winter meant no more calving, no pushing cattle to the sale pens and no more branding. He was going to have to wait until spring.

Jack's determination would not let him give up and he'd try to be patient until spring. He felt he really messed up things this time. He wanted to get back to ranching.

Damn!

CHAPTER 9

1927 - HOME

As Grace read the just received letter from Nellie, she could envision her taking a break with a cup in hand, sitting at their long kitchen table, and taking a pencil and tablet. The letter described their new home, and about how eagerly they awaited Grace's joining them. Days spent unpacking and arranging wore her out. The boys helped their dad set up his sawmill.

Grace immediately wrote back asking questions about the Whitewood area. She didn't mention her recovery progress which was slower than hoped. Yet she would still fight for release before winter.

Her dreams of going home for Christmas in 1926 fell in despair when the doctor decided that she was not ready to leave Sanator.

Grace couldn't blame anyone, just her own body. Her view of the hillside became bleak. Snow began to fall as softly as her tears. Her one friend at the sanitarium left in October to return to her home. Now Grace was alone with no one to talk to or who cared about her. She didn't even have her beau writing to her anymore. Her spirits slumped.

Grace wrote home telling her family that she couldn't be released yet and tried to be cheerful, but it was difficult. She sat on the porch watching the fields and hills speckled with white. Christmas was not worth celebrating since she could not go home and her family was struggling just to keep their heads above water, plus pay for her sanitarium bills.

Yet Christmas did come and go like all other holidays at the sanitarium.

Her letter home after Christmastime was a struggle.

December 29, 1926

Dear Family,

I was thrilled with my Christmas presents. Thank you so much. I love the sweater you crocheted, Mom. It is perfect and I'm wearing it right now. Dad, thank you for the book, "Winnie-The-Pooh". I will cherish that and read it to my pupils when I get back to teaching. To all my siblings, I thank you so much for the fudge. I shared it with other patients here who did not receive any gifts. You don't know the joy it gave those poor souls. Thank you for your generosity and love.

I am sorry that I could not send all of you something besides my homemade card. I will make it up to you when I see you.

The doctor said I am getting better and maybe by early spring I can leave. Please keep up the prayers.

Take care and may God bless you.

Love,
Grace

Her days inched by and spring seemed to arrive as slowly as a snail, but at a steady pace. The birth of spring brought new hope once again along with more determination to the Sanator residents. Grace did everything she could to continue her climb to good health. Her walks on the grounds grew longer and helped her gain lung strength. In June, she received the news she had desperately wanted to hear. She would be released and emerged into the outside world again. She was all smiles as she wrote her parents.

June 20, 1927

Dear Mom and Dad,

Good news! I get to leave Sanator and come home. I can't tell you how wonderful that makes me feel. Overjoyed is not enough to say. I can't think of any other words except thanking God for His love and giving me a new life.

Would you, Dad, or one of my brothers be able to pick me up and bring me home? If you are not able to take time from work, don't worry. I will see if I can get a bus to Whitewood. Just let me know as soon as possible. I am so eager to see all of you and be out of this place.

I will await your reply.

Your loving and grateful daughter,
Grace

She struggled to hold back the tears as she wrote. How hard to wait for their answer! What day would they come, or would she have to take a bus?

Mom and Dad's reply did not come until the next week. Dad would pick her up that Friday and her mother would be with him. The rest of the family would be preparing a big homecoming celebration.

Grace packed her suitcase that Friday morning and sat in a straight chair on the porch by the entrance with her suitcase sitting on the floor next to her chair. She would greet her parents at the front entry. Grace was happy they would not have to see the long porch filled with patients in beds hidden from the entrance. She had trouble concentrating on the book she was reading, and kept looking up to the drive, hoping to see her parent's car coming up the hill. At noontime, the staff brought her a sandwich and fruit juice. She anxiously prayed that nothing happened and her family was safe. Nerves almost conquered her before she saw an auto coming up the hill and into the drive, dust enveloping the car. Could it be them? She shaded her squinting deep brown eyes with her hand, hoping to see more clearly. When it got closer, her hand flew to her mouth. Yes! It was her parents. She could no longer hold back the tears.

Before her dad could turn off the engine, her mother was already out the door, almost running to her daughter. Grace jumped off the porch steps and ran to her. Her mother's arms wrapped her in a loving embrace. Then Dad took his turn and his bear hug almost made her lose her breath, but she laughed as he released her. They looked at each other for a few minutes smiling. Then they got Grace's release papers and paid the final bill.

The ride home was full of news and updates. She heard stories about each sibling. Most were silly things, others about how the children had grown and how they had been such great help. Grace began to tire while she sat in the back seat nodding her head until she finally lowered herself down onto the seat and fell asleep. Mom reached around and covered her with a shawl.

A jolt woke her. "Where are we?" Grace asked as she finally rose and looked around. She thought just a few minutes had lapsed with a quick nap, but it must have been longer. They were turning onto the main street of a small town.

Dad smiled. "This is Whitewood. We are almost home now, just a little more toward that mountain and we're there. Whitewood got its name because of all the birch trees around here. Of course, you can see the hills full of spruce too. We have plenty to cut for lumber," and nodded to the trees.

Grace looked around and wondered if there was a school. She still wanted to teach. "Do they have a school, a mercantile store, a church and other things?" Whitewood looked similar to many small towns she had seen before. A couple of sandstone buildings dominated the smaller buildings that displayed worn siding.

"We'll show you around another time," her mother answered. "We really like these hills. The neighbors are wonderful and they accepted us right away. Of course, your dad is the social type anyway, always introducing himself. The people keep his lumber business busy." She shook her head as if in disbelief. "Sometimes I don't see much of your dad except at meal times. He goes to bed early, exhausted. I'm not complaining, but you work too hard, Al," she said as she looked at her husband.

"Pshaw. Work never killed anyone," he replied gruffly. He had a business to run. He was going to do his best to keep his word with customers. Hopefully money would keep coming in. He also tried to keep his one remaining worker even when there was little to do except cut firewood. He changed the subject. "Gracie, have you kept up on what Prohibition has done to the country? Those politicians better wake up soon because that law just isn't working."

She replied that she read all about it. "Here it is 1927, seven years after the law was enacted. I think politicians are beginning to see what that created . . . more crime and more gangsters. Al Capone always seems to be in the news and he has his illegal businesses going regardless of the law. The federal government can't get proof to put him away. Maybe the government is about ready to re-think the liquor law."

Her father agreed even though he might be classified as a law-breaker since he made his own wine. After all, berries and dandelions were plentiful and their wine could provide medicinal aid. At least that's what he told the family. There were plenty of people who made wine or beer and had stills hidden. People were going to have their liquor one way or another. He didn't make much wine, only his family knew about this so-called medicine in the cellar and it was kept out of sight. Every so often, he enjoyed a glass of his homemade brew while he sat in his chair to read the newspaper or listened to their squawky radio and enjoyed smoking his pipe.

As they passed some homes, her father pointed to each and gave a synopsis of the occupants. He described what the husband's work was and how he knew the family. A few times, someone was outside and waved. He returned with a sound wave back and a smile.

Finally, they approached a house sitting on the mountainside in a small open field. Dad honked the horn several times. Grace's siblings were standing at the door of the two-story building that resembled her old home. They were waving frantically as the car arrived in a cloud of dust

Grace was overwhelmed and her tears flowed freely. Her siblings had grown up. Nellie and Laura were young ladies now while Fred and Robert were adults. She saw that her baby brother, Charlie, was no longer a little tot, but a shy seven year old. Tears flowed as she hugged each before they led her inside. The aroma of roast beef and rhubarb pie, combined with seeing all the familiar furniture, brought joy and peace.

I'm home!

CHAPTER 10

1927 and 1928 - LIFE AT A STANDSTILL

Grace felt the joy of finally being home with family. She helped her mother as much as she could, yet tired easily and took a nap once or twice a day. Every morning she took a walk around the grounds beginning to discover more berry bushes, wild roses and she found sprouts of rhubarb along a trickle of runoff in a ridge.

She still wanted to teach, but jobs of any kind were getting very hard to find. "I'm willing to take a part-time job right now," she told her mother.

Mom patted her hand and told her, "Well, when the time comes, it will be what is supposed to be." She hoped her daughter might find someone soon.

The warm days of summer helped the garden to mature. Some vines produced pea pods, some displayed rich red tomatoes and some held green beans. Hidden by the soil, other plants did not reveal their richness until picked. In between scant rain showers, the women hauled buckets of water to deposit in the furrows between the plants.

Grace remembered the watermelons Dad always planted by their old home. As a child, she often rode with him when he took a wagonload of watermelons to town to give to families who didn't have as much as they did. He sold other melons to families in the better neighborhoods or in markets. The thought of biting into one of those delicious watermelons almost made her mouth water. Oh! How she missed that.

Many of the family's conversations during meals brought information, gossip, laughter or just banter. During one meal, the Black Hills news was the center of the discussion.

Dad asked Grace, "Have you kept up on the stories about this massive sculpture the politicians want?" He checked the newspaper to be sure he had the right name. "A historian, Doane Robinson, wanted something big to promote tourism in South Dakota. I don't know if we need tourists, but we sure need more money in this state."

Grace had read all the articles on this issue. "The politicians are pushing for it. Robinson wanted it to feature our western heroes like Lewis and Clark, Buffalo Bill Cody and even Red Cloud. That didn't go over for some reason with politicians. They decided a bigger draw for the public should have a national focus, not just a western emphasis."

Dad nodded and tapped his pipe. "Well they got their wish. Our Senator Peter Norbeck helped to get it approved for federal funding and there's to be four presidents in this sculpture." He stopped to puff on his pipe, leaned back and looked out to the field by the house.

"When they had a sculptor come named, . . .what was his name? Oh yes, Gutzon Borglum, chose the site known by the Lakota Sioux as *Six Grandfathers*. The government renamed it after a prominent New York lawyer, Charles E. Rushmore. I wonder how that lawyer was lucky enough to get the mountain and all those sculptures named after him." He paused and shuffled the paper to read more. "Why the name *Rushmore*? I wouldn't be surprised if money didn't pass between hands for that." Dad wasn't fond of lawyers or politicians, thinking too many were arrogant and didn't always have the best morals. Oh, he'd admit that some were honest, and he gave them credit while disliking the crooked ones.

Grace smiled. "The project was approved by Congress two years ago and the carving began this year. It will take years. Just think of the enormous size. I read that just the face of Washington will be sixty feet high! Can you imagine that?"

Mom nodded, "If this gets done, we have to go see it. Can you imagine a mountain carved with the images of Presidents George Washington, Thomas Jefferson, Theodore Roosevelt and Abraham Lincoln?" They all nodded and finished their meal wondering what the mountain would look like.

Too soon, fall displayed the glorious hues of the season. It was always the time for canning the produce from their garden, nearby bushes and apple trees. It meant long days over the stove sterilizing jars, peeling, slicing, cooking or blanching. Many days Mom and Grace's arms swept over their foreheads catching drops of perspiration before they could land in the mixture. They sterilized jars, then filled each with the produce and put them in the boiling water to be cooked. Paraffin covered the jams and jellies before they screwed on the lids.

Grace and her mother also saved the seeds from the garden plants. They'd be ready for next year and able to plant without buying seeds.

Dad used five-gallon stoneware crocks to make his wine with chokecherries, wild raspberries, or dandelion blossoms. Grace washed the previously used bottles readying them for Dad. Some old corks had to be soaked to get their buoyancy and original shape back, or Dad bought new corks when needed. For several weeks, the large crocks, covered with cheesecloth, rested on the long timeworn wood porch table while the brewing worked its magic. The aroma of fruit and yeast wafted into the kitchen. Dad tested the wine often. On a warm sunny day, he lifted the cloth from the crock and spooned out a sip. "They're ready," he said one day. "Where'd I put the corks?"

Grace pulled them out and he began to strain the nectar into the bottles. A cork was set in place and each bottle set on the machine. Then Dad used his strength to push down on the lever and seal the cork. After all the bottles sat filled, a small amount still remained in the crock.

"Well that supply looks pretty good," Grace said with a smile.

"You ready for a sip?" he asked without waiting and tipped the crock to dip out enough for two glasses. He took a taste and smacked his lips. "I may have to have a glass of that tonight while I read."

Grace wasn't a drinker, but this wine was enticing. "You better hide those bottles before the authorities come checking, Dad."

"Aw. There aren't any law officers around here who would arrest someone for making their own. I don't think this Prohibition can continue much longer anyway. No one around here cares."

"We'll see," she said with a grin.

By October, most of the canning was finished and the cellar was full of color. Shelf after shelf was bulging with jars of various colors. Large burlap sacks and barrels filled with potatoes, onions and pinto beans sat on the dirt floor. Of course, the bottles of wine sat hidden in the back of the shelves.

Two industries seemed to keep making money while the rest of the country seemed to be in a downfall. Automobile production kept up a steady pace while the motion picture industry became innovative in finding new ways to entertain the public. People wanted to dream of better times, laugh and feel good for just a while before entering the bleak society of joblessness again.

Grace checked the latest newspaper and read that the entertainment industry came out with a part-talking motion picture, which was becoming a marketing success. She remembered that it wasn't that long ago that people had begun to enjoy the new silent picture shows. Now in October 1927, *The Jazz Singer* was a hit and the "talkies" gained in popularity. People wanted more of them to replace the silent movies. Technology improved all the time and they recorded sound on a disc called a Vitaphone. The movie and radio investors had the money to keep the industry going strong even with the poor economy. Grace wondered if she would ever see a "talkie" since she didn't have any money even if Whitewood did get one. If she hadn't contracted tuberculosis, Hobart or another gentleman might have taken her in his new auto to a picture show. She remembered when she sat on a bench in the park, with his arm round her and they watched the silent movies. Would she ever have that kind of life again?

The economy worried Grace as well as the whole family. She asked her father, "Are we going to have another recession or depression?"

Slowly he answered, "I think we're in for a big one, from what I read in the paper. We should be fine, but we'll have to cut back on our expenses." He tried not to worry the rest of the family, but he told Grace, "The lumber business is slowing and I'm about to lay off a boy who has worked for me since we moved here. God! I hate to lay him off."

"I'm sorry, Dad. He'll be alright because he's young and single. He doesn't have to worry about a family like you. You do what you have to do."

Grace's first Christmas since leaving the sanitarium arrived with a thin blanket of snow. On Christmas Eve, the family opened presents, mostly homemade. Gifts meant more when homemade now, such as shirts for the men and boys, aprons or dresses for the women or girls. Early on Christmas Day morning, they squeezed into their automobile and drove on the frozen dirt road to Sturgis for Mass at Saint Martin's Church. Very little snow had accumulated on the road and their full auto made its way down the hill, bouncing in and out of the frozen tire ruts. Parents delivered the children to the church early so they could practice their procession down the aisle singing Christmas carols. Mass was long, as usual on Christmas, while everyone was eager to go back home to their special meal. Many parishioners included prayers that their New Year would be prosperous.

The Lee family returned home hungry and grabbed the cinnamon rolls kept warm above the oven. A mouth-watering aroma of wild turkey roasting in the oven greeted them and stomachs growled. Before the bird went into the oven before dawn, Mom stuffed it with her own recipe. Potatoes soon were ready for mashing, while pre-baked dinner rolls sat with a towel over them to keep them warm. Grace set a bowl of cranberry sauce on the table along with a dish of churned butter. Nellie and Laura set the table around the pinecone, berries and a spruce branch centerpiece they'd made on Christmas Eve.

When the roasted turkey sat on the kitchen counter, Grace yelled, "Dad, we need you to carve the turkey now." Mom hoisted it to a platter to start making the gravy in the roaster. Dad was a good shot and dropped the wild turkey with one shot the other day.

Dad was sitting in front of the fireplace with his head tilted back and his mouth open, snoring. When he heard his name, he jerked his head, waking up. Only a few years ago he had a full head of brown hair. Now worry along with hard physical work had changed his pate to a mixture of white and grey.

Grace could almost hear Dad's mind saying, *I've got to teach one of the boys how to cut the damn meat so I can take a longer nap.*

When he came into the kitchen, he told her that six out of his eight children were home to celebrate, yet he missed his two daughters, Jeannette and Helen.

Following the grace before the meal, Dad took each plate to place turkey slices on it. Bowls of cranberry sauce, potatoes, stuffing, gravy and vegetables made it around the table. In between bites, they talked, joked, teased and laughed.

During the meal Mom asked, "Al, did you take milk, butter and a ham or chicken to the Bakers and to Widow Shultz?"

"I wouldn't forget," he replied. "Bakers got a big ham and Widow Schultz got the other wild turkey we killed and both got the jars of jellies along with potatoes." He always took what he could to help those two families. The Bakers were a family of eight and Mr. Baker could only find work occasionally. Mrs. Baker took in laundry when she could find someone able to pay her, or traded for meat or other edibles. Widow Shultz had three children under the age of twelve. Her husband died of pneumonia three years earlier. "I gave the children some of the cookies and candy you ladies made. The little ones thought I was Santa Claus. Maybe they didn't notice that I didn't have a beard," he laughed.

"Good," Mom said.

After everyone finished eating and patted their stomachs, they raised their arms to stretch and then yawned. Grace, Nellie and Laura cleared the table, washed and dried the dishes and pans. Mom decided to sit by the fire and crochet. After only a few stiches, her hook dropped to her lap and her greying head fell back. She was sound asleep.

Later on, everyone enjoyed apple pie with a glass of milk for dessert. With chickens and a milk cow, they always had plenty of eggs and milk. Cream rose to the top of the milk jar and enhanced the oatmeal breakfasts. Women also churned cream into thick butter. Their old butter churn made strong muscles in the arms of the churners. Mom churned longer and faster than her daughters did due to years of experience and muscle use.

The Christmas season ended and the days passed while Grace continued to get stronger. Then the New Year arrived with only a small celebration at home with chokecherry wine from the root cellar. An icy storm blew in and they toasted the snow and cold while enjoying the warmth of the fireplace. They all wondered what 1929 would bring.

After the continuing months of blustery, icy days, spring finally began to sneak in. The new season arrived with infant blossoms, rocked by gentle warm breezes.

With the warm spring days and improved health, Grace decided to go with her brothers to a dance one Saturday night. Her feet itched to step to the rhythm. Besides, just maybe she'd find someone interesting to talk to. She didn't tell anyone that she was lonely, but she'd love to have someone pay attention to her. When she taught, there were men who caught her fancy and vise-versa. Several courted her before Hobart came into her life. She wondered what he was doing now and if he had married. At 28 years old, Grace knew she could be considered a spinster. Even with all her family around her, she still felt lonely.

People piled into the dance hall in good spirits. The floor filled with dancers all stepping to the music played by a fiddler, guitarist and pianist. Laughter helped everyone forget their troubles and young girls searched for their dream beaus. Grace stayed in the background and helped pour lemonade. She didn't see any man who really interested her. They were too old, too young or appeared to be too bold. Even though she didn't find one of interest, she didn't stop swaying back and forth with the music.

"May I have this dance, ma'am?" asked one friend. Tom held out his calloused hand that gave silent testimony to his hard farm labor. He was married, but moved from one lonely woman to another, dancing with each. His wife didn't mind his dancing with various partners since she wasn't that fond of dancing and he loved it. He picked many widows or those whose husbands didn't dance.

Grace raised her arm to reach his shoulder, looked up to his clean-shaven, sun and wind-burned face and smiled. "Thank you, Tom. After this, though, you better dance with your wife again," she laughed. She was grateful for friends.

Tom was the type of man she'd like to meet. He was a hard worker, honest, religious, faithful to his wife, full of humor and generosity. She thought it was too bad he didn't have a brother!

The evening continued to pass with Grace dancing very little and not finding anyone of interest. Maybe next time. The musicians played the last song while the couples swayed around the floor holding tight to their partners. She stood back and helped clear the table of food along with some widows and a couple of spinsters. Then everybody began to walk to their car, tired, but happy to have had some fun, a break from the dismal times.

Grace looked out the car window and dreamed of that illusive someone she couldn't seem to find.

Will I ever find that someone just for myself, or am I doomed to never finding love?

CHAPTER 11

1929 – HOPE COMING

The hills produced many brilliant colors in the fall, yet not as bright as usual. Jack bagged another deer in October. Although not as large as the one he shot the previous year, this one would give the Ramser family and him plenty of meat. Mildred fixed various dishes with the deer meat, and often Jack's favorite was her roast with special spices.

Both men went turkey hunting for Thanksgiving and returned home with two large birds. Mildred told them that she was taking one to a charitable society that served turkey dinners to the poor—or to the men working the mines who had no family. "I'll decide later. We can eat only one of those fat birds."

By Christmas, the town sat covered in snow while the streets contained muddy ruts and brown puddles where auto exhaust melted the snow quickly. Jack drove the street bouncing with each rut or puddle and then swerving to miss another.

"We need the city to fix the streets," he spouted loudly as Mildred bounced along on the seat beside him. They were going to Deadwood to buy gifts for the three children. They had two teenage sons and a little girl about ten years old. Jack didn't mind shopping for the gifts because he had become close to them and knew what they wanted.

Bill worked the mine that Saturday because there was a problem with one of the tunnels. He didn't give Mildred details, but Jack knew she worried. The shopping would be a good distraction.

He laughed and said, "Your kids were pretty upset since you wouldn't let them come."

"Oh yes," she laughed as well. "I didn't want to tell them it was to buy gifts for them, but they probably suspect."

After purchasing the gifts, they stopped for lunch at a café attached to a motel. A woman, probably in her mid-thirties, brought coffee and took their orders. She was chatty and learned their reason for the packages sitting on a chair. She was a nice looking woman with a pleasant, friendly smile and a nice hourglass shape.

When the waitress left for the kitchen, Mildred whispered, "Jack she looks like a good catch. You should engage in a conversation with her. I'll quit talking, you take over."

The waitress refilled the coffee cups. While being poured, Mildred kicked Jack under the table and then gave him a nod when he gave her a rolling-eye expression. She decided to begin by asking, "What is your name? I'm sure it is Irish, right? I love your accent."

The woman looked up and smiled again. "Yes, I'm Irish and my name is Maggie." She smiled and almost added that they had the accent, not her.

"What a pretty name. Isn't it, Jack?"

Once again she kicked him under the table as he gave her a stern look this time. "It is a nice name. Could you bring some more cream for the coffee please?"

Off Maggie went and Jack said, "Knock it off. You're embarrassing me."

Cream arrived and the meal followed in a minute. She served them as if they were special guests.

Mildred was not about to give up. "So you're Irish. Jack, here, is of Scottish descent. I imagine you two could have a lot to talk about. Don't you, Jack?" She gave him a big smile and her eyes told him that he better begin a conversation.

He answered, "Well, I was born in this country and I don't know much about Scotland or Ireland." He paused to think what he should say next and just began talking. "Were you born in Ireland?" He looked up into her sparkling green eyes and held the gaze for longer than he planned. He really wanted to ask if she was married, but he couldn't just outright ask that kind of question.

"No, I wasn't either. I was born in New York City and worked as a maid there. My marriage was arranged and I had no say-so. When

I got married, we moved here and my husband is an automobile mechanic." She dropped her hands to her side and almost bowed before she added, "I will remain married." She spun around and walked to the kitchen.

"Damn," Jack said under his breath. He'd thought maybe he could get interested in her. Her age was close to his, he was sure. "Damn," he said again. His meal was ruined.

"I'm sorry, Jack." Mildred wanted him to find someone and she had been out of line. "I promise I won't do that again."

He nodded and said it was okay. "I should know better. Any woman her age and looking as good as she does, has to be married."

"Well, maybe someday you'll find one who isn't married, but would like to be. She will be just what you are looking for. Trust me, you'll find her."

That ended matchmaking and the days turned into months. Soon 1929 rolled in with a looming disaster. Farmers plowed up more native grass fields in hopes of planting more wheat and corn. Then, over time, too much surplus of wheat and corn caused a drop in demand and price for those crops. Now farmers also unwillingly greeted drought along with all the other troubles. Without more crops purchased and without rain or snow, the farmers were doomed.

Jack tried to find work on a ranch without success. He saw that the country was running into trouble. No rain and too many wheat and corn crops seemed to be leading to disaster. Somehow, this reminded him of previous rough times in the early 1900s. He remembered back then even though he'd been young at the time. Farmers and ranchers always struggled. Yet he knew this would bring some to their knees. He felt it.

Working in the mine continued and Jack wasn't enjoying life. The only thing saving him from giving up was living with Bill and Mildred and watching their children. They struggled with school assignments, the boys becoming young adults full of energy and the girl starting to change while becoming more moody. He enjoyed watching their excitement over a new friend, or table games, or outdoor ball games. Often he played games with them.

Mildred and Cora Lehmannn visited back and forth while the men worked. In the summer, the families and Jack often got together for a meal or a picnic.

When he didn't have any luck in finding a ranch job, Jack stopped joining them. He went to the saloon for a beer and listened to other men talk. Maybe he'd hear about a job on a ranch coming up. The only thing he heard was all the talk about their personal troubles or about the country's.

He was stuck working in the mine. There weren't any other jobs to be had, or that he could do, and he couldn't just quit. Next year he would widen his search for a ranch job. Even though he felt trapped in the mine, it wasn't as bad as it had been with Drake. He at least had his freedom when he was above ground.

Fall quickly became the death of hope for the whole country. When the stock prices dropped after the decline in wheat and corn prices, more followed. Then September 4 brought the 1929 stock market crash.

The effect of the stock market crash hit rich and poor alike. All crop prices dropped more while the drought increased. Dust storms hit the Midwest as well. Banks failed and some people learned that a banker either disappeared with their money or all money was gone—nothing to give back to depositors.

Farmers and ranchers couldn't pay their bank loans and certainly couldn't get new loans to plant crops. They hung on as best they could while their crops dried up. No rain came to allow crops to grow or to harvest and give the people capital to continue. Soon the wind grew stronger and stronger. Then the dreaded dust storms piled higher and blacker as they blotted out the sky. Darkness rolled over the country as if it were the black of night. Dirt and dust covered everything in its path and seeped into homes. Even the cupboards couldn't protect whatever was in them. Farmers had plowed up so much land that all native grass was gone and there was nothing to hold the top soil. Wind took the soil on wild rides and left barren fields that could no longer produce even a blade of grass.

"When are things going to change?" Jack asked a fellow miner.

Shaking his head, the other man could only speculate. "I doubt it ends until we get lots of rain and it continues . . . or if the government steps in and can change the economy somehow."

The arrival of 1930 brought little hope for a better year. "Maybe with the elections coming up we can get a change," Bill said one evening.

Jack rolled his cigarette, lit it and thought for a moment. "I sure hope so. I've got to study what the candidates are saying they'll do. Otherwise, it's just gossip. Wish we could see a candidate talk and get a better idea."

Bill could only nod and agree. "I'm thankful I have a job at the mine. It seems to be the only business not struggling around here. I think I'll be okay."

"Guess I should be thankful too." Jack flipped the cigarette ashes on the ground. "I hate going underground, but at least I got some money coming in. Look at all the poor folk not able to feed their families already. The hell they have to go through!"

That ended their conversation and another day below ground was looming. Jack wasn't excited, but wasn't going to complain. He still dreamed of his own home and family even though he was close to 41 years old.

The year passed slowly. Finally, the Ramsers, Lehmanns and Jack toasted 1931 arriving. The men found a place to supply them with whiskey and weren't worried about being caught as long as they only drank in their homes. This year they celebrated at the Lehmannn's home.

Everyone was tired of driving through the ruts or slush. Besides, the cost of fuel was rising as well as the cost of food. They were all glad they still had some coins in their pocket. Jack always gave nice gifts at Christmastime. He gave to the Ramsers, the Lehmanns and their children. His enjoyment was in deciding what to give each child and maybe even trying the gift out first. Then on New Year's Eve, he brought home store-bought sodas for the children and a new game called Monopoly. Everyone had a laughter-filled day playing that game.

"Finally the snow is melting and disappearing," Jack said to himself one day as he drove through town. He was going to look one more time for a ranching job. This time he headed to the Frawley Ranch, a big organization that didn't seem to be suffering too much from the god-awful depression.

When he arrived, the boss was in a stew. He just fired a man who couldn't seem to do anything right. By the time he was done talking to Jack, he'd calmed down and said maybe there was hope after all since Jack seemed to know what he was doing. He hired Jack right then.

Jack drove back to Lead and told Bill and Mildred that he was moving out. They were disappointed to lose him, but said they felt it might have been coming. He had become like a brother to them and an uncle to the children. Then they smiled because it was what Jack had been wanting for a long time.

"Well, man. Keep us informed, especially if you find a good woman." Bill could never resist the chance to tease. "Mildred can clue her in on your shenanigans." He laughed heartily.

Jack also laughed. "Well, if I ever do find someone, you sure aren't going to get a chance to tell her about my past."

When he packed his belongings and walked out of the Ramser home for the last time as their tenant, he felt a little sad. When he opened his car door, he looked up at the bright blue sky, then to the hills blossoming into color and smiled. He started the car, gave a wave and chugged down the hill.

He was eager to be going above ground again. He felt good and sure it would be a good life now. Wouldn't it?

Damn!

CHAPTER 12

1929-30– COLLAPSE

Grace's days passed normally with the usual routine. Housework, washing, ironing, cooking, watering and weeding the garden, feeding the chickens or doing any other work that came along had to be done. Routine brought boredom, not relieved by the newspaper or radio programs.

On a lazy sunny day, Dad dropped the newspaper on his lap and bellowed, "Listen to this, Gracie. On February fourteenth the gangster, Al Capone, and his army of men allegedly killed seven rival gangsters. The news called it the 'St. Valentine's Day Massacre.' The government better do something pretty soon or Al Capone is going to rule the whole country."

"He'll get his comeuppance one of these days," Grace replied. She knew the government was trying to get Capone any way they could to prove guilt and put him in prison. "The government is working on it. He'll get caught someday."

Then in August, the radio premiered a comedy called *Amos and Andy*. The family listened each week, laughing throughout the broadcast as the radio squawked and crackled. It sat on the side table with the volume turned high. The program became a favorite in many homes and the talk in town. *Amos and Andy* provided a needed diversion with laughter during the rough times everyone was experiencing.

One evening while sitting in his chair and listening to the radio, Dad yelled to the kitchen, "News is broadcasting that the Dow Jones Average peaked with a record high of 381.17 on September third and they're hoping it will continue to grow for the rest of 1929." Dad didn't usually pay too much attention to the stock market, but this was big news.

A month passed with no rise in the stock market and on Tuesday, September 4, radio stations sadly broadcast the *Wall Street Crash*. The continual coverage revealed that the stock market collapse wiped out more than thirty billion dollars from the New York Stock Exchange.

Radio announcers described the panic that hit with a fierce blow throughout the country. The broadcasters' cracking voices revealed their shock as they reported this "Black Tuesday" disaster. Investor after investor began to tumble. News of men committing suicide became commonplace.

Dad shook his head, and Grace wondered if he was thinking how this disaster was going to affect his business.

He moaned, "There are runs on banks and they're closing at an alarming rate. God Almighty! Here we go again. I'll bet my shirt that we're going into a deep depression. And this time we have the damned drought along with it."

Grace didn't look at Mom. She knew worry lines were growing. Mom and Dad had been through a depression before and survived; they would have to do it again. She prayed that her parents would survive one more time even though it would be harder this time since they were older than before.

News continued daily regarding this disaster. "My God," Dad mumbled again, "Look at these pictures in the paper. People are jumping off skyscrapers to their death. Look at these pictures. God Almighty, what is going to happen to the country?"

Grace and Mom shook their heads in horror as their eyes scanned the pictures in the paper. "Lord, help them and help us," both replied in unison.

Dad went on, "We're hitting bottom." His business was slowing and he prayed his family wouldn't end up in disaster. He'd never commit suicide, but maybe he'd want to, if things got bad enough for his family. He'd fight to keep them safe, have shelter and food.

Grace knew her father was struggling to keep his few final workers on, pay the bills, while drumming up business. She saw furrows on his brow and around his mouth increased as his mind worked on ways to survive. At least he didn't have a mortgage on his property or their home, but construction had drastically fallen 80% and definitely less lumber was now needed.

Not many celebrated when 1930 rolled in. Unemployment had grown to 3.2 million people nationwide. Those out of work were desperate and wandered anywhere and everywhere to find work. How many would survive? Grace prayed for them, especially the families with children.

She told Mom on a bitter cold day, "We don't have to buy bread; at least as long as we can get flour. The price for a loaf is eight cents now while flour is three cents a pound. We'll pay for the flour and continue to make more bread loaves than we can buy for that amount. We'll stretch the best we can." She was determined to do her part on conserving with baking rather than buying. "I'm glad we have our own cow since milk has gone to fourteen cents a quart and the way our family drinks milk, we would go broke."

Mom laughed and agreed. "We can sell butter too. It is going for twenty-five cents a pound; we have extra that we can still sell cheaper. Dad will make sure some goes to Widow Schultz and maybe a couple more."

Grace nodded. "There won't be too much left, but we can try to sell it."

Supply and demand was out of balance. Grace told Mom after reading the newspaper, "Drought is starting in the Great Plain states; no rain, along with no seed money, means unplanted fields. This drought just tops off the misery for farmers with all the banks that closed. The fields they plowed are bare—just the topsoil blowing with the wind." She stopped to refresh her memory. "Then the grasshopper invasion last year left no vegetation, and only dead stalks stood on the South Dakota plains and other mid-west states. So much misery!"

Mom just nodded and went on with her baking. Her jaw was set tight. Would they suffer as well? "We don't know God's plan and we will have to have faith and just live through this."

Dad came in for lunch. Before eating, he listened to the radio to see if there was any news on politics. When he came to the kitchen table, he said, "Well, the Republicans have regained the state legislature. Now with that farmer, Warren E. Green, from Hamilton County elected as our new governor, I wonder if he can do any good for South Dakota."

"Dad, he's going to reduce the educational institution and salaries by 10% below the last budget. That is going to hurt education even more. Government is forgetting that education is what will make our future. What's going to happen to these children when they grow up and don't know how to solve problems and better themselves?"

"True, Grace. I guess we just have to wait and see what happens. Maybe in tough times the youth will learn better, understand life and know how to survive."

Grace nodded. She knew the children were going to suffer without teachers or supplies. It seemed that Congress always wanted to make cuts in education. They needed to remember that the children were the future of the country. If they allowed ignorance to prevail, the country would suffer because the new future would be a disaster.

Why do they not see that the children of today are the country's future?

CHAPTER 13

1931 - MISPLACED

New Year's Day 1931 arrived with people's morale as low as the economy's. Many people could not afford to celebrate the arrival of a new year. Instead, they were searching for food or work and hanging onto what little hope they still harbored. Almost five million people were now out of work and the number kept growing every day. Countries throughout the world were seeing the same decline and devastation. It was not just the United States suffering; it was a worldwide Great Depression. The Midwest states in this country also suffered with the god-awful dust storms while drought reached every state from Canada to Texas.

On a bitter cold day in the beginning months of this gloomy year, Grace wondered who was driving up to the house in an overloaded dilapidated automobile.

"Good God! What are they doing here?" The adult faces peering out of the auto windows looked as dry as shriveled up apples. Grey bags hung below exhausted eyes sitting on sunken cheeks.

Her mother looked out, "Dad's walking to the auto. He'll take care of it." She saw they were a desperate family like so many they read about in newspapers or heard about on the radio. Immediately going to the kitchen, she began pulling out pots and skillets.

"Grace, we have to fix those poor people a meal. I'm going to run out back and catch a couple chickens." Mom was quick in seizing and chopping off the head before a chicken realized there was danger. She was also adept at plucking and scalding. Back inside, she quickly held two headless stripped chickens by their legs, ready to use her butcher knife in cutting the pieces.

Grace watched as Dad greeted the group. After a short discussion, he waved for them to follow him. Walking into the kitchen, he told the visitors, "Come sit by the fireplace while my wife and daughters fix you something. This is my wife, Isabella and these are my daughters, Grace and Laura." He motioned to one, then the other. Holding his wife's eyes for a second longer, he silently communicated the need to help the poor souls.

"Nice to meet you," the oldest man replied. "I'm Jeff Warren and this is my wife, Carrie, my son, Junior, and his wife, Beth." He quickly rattled off the names of the five children, nodding to each as he said their name. The youngest was in Beth's arms hanging tightly to her neck.

Grace immediately smiled. "Please, do come in. I have a big pot of coffee on the stove about ready. In a minute I'll bring you a cup." She bent over to eyelevel with one of the younger ones. "For you children, how would you like some hot chocolate?"

Big smiles appeared and they all nodded and re-nodded their approval. She had saved to buy cocoa to bake a cake, but this was for a much better cause. "We're fixing dinner and would be pleased to have you join us." There was no refusal.

"May we help?" Carrie and Beth said at the same time.

"Oh no, you enjoy the fireplace and coffee. I think you could use a rest," Grace replied with a smile. She rushed around, served the drinks while her mother began cutting up chicken, then dunking each piece in her seasoned flour. The hot grease sizzled in the cast iron skillet as the pieces slid in, and the tantalizing aroma drifted through the home heralding a delicious meal to come. Laura peeled potatoes, quartered each and dropped them into a large pot of boiling water. The smell of the food caused a few of the visitors to have loud rumbling in their stomachs. Grace or Laura refilled coffee cups when needed while passing around the cream and sugar.

All of a sudden, a little tot was pulling on Grace's skirt. She looked down. He held out his empty cup and the sweetest big brown eyes she had ever seen were pleading with her for more. Smiling, she took his cup and said, "I'll make some more right away. Give me a few minutes while you sit at the table and draw me a picture." She quickly found a paper and pencil.

Carrie immediately rushed in stating, "Oh, I'm so sorry. Little Wally got away from me. You don't have to do that."

"Oh, it's no problem," Grace answered. "He'll be fine just sitting there drawing. You go on back and don't worry."

"I can help", she replied.

"Thank you, but we're fine. Anymore women in this kitchen would create havoc." Grace laughed.

Carrie nodded with a smile and retreated just as Charlie suddenly bounded up the porch steps and into the kitchen.

"Who's here? What's going on?" The ten year old tried to wipe his dirty hands on his pants and immediately heard the familiar reminder to wash his hands and face. After draining the kitchen sink to get rid of Charlie's muddy water, Grace introduced him to the group. Charlie took the two older children to a corner and they played card games while the adults visited.

It was a good thing that they had an extra-long kitchen table that could accommodate everyone. Dad said the blessing and then the bowls or platters of food passed from one to the next. The chicken, along with a huge bowl of mashed potatoes, a bowl of gravy and home-canned green beans soon silenced the growling stomachs. Adults took only small portions to make sure the children had plenty. The children grabbed the homemade bread slices as soon as the plate arrived at the table. In an instant there were only crumbs left on the plate. Mom ran to the kitchen and sliced another loaf. The family left only the bare chicken bones on their plates, giving huge smiles with thanks.

Grace smiled when watching one little boy lick his plate so he wouldn't miss some unseen morsel. Yet, she was sad thinking all they must have been going through. She wondered how many more families were like that in the country. How many even got the chance her family gave to these people? She almost whispered aloud for God to help them all! She prayed that her family never would have to go through anything like this.

The Lee family learned the group included another son's two children. That son died when a tractor overturned on him. Carrie wiped tears away quickly as grief engulfed her and when her husband said the son's wife disappeared, leaving the children with them. Silence filled the air for a minute.

Then Jeff cleared his throat and continued, "We owned a nice-sized farm, but the bank took all our money when it closed and the banker left town before we knew what happened. We were forced off our land by foreclosure and became drifters traveling wherever we could find work." Farming was out of the question because of more foreclosures and the lack of rain.

Jeff stopped for a second to clear the lump in his throat. "We worked at various jobs here and there, taking whatever we could get. We slept wherever we could. Usually the children slept in the car and we adults slept underneath on the ground. Occasionally we found a vacant house to use for the night." He hung his head in despair and shame.

His wrinkled hands displayed calluses and he moved slowly due to swollen joints from arthritis. His sunken shoulders were those of a drained and suffering man. Carrie wasn't in any better shape. Junior looked only a few years younger than his father did. His broomstick-thin wife, Beth, stood tall in pride and determination, yet thin as a pencil. She whispered to Grace that evening, "We adults don't always eat. We make thin soup when we can find a potato or a vegetable. The children get most of it. Sometimes we catch a rabbit or a fish."

Grace could see how the well-worn patched flower-patterned dress hung loosely over Carrie's skeleton. The children held onto the love and trust in their parents and grandparents who did their best to provide for the little ones. Yet, love did not nourish their bodies.

Dad listened to the men tell their story. Then he dropped his head in disbelief, shaking it back and forth, "My God! You've been on the move all winter?"

"Yes sir," the son answered. His eyes glistened as he sniffled before getting control with a deep gulp. "We tried to get work in Whitewood, but couldn't find any. Someone told us to see if you had any work."

"Lord, God Almighty. We'll come up with something. We'll work it out," he said as he nodded for reassurance not only to the man, but also to himself. He had no idea how he could support that many extra people, yet he couldn't turn them away.

Maybe the men could kill rabbits or some wild fowl to help with the food, or maybe fish from the creek. Poaching was commonplace with many during these tough times. The women also knew how to

70

stretch the meals with many soups and noodles. The root cellar still held enough produce—for how long, though, he didn't know.

Grace could see that her mom already knew they'd need to arrange some kind of sleeping quarters. Then they both remembered the little clapboard cabin, used by a previous worker and his family. It was empty, but would be a workable accommodation.

Dad must have been thinking the same thing. He announced, "We have a cabin that you folks can use for now. It's not much, but it'll work. We do have a spare bedroom upstairs if you, Will and Carrie, would like to stay in that." He glanced at his wife, saw her smile and nod.

Actually, the bedroom was Grace's and Nellie's, but since Nellie was away at nursing school, the Warrens certainly could use it. Grace would move into Laura's bedroom with her.

"God bless you, sir!" the adults exclaimed in unison. A new sparkle in their eyes seemed to acknowledge that their hopes and prayers seemed answered. "We'll do whatever needs to be done. I don't know how we'll ever be able to pay you back, Mr. Lee."

"You don't have to pay me back. When your life changes for the better and you see someone who needs help, just pass along what you can to them. That's your payback to us."

They nodded and Jeff added, "You bet we will. I think we'll call it the Lee passing." That brought a smile to everyone's face.

Grace and Mom bustled around to find bedding, linen and other things needed. The other women began to clean and arrange the cabin, telling each child the bed assigned to them—two and three to a bed. Their bedrolls could rest and be aired out while using the bedding provided by the Lee family.

The family stayed busy. Will and Junior helped Dad with cutting lumber. They cleaned the sawmill tools as if each had been their own. Extra hands gave Dad a chance to relax a little and not work as hard. Jeff was a good shot and brought many rabbits for meals. Plenty of milk helped even though there was no leftover cream to make butter to sell.

Soon, it was time for them to move on.

"We will always remember your kindness," the adults said as they gave notice they were leaving. Jeff obtained a job with the dairy farmer up by Crook City. He'd be able to rent a small home for his family and smiled with pride when he told the Lee family. Carrie and

Beth cleaned the cabin to a spotless condition, washed the bedding and had the cabin ready for anyone else needing shelter. As they drove away, the children pressed their noses to the car windows and waved.

Mom told Grace, "May God help them. I must say we sure have done a lot lately. I think I'll just sit and do nothing today. I can catch up tomorrow."

Grace nodded. "Good. You rest. I think I'll take a break to write Jeannette and Helen. I sure miss my sisters. Maybe someday they can come here to visit." She worried about her family.

She knew her father didn't speak of his business and always said, "That's not for a woman to worry about." Nevertheless, he struggled to keep up the lumber sales. Grace noticed his accounting books open on his desk one day while dusting. Her natural curiosity took hold, so she looked the numbers over. Her eyes widened and her shoulders drooped when she saw the figures and worried if he would not be able to keep his business going. What would happen to them? Would her family be like the Warrens whom they helped? Grace didn't tell anyone else and prayed harder that maybe they could survive. She resolved to scrimp more where she could. Maybe a little less sugar in the cooking or baking, or less coffee beans in the grinder would help. Dad's good horse-trading ability often helped him in buying gasoline for the vehicles, machinery, kerosene for the lamps, and any medical expenses for his family.

The fall of 1931 brought the usual canning process. Grace and her mother had expanded their garden and they picked berries by the basketfuls from the bushes nearby or by the stream. They dried apples, sliced them thin, placed them on a board and then put a screen over the top. When dried out, the slices were stored. They did the same with strawberries and also made applesauce and apple butter. Canned carrots helped as a substitute for sugar in some recipes because carrots are sweet. The main things they had to buy were flour, salt, sugar and beans. Mom kept a jar with leftover change, which usually totaled enough to buy a 50 lb. bag every so often, especially if she could trade something for the balance due, if there wasn't enough money in her jar. Sometimes there was no sugar left and little flour before she could afford replacement. Flour was always needed for bread making.

Grace's family did not buy soap even though she would have loved to use a lavender scented store-bought bar on her face. The women used a large round metal tub to make their own soap with lard, water and lye. The tub sat on the porch in warm weather and they hoped a breeze would keep the fumes to a low risk. The two women took turns stirring the mixture for about an hour until it became thick like pudding. Then they could scoop it into molds until hardened. They used their soap to wash clothes, dishes, and themselves—no need to buy soap when they could make their own and they always had plenty of lard.

Grace came in one day saying, "Dad and the boys killed a hog and are going to gut it and hang it now. That will give us plenty of bacon, ham and pork. We'll also have plenty of meat for this winter. Thank God our sow gave birth this year to a good batch of babies." She didn't add that her father gave a couple of babies to the families down the hill.

"I hope we have enough feed for the pigs as they grow," Mom sighed. "We can make pickled pigs feet tomorrow: I'll use the ears and tail for a pot of beans or in a stew. We'll have to clean the intestines to make sausage from the trimmings." She stopped to rub her back, thinking of the all the work to be done. "I'm glad we can hook a hose to the faucet on the pump and clean them out. Let hope that cleans them well, or we'll have to turn the intestines inside out and scrape them. That's a chore." Many times, she'd done this and was quick at cleaning the intestines then stuffing them, but not pleased in doing it.

Grace nodded. "Maybe someday we can buy a machine that does that. Dad will smoke some ham hocks in the smokehouse. He knows how to get a good smoke with a cool fire. We don't want the meat to be cooked, just smoked."

Her mother smiled. "We just finished canning the chickens. This spring we had plenty of chicks too, so we still have the hens to keep us going. I think I'll give a couple of the chicks to Widow Schultz. That poor woman really struggles."

Grace smiled. Her mother and father certainly were good about helping others. She, herself, offered to tutor, without pay, a couple of young children. She wished she could have gotten a teaching job in town. Her thoughts drifted back to her old school. How she missed teaching. She also remembered all the dances and fun she had with friends and boyfriends while she was teaching.

Oh how she would like to have her own family and her own home! Why did Hobart not wait for her? The Great Depression put her into a deep depression as well.

Why couldn't my life have been like I dreamed—teaching, Hobart and my own home?

CHAPTER 14

They gave each other a smile with a future on it.
Ring Lardner

Jack arrived at the Frawley Ranch in good spirits. He settled in and met the others who shared the bunkhouse. He quickly learned about his new dwelling.

The ranch was close to Spearfish and the cowboys came from various counties and states; most were hard workers. Ranching was tough and the price of beef was low. Many owners reduced their herds to stay alive during this depression while others gave up. Henry Frawley had hung on through rough times before, in the late 1880's, and he'd do it again. By the 1930s, he still held around 4,700 acres, which included four ranches: the upper, lower, middle and east ranches. His cattle and farming businesses were well-planned and involved shrewd management lasting through the decades—a combination that had kept him in business for decades. He knew many men were looking for work and got his hands cheap. Yet he was fair with all who gave him a good day's work. For single men, he provided a bunkhouse and board. Each received a small salary, accepted with gratitude during these hard times.

Jack enjoyed the work and had acquired a good deal of ranching experience in the last 25 years, which helped him stay on the good side of the boss. As a loner, he didn't trust most people, but some ranch bosses, he did. They never lost their temper with him and they kept their word. Jack shied away from any confrontation with other men, never wanting to fight. Exceptions happened when he saw someone being vicious, particularly to an animal or a child. Then his temper erupted. He could not stand violence of any kind, especially if it involved a whip. Usually the offender got the worst of it because Jack's strength increased when it came to fighting for the defenseless. While working at the Frawley Ranch, Jack hadn't found any men to raise his ire—yet.

Occasionally the Spearfish, Deadwood or Whitewood town halls opened for a dance and the cowboys always heard where and when. A dance meant pretty girls and to see where the evening went. Prohibition meant no alcohol allowed. However, men knew where to buy a bottle of moonshine or they made their own. The breaks at their autos caused some to come came back inside the dancehall feeling a little happier than before.

"Come on, Jack, it'll be fun," one of the ranch hands stated while raising his arm in a swooping motion toward the door of the bunkhouse when the group left for a dance. "We're goin' to the dance to see the pretty gals. Come along."

"Not tonight. My feet are tired. You young whippersnappers dance for me." Jack declined each time claiming that he was tired or wouldn't enjoy dancing. He'd read his dime Western novel instead. In truth, he loved dancing, but he wasn't ready to meet any women. He remembered his near-death experience in Nebraska and gave a slight shudder. Paying attention to the wrong woman could bring a beating worse than a whipping with a bullwhip—and he knew both.

On the Saturday of the dance in Whitewood in1932, Jack finally decided to go. His feet itched to be on the dance floor. He also needed a woman's company and it had been far too long. He felt lonesome. A spur-of-the-moment decision was made. He'd go.

As the men were ready to get in the auto, Jack yelled, "Hang on a minute. I'll be right there." He quickly donned a clean light blue shirt with only a few wrinkles visible under his Levi jacket. His jeans received a quick brushing by hand to remove as much dust and dirt as possible. "I'm coming," he yelled as he looked in the small wall mirror and combed his wavy strawberry-blond hair. He was a young looking, handsome 42 year-old with a tanned, firm-muscled body. Many of the men wondered if he was married or had been married. Jack wouldn't answer questions about his past and mystery created more questions. They all figured since he was older he probably had at least one woman in his life, but they had no proof.

The hall filled up with folks from all around. The ranch hands began to point toward which girl they chose to dance with them. "Which one you pickin', Jack?" one young man asked.

Jack answered with a laugh. "There don't seem to be many over twenty-five years old, except the ones with grey hair." He looked around and suddenly his eyes fell on a woman who appeared to be past twenty-five years old. Her brown eyes encircled by long, dark eyelashes and her dark hair felling neatly around her unblemished face captivated him. He noticed that she seemed to carry a smile when she talked to the women with her. He felt a stirring inside and thought he'd see if she wanted to dance when the music started.

The woman looked across the room and her eyes found Jack's. He didn't break the gaze and she smiled. Rattled, she forced herself to turn her head while her cheeks became more than rouge-pink. She whispered to her friend and nodded toward him. Was she asking who he was, or what? Did she think he was a threat, a womanizer? Or what?

The friend looked at him and saw that he was still looking at her friend. She talked again while nodding his way. What was she saying? She grinned and nudged the interesting woman in the arm. Then she boldly walked across the room before her friend could pull her back.

Jack saw her coming and started to back away toward the door. The woman looked determined as her heels clicked on the polished oak floor while her skirt swished back and forth with each step. Edie didn't stop until she was right in front of him.

"Hi. I'm Edie. I thought you might want to meet my friend. Who are you?"

"Ah—Jack," he replied with a puzzled expression. "I didn't mean no harm. Is she married? I don't want any trouble."

Edie laughed. "No, she isn't married and you aren't in any trouble. Now, if you'd been looking at me that way, my husband would have given you more than trouble." She laughed.

Jack let out a sigh of relief. "I just thought I'd ask her to dance later." He was flustered, moved from one foot to the other with his hands in his pockets. Then he looked across the room. Grace wrung her hands and looked at him with shyness written all over her face. Quickly she dropped her eyes and busied her hands with her skirt, smoothing the flowered cotton fabric she ironed stiff with starch.

All of a sudden the music started. Edie took Jack by the arm and started to guide him across the room. "Come on. The music is starting and you can ask her to dance now."

They stepped quickly and in a couple of seconds, Jack stood before Grace. Edie let go of his arm and introduced the two. "Jack, this is Grace. Grace, this is Jack. Now I believe you two can carry on. I'm going to find my husband and drag him out on the floor. Enjoy." She grinned at Grace and winked as she turned to leave.

Grace had not danced much since she left the sanitarium. Most men at the dances were looking for a younger girl. Even though TB had taken its toll on her, she still loved to dance—even if it was mostly with friends' husbands or with her brothers. She could see that Jack was at least in his late thirties, maybe older. "Hello, Jack," she said in a soft voice as she raised her eyes to meet his. She liked his name.

"Hello, Grace." The name fit because she appeared graceful in her movements when he watched her across the room. "Would you like to dance? You don't have to, if you don't want to." His body was prickling with a feeling he'd never had before.

Grace looked into his sea-blue eyes and smiled. "Yes, I'd love to."

He took her arm and led her to the floor. The slow dance suited Jack and he led his tiny partner in his arms. Conversation was nonexistent because neither knew what to say. They moved like a team from the first step and seemed to meld together as the music played.

When the dance ended, Jack led her back to her previous spot. "Thank you, ma'am. I really enjoyed it." He didn't know what to say, but just stood there not wanting to leave.

"Why thank you. I haven't danced in a while and it was a pleasure. I love to dance. You must too because you moved so easily to the music." She didn't want Jack to walk away either. Her smile mischievously curved up higher on one side.

"Oh, I've danced quite a bit in my travels." He didn't want to say too much about his past adventures with dances, especially the one episode in Nebraska.

"Oh." She paused for a minute wondering where he had been, and curiosity took over. "Where have you traveled and where do you work?" She couldn't resist asking.

"I've been all over. I work at the Frawley Ranch now . . . the upper ranch. I worked at the Wasp One Mine at Lead, but quit that. I'm used to the outside air above ground, not underneath the earth in some hole. I hate the cold, wet, black in those tunnels. I prefer to ride the range and just talk to my horse." He stopped and frowned. "Ah, I don't mean that I don't like to talk to people, I just don't like some people yapping all the time."

She smiled. "That's alright. I get tired of some people as well. Now where all have you worked before the Frawley Ranch?"

I've worked on quite a few before the Homestake Mine and decided to do it again." He quickly changed the subject. "Do you work?" Many women were working now, especially since the country was changing after World War 1.

Grace paused. She wished she could say that she was working. "Umm . . . I'm not right now. I used to teach. I'm staying with my parents near Whitewood and haven't found a job yet. Teaching jobs are scarce." She knew that in some places, the teachers hadn't received a paycheck for months while others were forced to quit because the school district went bankrupt. There was little hope of a teaching job for her during this time and all she could do was help her parents at home the best she could.

She wanted to talk about something else besides herself. "Maybe you know my brother, Fred Lee. He worked at the lower Frawley Ranch for a short time."

Jack frowned for a moment, scrunching his lips tight while thinking. "Hmm, I don't think so. I work at the upper ranch and we don't always know the others." He was talking to a woman more than he had in a long time.

"You taught school? That's great. I never got past the sixth grade and had to quit then."

She felt his tone revealed a hint of a deep wound.

"I'm sorry to hear that." Grace's mind wandered and she silently questioned if he was, or had been, married. If he was married, where was his wife? She definitely would not have anything to do with a married man, nor ever court a divorced man either.

She just looked down at the floor wishing that Edie would appear and take over the conversation. Another thought entered her mind. Why did he have to quit school after the sixth grade? Did his parents need him to help with a farm or business? Where were his parents now? She wanted to know more about him.

Silence seemed linger since neither was sure what to say. Then the music picked up again and he decided to ask for another twirl. "Would you care to dance again?"

She didn't see Edie come up behind her. Edie answered, "Yes, she'd love to." She nudged her friend, pushing her closer to Jack with an impish smile.

"Ah, yes I would," Grace answered shyly while looking into his blue eyes which she considered enticing.

He led her to the floor again and held her close as they kept time to the music. He hinted that he could dance with her all night! She was so small and enticing.

Grace couldn't resist as he pulled her closer. Their steps matched the beat of their hearts. She wondered what to say in order to find out more about him. He was so handsome and danced like a dream. A warmth rose inside her making her feel safe and she hoped she might possibly be glimpsing her future.

Neither seemed to need conversation, just the closeness was enough for them. Then the music ended and they had to separate. When Jack led her back to her spot, a man stood with his arms crossed over his middle and looked at him with a frown. Jack recognized the face and was sure that he had worked at the ranch. Was that Grace's suitor, her husband, or ex-husband? Who was he? A fight wasn't necessary. If that man wanted one, Jack would back off. He didn't mean any harm and definitely not another Nebraska scene.

He quickly thanked her and turned to retreat to the other side of the room.

Fred asked Grace, "Who was that? I think I know him."

"His name is Jack. I don't know a last name. He works at the Frawley Ranch—the upper ranch, he said."

Her brother nodded his head up and down once. "That's where I've seen him. Where's he from? Is he married?"

"Oh, for heaven sake, Fred. I didn't ask him a hundred questions. We just danced a couple of dances. Don't worry. He's not interested in me anyway."

"Ha! You should have seen the way he looked at you." He shifted from one foot to the other while his arms stayed crossed on his chest looking like a protective father instead of a brother. I'll see what I can find out about him."

"Where's Frances? You shouldn't leave your wife to run over here and mind my business. Go dance with her."

Fred laughed. "She's gossiping with some of the church ladies. She's fine. Now, you behave while I'm gone." He nudged her arm and walked away.

Grace noticed Jack asking some other women to dance. He must have thought that Fred was her beau. He appeared to be enjoying each new dance partner. She hoped he was still thinking about her, though, and kept stealing glances at him. He did the same.

She was on the dance floor only a couple of times and otherwise tried to hide in the background. Her envy couldn't be contained when she saw the other women dancing with Jack and wondered what Fred had found out. Her heart was still aflutter and she would so love to be back in Jack's arms again. She wondered what was going on inside her. None of her previous boyfriends affected her like this man, not even Hobart, her old beau.

Far too soon, the dance was over and people started to leave. Fred said he found some men from the ranch he knew and the questioning began. None of the ranch hands seemed to know much about Jack. They said that he stayed to himself most of the time and didn't talk about family. He had never talked about a wife, and as to whether he had ever been married, they didn't know. One fact remained the same with each ranch hand. Before the Frawley Ranch, Jack worked at the Wasp #1 Mine near Lead and he came from Nebraska before that. They said he was a good worker and that's all they knew.

Grace's curiosity tweaked and she wanted to know so much more about this Jack. Would he be at another dance? She hoped so.

Jack looked to see if the captivating woman left with the man who seemed ready for a fight. His eyes fell on Grace and saw that she was indeed walking with him. However, another woman wrapped her hand around the man's arm with possessiveness. Who were they? Was the one hanging onto that man his wife? It looked like Grace might be by herself and his heart gave a sudden jolt.

He met his ranch friends and they started on the drive back to Frawley's. The men were talking about one girl or another. Jack didn't join in; he just gave a slight grin and thought of Grace. A prickly tickle went up his spine. He didn't get that way over a woman and especially not over one he'd just met. He tried to get control of himself. He wondered if he'd see her again. He had to!

Grace was listening to the chatter of the group as they walked out to their car. Her eyes searched for Jack and saw him looking at her. The red began to creep up her neck to her cheeks. She was glad that only the moon shone on her. Giving a shy half-smile, she nodded at him. He smiled and nodded back.

At home and in bed, she relived dancing with Jack. She looked out the bedroom window and saw the full moon glowing bright. Would she see him again? The moon reminded her of a verse in one of Shakespeare's poems:

> *How sweet the moonlight sleeps upon this bank!*
> *Here will we sit, and let the sound of music*
> *Creep in our ears: soft stillness, and the night,*
> *Become the touches of sweet harmony.*

CHAPTER 15

1932

Life is a dance. Love is the music.
Author unknown

Grace hoped to see Jack at the next dance, yet time seemed to crawl while she wanted it to race. If only she knew whether Jack was or had ever been married. Her mind twirled with various scenarios.

Weeks passed and finally an announcement tacked up on the bulletin board at the post office announced another dance. Fred and Bob decided to go and have some fun and get their minds off all the financial worries and trying to find work. They fueled the auto from the gasoline tank that Dad kept on the property. Gas purchased in bulk was cheaper and they used it for Dad's sawmill.

The women would also go, thankful that they could enjoy life a little, even without new clothes or a new car to get them there. However, Grace, Frances and Laura wished they could afford new dresses, or even have some new material to sew their own dresses. Dreams were all they could have; there was no extra money for vanity.

Grace knew that Bob wanted to go to the dance so he could see Clarice again. He told Grace he was struck by her quiet beauty and thought maybe she would be the one for him though he still wasn't sure.   Besides, he didn't think that he could support her decently, and he wouldn't have her live in poverty. The economy interrupted too many romances.

Spring was arriving. Trees began to show buds and tiny green leaves were peeking out, ready to meet the sun. Fields began to lose the drab straw hue and overtaken by the fresh green grass. Wildflowers were also popping up throughout the grassland. Crisp nights turned to warm days. Everyone wondered if there would soon be rain, or would the hot, dry weather persist? They longed for moisture. In fact, all the Midwest was desperate to see pregnant clouds carrying gentle, steady rain.

The Sunday before the dance, the Lee family returned home after Mass in Sturgis. Dinner was almost ready. This time the meal was beans with ham cubes, but there was no dessert. Mom was afraid she'd run out of flour and sugar before there was money to buy more. She estimated she had enough flour to make bread for now. Even without dessert, her meals were always nourishing. Homemade bread, churned butter and jam from her last fall's canning, were plenty dessert.

The men discussed the dance again during dinner. When Dad heard about it, he said they should all go. "Gracie, you go too. You need to have some fun." She missed so much in life the last few years and he wanted her to enjoy herself as much as she could.

"I may go." She tried to act indifferent, but she hoped Jack would be there again so she could get more answers. At his age, he had to have been married and she would not get involved with a man who was married. On the other hand, maybe he had been married and lost his wife to some illness or disease. It could happen. Maybe he was divorced, or maybe he had more than one wife since he traveled around. All the different possibilities kept running around in her head and she had to know the truth. She couldn't keep her mind off him.

Fred popped up, "Sure, Gracie you ought to go. Maybe you'll see that Jack again." He grinned slyly.

"What? Who's this Jack?" Dad's head rose and looked from one to the other. His knife rested in the air while his fork remained speared in the meat. He hadn't heard anything about a Jack.

Mom continued eating, but raised her eyes and looked at Grace who seemed to be flustered. The last time Grace was interested in a young man had to have been several years ago, before tuberculous.

In no time, they learned about Jack. Fred gave what information he found out about him—not much, but some. Bob said that Jack seemed to respect Grace.

Last to comment was Grace. "Well, he seems very nice and he's an excellent dancer. What's wrong with my dancing with him?"

Dad thought for a second while he frowned at his plate. "Nothing's wrong with dancing with him." Then he told the boys, "If Gracie goes, Fred and Bob, you keep an eye on her, but let her have some fun. If this fella respects Gracie, let her be. Oh, and keep an eye on Laura." His youngest daughter, nineteen years old, was out for fun and could be more of a worry especially with that mischievous twinkle in her eyes.

That settled it. Grace would be going to the dance.

When Saturday arrived, she took extra time grooming and fretting about her plain older cotton dress, but it would have to do. Once it had been a favorite dress; now it looked like a washed-out limp blue rag. At least she could add her mother's new crocheted white collar to brighten up her attire. She also brushed her dark hair until it shone as if wet with sparkles here and there.

On the ride to the dance hall that evening, her hands fidgeted and she kept smoothing her hair, then her skirt. She bit her lips gently to give them more color. The rest of the group grinned, seeing Grace excited for a change.

Jack and his friends were always eager for another dance. It was calving time, yet he managed to switch shifts with another man who didn't care to go to dances. Jack polished his boots to a slick shine over the scuffed marks. He made sure he had a clean shirt to wear and took extra care with his appearance, hoping to see Grace again. Finally, the auto was loaded with the ranch hands and off they went, the tires spitting dirt.

The fiddler was already playing a slow number when they arrived. When the group walked in, Jack immediately looked for Grace. His eyes found her helping a couple of the women get the drinks ready.

Grace suddenly looked up to see Jack across the room. He grinned and nodded. She did the same and turned her head back to the table. Her cheeks had more color than usual.

Edie noticed and then spied Jack. "Ah ha. Your love is here," she nudged Grace and smiled.

Jack look around for the man who seemed possessive of Grace last time. That man was busy in conversation with several local men and his back was to Grace.

Jack walked over and smiled at her. "Care to dance, Grace?"

He remembered her name! All she could do was nod while her tongue tried to untwist. Finally, a weak "yes" came out as she looked up into his sparkling blue eyes. He smiled and held out his arm, which she took as they walked to the dance floor. Then he took her hand and gently pulled her close. The two danced together as one. He commented on the sweet scent of her hair. She loved his manly scent mixed with soap and some type of cologne . . . maybe just a dusty greenery aroma from the ranch. Whatever, she liked it.

"How're you?" Jack asked as he looked down into her lovely brown eyes.

"I'm fine. How are you?"

"Fine too. Now that we're over that, will you tell me your last name?" He felt bold, wanting to know more about her.

"It's Lee, Grace Lee. My father's name is Alfred Lee; we live a couple of miles from Whitewood. And you are Jack who?" She wanted him to know her father's name in case he wanted to find her.

"Oh, I'm not Jack Who," he teased. "I'm Jack Morris. Actually it's Jackson Morris, but I go by Jack." He would have to work on getting to Whitewood. He sure wanted to see her again, and again, and again. There was something about her eyes, her sweet smile and her tiny figure that captivated him.

Grace grinned when he joshed. "Where do you come from Jackson Morris? You haven't been in South Dakota that long have you?"

He paused not sure how much to tell her. He wanted to tell her all about his life, only decided he shouldn't unless their conversations continued for more weeks or months or longer. "No. I've only been here for a few years I guess. I used to work ranches. So Frawley's was a good pick especially with this poor economy. I think this ranch will survive."

"Where did you come from before you worked at the Homestake?"

His eyes never left hers. "I worked on a ranch in Nebraska and some other places." He shrugged not wanting her to ask too many questions, not yet anyway.

"And where did you teach?"

She answered with a smile and then a questioning look if he changed the subject on purpose. "I taught in the southeastern part of the state. My family moved here in 1927."

Grace paused, afraid to say that she'd had tuberculosis—that would surely scare him off. She was embarrassed to tell anyone about her stay at the sanitarium. No man would want to be around a physically weakened woman.

The music ended and Jack led her back to her side of the hall and lingered, making light conversation. When the band started again, the beat was fast and Jack took Grace's hand again leading her to the floor as a smile spread across his face. The music wasn't a Charleston, but some dancers tried it anyway. Jack didn't attempt that and quick-stepped around the floor. He wanted to lower his head to rest beside hers. Of course, she was so short he might have looked ridiculous. After many quick steps, Grace was out of breath. She missed a step and her body seemed to droop while her complexion changed to a pale blue-grey and her shoulders sagged. Jack saw that something was wrong and stopped, slowly helping her to a chair, almost carrying her with one arm tight around her waist. He sat beside her and kept his arm around her while he worried. "Grace, are you all right? Do you want me to get help?"

She shook her head and took a deep breath. "No. I'll be fine." Then she took another long gulp. "I overdid it and shouldn't have tried that fast step. I'm fine; I just need a minute to catch my breath." She was embarrassed and then realized that he still held her, which brought a smile.

"You want me to get you a drink, Grace, water or lemonade?"

She liked the way he said her name and how he had reacted. "That would be nice. Water please. Thank you."

He jumped up and returned quickly sitting by her again handing her the glass of water. The man he'd faced before was approaching with the woman he danced with all night. Then another man and woman came. Then Edie and her husband came. What was going on?

"Gracie, are you okay?" asked Fred. He glared at Jack. "What did you do to her?"

Jack rose while he planted his feet ready for a fight, if he had to. His Scottish temper seemed to burn. "Not a damned thing. She lost her breath and I've tried to help. Who are you anyway?" His jaw was set, lips tight and his back stiffened while his hands balled up into fists at his side. This had better not be like the last walloping he took when the husband came home.

"I'm her brother, Fred, and he's her other brother, Bob." He nodded toward Bob and then shifted his head again. "Grace shouldn't do the fast dances. You don't ever do that again. You hear?"

Jack bristled sure there was more to the story. "Yeah, I hear. Do you mind if I sit with her for a while?" His sarcastic tone fell with determination. He didn't want the brothers to think he'd harmed Grace on purpose. "I won't hurt her," he growled.

"Okay, but Gracie that's enough dancing for you tonight. Dad would have fits if he knew about this." Fred began to calm down.

Grace slowly gained color back in her cheeks. "Oh, for God's sake, Fred, don't tell Dad or he may not let me come to any more dances again," she begged.

Fred's wife pulled his shirtsleeve. "Don't tell. She's fine now. Let's dance."

Soon they all left since Grace seemed back to normal.

Jack glared at the two brothers as they left. He would never hurt Grace.

His attention went back to her.

CHAPTER 16

1932 – LEARNING MORE

After Grace's brothers and friends went back to dancing, she looked at Jack apologetically. "I'm sorry. I should have told you that I have problems breathing sometimes . . . too much activity and too much excitement. I just love to dance, especially with someone who is as great a dancer as you." She smiled and looked into his eyes, which showed so much concern for her.

"God! You scared me, Grace. I won't do that again. I promise. For the rest of the night, we can just sit and listen to the music. I don't have to dance. I just want to be with you." What a confession! He hadn't planned on saying that, even though it was true.

Grace almost laughed with pleasure. "Thank you. I like being with you too. Tell me about some of your ranching experiences." She hoped he didn't notice her cheeks beginning to deepen in color.

He looked off in the distance of remembering. "Ranching's just ordinary work. There's cattle, roundup, calving, breeding, fence mending, feeding and all that. Once in a while there's something that breaks the monotony. Like when I was young and learned to be a trick rider. I don't do that anymore though. Age has shot me down." He laughed.

"Trick riding! My, that must have been exciting. I love horses. Where did you learn to do that?" She was impressed and tried to picture him doing all those fancy maneuvers. She thought what a handsome young cowboy he must have been.

Why did he stall and not continue right away? Did he think she only considered him a bumbling cowhand? She certainly didn't and wanted to know more about this interesting man.

He finally looked up from his hands and began, "I was just a kid when I wandered onto the Pine Ridge Reservation. Black Elk, a Lakota Sioux, took me in for a while. I liked him and he showed me how to break a horse, to rope, to do some trick riding, plus other survival things. Indians are expert horsemen. Ben also told me to live for the present and not to live in the past. I find that kind of hard sometimes."

Jack shifted and looked out at the dancefloor. "I can still picture that proud man sitting on his horse. I think Black Elk saw a young boy needing some guidance when he saw me and he gave what he could." He stopped to look at her and see if she cared what he was saying.

She was and leaned toward him. "Jack, keep talking. I want to hear more."

"Well I learned that Black Elk worshipped the spirits of Mother Earth and it seemed the right way to worship. I looked up to that wise, generous man. His son, Benjamin Black Elk, was about the same age as me and we became good friends."

Grace glanced up at him wondering if he had taken up any Indian ways. "You lived with the Indians? Lord, weren't you afraid of those savages?"

Jack's laughter was loud and it took a moment before he could answer. "Nope, not ever. Indians aren't dangerous. The Whites left them lousy land to live on and got them addicted to whiskey. They aren't savages and I got along with them just fine. If you deal fairly with them and respect them, they'll respect you. I wish the Whites would see how resourceful and peaceful they are."

"How long did you stay with the Indians?" She didn't know what to think of that.

"Oh maybe about a year or less, I don't remember. After I left Pine Ridge, I went to Lander, Wyoming. I learned that the town was known as the "Cowboy Line" of the Chicago and North Western Railroad. That started the slogan, "where rails end and trails begin" and it was the home of the first world professional rodeos. I watched the rodeos a lot when they were in season and I decided to try trick rope riding." He paused.

Grace saw that his mind traveled back in time. Maybe good memories surfaced and he felt he was back there. His eyes drifted above the dancers and to the wall across the room seeing his bygone days. He must have been quite young then, only in his early twenties?

"Ben Black Elk had taught me well on the use of horses and roping. I knew I could do as much or more as some of those fellows performing in the rodeos. I practiced at the ranch where I worked."

He stopped and looked at Grace. As much talking as he was doing, he began to squirm. She loosened his tongue like a waterfall. "I've never talked to anyone about those days and here I am with my tongue wagging like a puppy's tail."

She laughed. "Well, keep talking. I love it."

He smiled and then seemed to lapse for a minute back to his rodeo days. The towns didn't lack for saloons and his group of ranch hands received plenty of liquor and attention. Before Prohibition, the saloons were busy and liquor flowed freely. He didn't drink much and always remembered what alcohol could do. He probably never failed to find a willing partner; he was a good dancer too. Like all the rest of the boys, he must have needed a woman's attention every so often; many of those girls were ready and willing to oblige. Jack almost blushed when he pictured those days. He'd never tell Grace.

Grace's family didn't know any Indians, she told him. Her family stayed away from them because she often heard about her great-grandma's sister who the Indians almost kidnapped. The older sister fought off the Indian woman and saved the child. That was enough for Grace not to want to be around Indians or to trust them—they were dangerous. Besides, her church considered them heathens or savages and tried to convert them.

Surprised at Jack's answer, she thought about treating an Indian as an equal. Of course, they were humans the same as she. She also wondered what past life Jack was hinting at when talking about the reservation and Indians. What else was there?

She noticed that Jack was in a different world while telling her about his past. Oh, to have seen him as a young handsome cowboy! She pictured him in his well-worn denim jacket and jeans with his dusty and sweat-worn Stetson shading his eyes. He'd be sitting on a horse surveying the cattle or galloping across a prairie. Picturing him as a trick rider was harder since she had never seen one.

"Keep telling me more. Trick riding must have been so exciting."

He smiled. "Those were the good ol' days. My first try at standing on Gypsy was a catastrophe. That sweet horse belonged to the ranch owner, but I always picked her to ride. She was such a beauty with a great personality I was sure I could stand on her while I roped. I planted my feet in front of the saddle horn with my toes pointing downward. Then I clicked my tongue on the roof of my mouth, like you probably did to get your horse to walk." He smiled at Grace noticing her color had returned; she seemed completely recovered and listening intently.

"When Gypsy took two steps, I lost my balance right off, landing on the ground hard. My rear hit first, then my legs while my arms flew up. I landed hard on my behind while dirt and dust coated me. I said some words that I won't repeat." He laughed and could almost see how he rose, leaned over, trying to get some of the dust off his pants, swearing to himself and rubbing his hand over his nose to prevent a sneeze.

Grace saw him imitate his fall with his arms and legs stretched upward while he leaned back in the chair. The image was vivid and she laughed.

"Oh, I'm sorry for laughing, but that must have been quite a sight."

He smiled and sat back up straight. "That's alright. My buddies roared, clapped and yelled, 'Do it again, do it again!' and wouldn't quit laughing. So I grabbed my hat from the ground and swiped it back and forth on my leg, put it back on, grabbed Gypsy and jumped up on her again. It didn't work and I fell off again . . . and again."

Grace's eyes glowed with amusement while listening. She loved to hear his soft voice, his way of telling a story, his animated imitation of movements. Her eyes stayed on him throughout his storytelling.

"Try after try and I finally figured out what to do to keep my balance and then I got it down pat. Finally, I began to get the feel of Gypsy's canter and she began to get the feel of my rope and my maneuvers." He stopped to look at her to see if she was interested. She seemed so engrossed that he decided to continue.

"Then Gypsy trotted 'round the arena and I did different stunts with and without the rope. One trick without a rope was putting one foot in the stirrup while keeping my body horizontal to the ground and my head even with my body. I pulled my other leg close to the one in the stirrup. All the while Gypsy trotted without missing a beat." He tried to demonstrate, leaning in toward Grace while trying to get his feet together.

"Then I swung up and sat up in the saddle." He straightened up realizing how close he was to her. "While galloping, I held onto the saddle horn with one hand and dropped to the side of my mare. I lowered my head and raised my feet straight up so I was bottom side up. Next, I stood in front of the saddle horn and kept my arms out on each side while Gypsy trotted around the arena. Pretty soon I could stand on one leg with the other rising out to the side. A few tricks I learned from Black Elk, but without a saddle. That was another experience with only the horse's mane to hang onto!"

He laughed remembering his falls and Black Elk and Ben laughing then. They always told him he could do it and to try again.

Grace was attentive not wanting to miss one word. "I so wish I could have seen you. I've never seen a trick rider. You must have really been good."

He smiled broadly. "I wish I could show you, but those days are long gone. After I got good enough, I did trick rope riding at some county fairs. It was fun, but I sure couldn't do it now," and he gave a deep laugh while shaking his strawberry-blond head.

She laughed with him. "Yes, I know how that is. I sure wish I had the energy I had when I was twenty years old." She thought back to her days *before*.

"Me too—the good ol' days."

He asked Grace, "You want another drink, maybe some lemonade?"

"That would be nice. Thank you. Lemonade would be good." She watched him walk away admiring his easy gait and perfect physique with broad shoulders and narrow hips. She blushed while staring at his body.

When he came back, the conversation continued only now it was her turn to tell about her life. She talked about her youth and growing up in a home full of love and laughter.

Jack so longed for that kind of life, and when she talked about her childhood, his heart ached. Why couldn't he have had that?

Too quickly, it would be time to separate and go home. When the band announced the last dance, Grace's eyes pleaded with Jack. He smiled, rose and extended his hand to see if she would rise and walk to the floor. She did. They danced slowly while he hummed softly to the tune in his tenor voice. She felt the world was perfect. Then the end came.

The band thanked everyone for coming. Some of the local folks were able to put a few coins in a cup for a donation to help the band. Ranch hands gave generously since most had no family and plenty of coins in their pockets. Every penny helped. A loaf of bread was eight cents, butter was twenty-five cents a pound and sugar as expensive as the butter. Any coins received helped to benefit the band members' families and the town.

Jack gave Grace a smile. "I hope to see you again soon, Grace."

She softly told him that she hoped so too.

He walked over to his friends and the next time he looked, she was walking out the door with her family and friend. Edie appeared to be talking to her a mile a minute. When was the next dance? It couldn't be soon enough.

As he watched her get into the automobile, his throat tighten, thinking about not being able to see her the next day. Finally, he piled into the ranch hand's auto with the rest as they talked about the girls and compared notes.

Jack didn't talk; his thoughts were private. Grace had gotten under his skin. He'd bet her brothers didn't think he was good enough for her. She was educated and refined and he was just a stupid cowboy. He wondered what she thought of him. He wanted to see her again, but did she want to see him after all his talking? He might have talked too much.

Damn!

CHAPTER 17

1932 - DANCING TO A FUTURE

Jack was surprised how Grace prickled every nerve in his body. None of the other women in his past shook him up like this petite lady. A spark coursed through his body every time he thought of her. His lack of education and his roughness didn't seem to bother her and she gave the impression she was interested in him.

He wanted to know more about Grace and remembered his father telling about his mother being an English lady. Was that it? Had he found a woman like his mum? If only he could talk to his dad—he sure couldn't talk to anyone else.

He thought of his "Lady Grace" every moment, especially while riding the range. He dreamed of holding her in his arms.

Miles away at the Lee home, Grace remembered feeling special when she was with Jack. She didn't feel damaged or like someone who had gone through tuberculosis. Jack seemed to be genuinely interested in her, but she had many questions. Maybe next time she would ask more about him.

A warm feeling crept up her body every time she looked into his eyes. She'd never responded to a man like she did with Jack and wondered how he could affect her so much. Was it possible that he was the one she had been praying for? Maybe she should ask her mother how she'd felt when she met her dad.

Jack's association with Indians bothered her somewhat. How could she find out the reason he was on the Indian Reservation? She felt he could not be part Indian since he has such a light complexion, strawberry blond hair and blue eyes. Who and where are his parents? Grace's mom certainly didn't like Indians and maybe her family was prejudiced because of the past history. The older generation still thought of them as savages, almost lesser beings. The younger generation gradually began to change their feelings. Maybe old ways did die hard, but they needed to change. Yet why was Jack so familiar with the Indians?

She dreamed of him all the time during the next weeks. Grace often looked out the window smiling and dreaming of her "Cowboy Jack".

While Dad passed the evening reading the newspaper, he shook his head back and forth. "Unemployment is up again. It has gone from three percent a few years ago to twenty-five percent and climbing. Incomes have dropped about forty percent, from what the news says." He scrunched up his mouth along with a frown while thinking for a second.

"For so many, income has gone down one hundred percent . . . no work, no pay. The farmers and ranchers have really been hit hard in the Midwest. When is it ever going to end?"

Grace chimed in, "Deflation has hit hard. Prices of crops are down again while foreclosures are up." She remembered another section.

"The Great Plains is in such a severe drought and those blasted dust storms keep stripping topsoil and blowing it to China! Farmers have no money to buy seed because the banks won't loan or they have closed. It wouldn't do much good anyway unless rain puts an end to this drought. Fields are without plants and the soil races away with the brutal winds. It's terrible!"

"I worry about Jeannette and Steve," Dad said as his voice dropped lower. "I hope they aren't hit too hard."

His daughter rarely wrote and when she did, she didn't give many details as to how they were managing. Their farm was near the Missouri River and they may have been a little better off than those who farmed on the open plains. Yet, the level of the Missouri was way down, just like all rivers. Creeks and lakes dried up as well. Water was at a premium and moisture was nonexistent.

"They'll be alright, Dad. They'll make it through this. Steve is smart like you. He's a good manager. He saved and knows how to make it through." She didn't add that she prayed they could truly make it through.

He nodded while Grace felt sure his mind was saying that good management saved him and his family so far, but he didn't know if it would continue. Dad's sawmill business income was way down since construction dropped by eighty percent. At least selling firewood would help him hang on and take care of his family. What else could he do?

Summer always meant more work for Grace and her mother. There was hoeing, seeding, weed pulling, hauling water to the garden, and picking fresh produce for meals. They thanked God their well continued to give them plenty of water. They hoped this summer would bring an abundance of their garden produce when September and October came.

Dad went to town often to market his business. If he heard of someone needing lumber, he'd be at their doorstep to introduce himself—the same if someone needed firewood. Some evenings found him falling asleep in his chair, too tired to read the news.

After a trip looking to round up business Dad announced, "Deadwood is going to have another dance." Only a few miles from Whitewood, nevertheless it meant more gas used. Grace begged her brothers to take her. They teased her, knowing why she was so eager to go.

Fred scrunched up his face for a second and then said, "I don't know. I'm getting worn out with all the extra work just to make a few cents. Although, I guess a dance would be good for us."

His wife, Frances, wanted a break from the daily chores at home and their baby son was a handful. "Maybe we should go."

When they all gathered at the folk's house for dinner, they discussed the dance. Mom agreed to take care of the baby for Frances so they could go. Dad felt too old to dance anymore.

"I'm tired to the bone; no dancing for me." He couldn't afford to hire help and managed the best he could. The depression was robbing him of good help and good health. "You young ones go and have fun; it'll do you good."

Saturday came and they eagerly climbed into Fred's auto. Frances and Robert sat in the front seat with Fred while Grace, Laura, Edie and her husband, Tom, sat in the back—a tight squeeze, but no one complained. Edie sat closer to her husband.

Tom gave Fred a few coins for gas money, "Gasoline is anywhere from ten cents to eighteen cents a gallon now, depending on where you buy. So we want to do our share."

Edie piped up, "Yes. We really appreciate this. Besides it makes for a cozy ride, doesn't it," she laughed. "At least we don't have anyone sitting on our laps."

Fred gave a thank you nod to Tom and added, "Since we get our gasoline by the bulk at Dad's sawmill we pay less than you do at the pump. Now if my ol' buggy will just keep running; I sure can't afford a new one now." Fred's old Packard chugged along from Whitewood to Deadwood while the sun shined brightly before dusk, giving warmth as it continued its journey. A breeze blew the tall swaying grass like waves on an ocean, while the Canadian thistle showed off its pink blossoms along the roadside.

"Gas prices will never go down," Grace said. "Thank God you all have some work. Did you read that unemployment in the United States is up to twenty-five percent and more than four thousand banks have closed?"

Everyone nodded solemnly remembering the friends who were out of work or who had lost their homes when their bank closed.

Edie added, "About the only thing that seems to be doing well is the Hollywood film industry. At least it's a good way for the public to forget their woes. Folks scrape their pennies together once in a while to afford seeing the other side of life on the screen. I read that a few popular cinemas are *42nd Street*, *A Night in Cairo*, *The Bowery* and *The Invisible Man*. Maybe sometime we'll be able to see them."

Soon they joined a procession of other well-used dusty, dirty autos also heading to the dance, each vehicle filled with other people hoping for a good time. The chorus of sputtering and grinding autos echoed throughout the hills. When they rolled down windows, white-grey puffs of exhaust surrounded them and filled their lungs.

As autos began to descend the hill, they drove along the bustling Main Street. The town sat in a valley along Deadwood Creek. Lavish brick or stone buildings revealed the good old days of gold mining and rich investors. The town's old saloons displayed the famous western heritage when days of mining were the lifeblood and boisterous laughter, music echoed along the Main Street, or maybe a gunshot echoed through the town. Present day showed gold, still in demand, made gold mining one of the few businesses able to survive the economy, other than the film industry.

The large dance hall became lively with people ready to enjoy the celebration of the approaching harvest. That is what harvest the parched soil could yield. Fred told his passengers, "Start looking for a place to park as close to the hall as possible. If we have to park too far away, we'll get too tired to dance after walking up the steep streets to the hall." He laughed.

They lucked out and parked a block away. When they entered, the music was just beginning while many voices filled the air as well. Cigarette smoke was already drifting toward the open windows.

Grace and Jack danced and danced, just the slow dances, no fast ones. They took breaks in between and sat talking. The dance hall was full of music, laughter, talking and every so often, a whoop from an over-excited man would interrupt the din. Grace and Jack's conversations were mostly generic in the beginning, although it escalated quickly. She mentioned Thanksgiving was coming soon. Jack asked about her family's holiday.

"My parents always have a wonderful turkey dinner with far too much food. We usually had turkey or pheasant when we lived down in the southeastern corner of the state. The men always went pheasant hunting for wild turkeys too. Then Mom taught us girls how to make cranberry sauce and her special gizzard stuffing. We end the Thanksgiving Day as stuffed full as the turkey was when he was put in the oven." She laughed. "How were your Thanksgivings?"

How could he answer her? His past contained no holiday celebrations until he was ranching and then it was only that the men ate their own fowl and trimmings in the main kitchen on Thanksgiving Day or any holiday.

"Um…mine weren't as much fun as yours and I like to hear about your family." He tilted his head and gave a weak smile. "So tell me more."

Grace wondered what was wrong and if he had not had a normal family life? "This year the boys, I mean my brothers, will hunt for a wild turkey. If they don't get one, we may have to kill a couple of our chickens. I'm sure they will find one because they are good hunters. This year, though, there are more people desperate to get any kind of meat they can for their family and they are out hunting often." She knew hunting was not legal without a license, but no one worried about getting caught. They were much too hungry.

"So, anyway, we'll see and we'll still have a good Thanksgiving, turkey or not." She was inclined to ask Jack to join her family for Thanksgiving dinner, but decided she had better wait.

Jack just nodded. He couldn't remember any Thanksgiving or other holiday dinner with his father because he was either out trapping or logging. His mind shifted to the man who took him in when he became an orphan at ten years old. His father's friend, Malcom MacGreagor, came from Scotland like Jack's father, both with their wives. The MacGreagors were kind, took him as their own son and traveled from Washington to Indiana where Mac's brother and he had a farm. Jack didn't stay long enough to have any holiday meals with them. He ran away still heartbroken over losing his father, not wanting a substitute. He didn't want a new family or to be in Indiana. He only wanted to be back in Washington. Jack wondered what his life would have been like if he hadn't run away.

He remembered that time so long ago, riding on the train with Mac and his wife when they left Washington, his first time ever on a train. The feel of the rails whining as they passed over them felt so strange. They went through Montana, North Dakota, Minnesota and finally on to Indiana. He never saw such vast country before, or huge cities like at the big city train stops. He only knew the little area around his dad's cabin in the mountains and the little town they walked to sometimes. He shook his head wondering why he ever ran away from the MacGregors. He sure paid for that mistake.

He needed to stop thinking of his miserable life or he'd be telling Grace about it. Then, what would she think of him?

Jack asked, "What was your school like when you were little? Did you like school?" He needed to know what a normal childhood was like, with a normal family.

"Oh, I loved school. My dear uncle taught me my ABC's and some math before I was old enough to go to school. Then when I could go, Dad took me in his buggy." Grace told him about a childhood memory that had always stayed with her.

"When I was about eight years old, Dad let me take myself and my sisters to school in the buggy, which was several miles from home. I sat perched on the seat in the middle of my two sisters. I was so proud to be driving. I did have one big disappointment, though," she shook her head and twisted her mouth up on one side.

Jack nudged her, "Well, what was it? Did you run the buggy into a ditch? And your father wouldn't let you drive anymore?"

She chuckled, "No, I did not run it into a ditch! I had the laziest horse anyone could imagine and I had to use the willow switch constantly to get old Blackie to keep moving or he'd fall asleep!" She hated that horse.

"One day I heard a chug, chug. Then an automobile appeared at the top of the little hill ahead of us, with dust flying behind. When they saw our buggy, a man jumped out and ran to meet us. He told us not to worry that he'd hold our horse's reins tight so it wouldn't balk or try to run when the auto passed.

"I was excited thinking it would be a thrill to tell everyone how Blackie had tried to rear and run." She stopped a minute and could still see that scene.

"So did Blackie need to be restrained?" Jack asked with a grin assuming there was more to her story.

"No, he sure didn't. That lazy half-dead animal fell asleep as the auto sputtered and putted past us. I was so humiliated! I could have killed that horse." She laughed and threw up her hands as if giving up. "If I'd had a rifle, I might have killed him. I was so mad."

Jack laughed, enjoying the sound of her voice. It seemed so eloquent to him. She caused a hankering to run through him when he listened to her. Her hands always remained at her lap unless expressing herself; not like some of the saloon girls who caressed and teased him.

A waltz began and they decided to dance. In silence, they moved in unison and melded together. Words weren't necessary. They didn't seem to notice anybody else and were in their own world.

Grace didn't know when she'd see him again. "May I write you a letter?" she asked him. Immediately she blushed wondering if he thought of her as a fast woman

Jack was surprised and smiled from ear to ear. He'd never received a letter before except from the government, never from a woman! He gave a broad smile and then quickly answered, "I'd like that, Grace, but I'm not good at writing."

He lowered his head sure that if she saw his handwriting, she'd probably drop him like a hot pancake. He didn't want to tell her that his penmanship was limited, the same as his vocabulary. He was sure she'd laugh at his writing.

"Don't worry. If you just say hello and that you plan to see me again, it will be enough. I'll know that you didn't get hurt rounding up cattle, or that you are still at the ranch." She smiled, while silently adding that she would know he cared enough to write her. She already knew that his caring and worldly knowledge made up for his lack of schooling. What was education anyway? Reading the classics? Knowing the proper usage of words? Or was it being able to quote poetry? She decided the person's character was more important than his book learning if he were considerate, respectful and a gentleman toward her, then what else could matter? Of course, being the most handsome man around didn't hurt either.

"If you write, I'll reply. Don't expect much, but I'd like to get your letter," Jack smiled down at her. That was all she needed.

The night ended and they parted after the last dance. The ride home for each filled with dreams of the other.

Jack felt young and vigorous again. The opening of his senses for the first time in years allowed him to smell, hear and feel the life moving around in the world once again. Grace made him feel so alive.

Damn!

CHAPTER 18

1932 - A DIFFERENT DEPRESSION

Winter arrived as if with a vengeance eating away at so many people. The icy wind didn't bring much snow, but came with enough artic cold to make a preacher swear. Work slowed in one way and became harder in other ways. The stoves had to receive fuel and animals needed to be fed and watered; no matter if any moisture came or how hard the wind blew horizontally biting into a person's face, freezing noses, fingers and toes. As it melted on a warm body, it gave a fresh clean scent, rarely appreciated at the time. People were stretching their food in hopes it would last through the season.

The Black Hills and all the land throughout the Midwest suffered from the lack of moisture. Darken clouds did not provide decent snowfall to quench the thirst of the soil. Fierce winds produced tall black walls of dust fifty to eighty feet high rolling over the land and covering everything in its path. The fields were bare and the soil parched; it resembled a flattened, torn, useless gunnysack with frayed edges flapping in the wind. Heavy hearts were common especially with farmers. At least the pine trees in the hills broke up the fierce winds and the Lee family did not suffer like those on the prairieland.

For far too long dances were not scheduled. Time crawled at a snail's pace for lovers eager to meet again at the next dance.

Grace decided to write a note to Jack. Boldness conquered. She had to know if he was interested in her even though she was sure he was, but then she had been wrong before.

December 1, 1932

Dear Jack,

How are you? This bitter cold must freeze your bones when you are out on the range. I do hope you have not caught cold and are able to stay warm.

We are starting to think about Christmas. We plan to give a ham to two different neighboring families who we help when we can. I will make some kind of a sweet for the children. They are so adorable.

I must go help get supper going now. I hope to hear from you.

Your friend,
Grace

Grace made sure that she had the return address printed neatly. She wanted him not to miss it. After her dad took the letter to the post office, she began to worry that Jack might think she was brazen. What if he got the wrong impression of her? She didn't want him to think she was a loose woman. Yet it was too late. Living with the consequences was all she could do now.

Her shoulders drooped every time she went through the mail. When she didn't see a letter from him, she became quiet and moped for hours. It had been improper for her to write him, but she had. Now he hadn't written back and she was sure her blunder had probably caused her to lose Jack. There was nothing to do except go on living a lonely life.

Could Jack have smiled when her letter arrived? Or did he think poorly of her? Yet maybe he could not force himself to write back. When spring came, would he go to the dances and be glad to see her? Did he want to see her again or not?

Grace heard Dad yell, "Listen to this!" while listening to the radio on a November evening. Mom and Grace came in and sat close to hear through the static. The announcer said Franklin Delano Roosevelt won the Presidential election over Herbert Hoover by almost a landslide. FDR won the electoral vote by four hundred thirteen and the popular vote by close to seven million. The radio reverberated with the announcer's excited voice.

Dad slapped the arm of his chair and yelled, "Well, I guess it shows that people wanted a change and squelch this damned depression. FDR can do it and 1932 may be the year."

Mom frowned. "Roosevelt's had polio and can't walk except somewhat with crutches. I wonder if he'll be able to keep up. His wife, Eleanor, certainly has been in the news and seems like she will push to keep him going onward to better times." She paused for a minute and raised her index finger to stress a point.

"You know she has had to put up with his shenanigans with other women. They have tried to keep it quiet, but there are too many rumors. Still, Mrs. Roosevelt has been loyal to him. I wonder how loyal he's going to be to the country—probably more so than to his wife." Mom just shook her head.

Grace nodded and added, "I think Roosevelt can get this country back on track with his New Deal program. He has got to. Congress is as desperate as the rest of us to get something going. The newly elected in Congress had better get it done. The country can't stay this way, and everyone is willing to try anything."

Dad continued, "Our Senator Norbeck was re-elected by over twenty-five thousand votes. The Republicans lost many of their seats in Congress. FDR will get it done now. But we'll just have to wait and see what happens."

Grace said, "Well, maybe Roosevelt can get his plans through to move us back on track. I also heard that the song *Happy Days are Here Again* has already become a hit. FDR used it on his campaign. I'll pray his plan will give us happy days again."

"When he's inaugurated in March we'll see what happens. Nineteen thirty-three can't come soon enough for me," Dad added. "Let's get people back to work, have more money flowing and give me a break. I sure could use some help, sit on my duff and give orders for a change. This ol' body is wearing out," he laughed.

Grace could see the decline in Dad's strength. Dad had aged ten years in the last four or five. He was only fifty-six years old and looked much older. Age combined with the hard strain on the body ate away the months and years. Mom felt that strain as well.

Both women stated in unison, "Now if only rain comes, everyone will be happy."

The next days and weeks filled with new hope. People had more confidence and many in Whitewood were smiling more often. Time would prove this New Deal Program either good or trashed with no hope for Roosevelt to be re-elected for another term. No one wanted this one to fail. Lives were at stake.

The Christmas season arrived with a happier atmosphere among merchants and hopeful purchasers since Roosevelt was ready to initiate his program as soon as he put his hand on the bible and officially became President.

Families received cards or just a letter from all the relatives who could not afford to send gifts. Christmastime brought news about grandparents, aunts and uncles, as well as from Grace's sisters. Jeannette's little one was now two years old and heading to the barn to help her father when she could get out the door. There wasn't much written about the dust storms and everyone hoped Jeannette's family hadn't been hit too hard. She hinted that she was tired of constantly trying to keep the house free of dust and dirt, but no hint of how bad it was.

Grace saw Mom shed a tear when she read about Jeannette's little one. Since she lived about 400 miles away, Mom had not been able to see the two-year-old baby yet. It hurt.

Helen and family were in the town of Bonilla, and not near enough to visit the folks except in the summer months, if there was enough money for gas. Her husband, Ralph, was Superintendent of the school there. Helen wrote, though, that Ralph had obtained a position in Sturgis for the 1933-34 school season and they would be closer. She also wrote about the dust storms with dirt covering everything. Helen's daughter was also two years old and demanding someone read a story to her. Helen said she was busy all the time and especially trying to get the dirt removed after a dust storm.

Mom stated, "Jeannette and Steve gave neighbors a portion of their slaughtered pig and they helped Jeannette with canning last fall. I'm glad neighbors help each other."

Grace added, "Helen has good neighbors as well. They survive by helping each other."

Before the big holiday, Fred picked up mail from town and returned to give Grace a square envelope, "For you Ma'am." He bowed as he handed it to her with a smirk.

She took the envelope from him and tried to slap him on his shoulder, but he dodged too quickly and he bounced off to the kitchen. The smell of fresh baked bread was a sure way for him to visit with Mom.

Grace looked at the envelope and gasped in a whisper, "Oh! He sent me a card!" She opened it and saw a store-bought Christmas card with a hand-painted Christmas tree with candles and popcorn strings on it. The inside contained a sweet message and Jack added, *Have a Merry Christmas, Grace. I hope to see you soon.*

All she could do was grin the rest of the day. The card sat on her bureau in her bedroom. When asked whom it was from, Grace replied, "It's just from a friend."

Grace sent Jack a homemade Christmas card. She found some heavy paper in her school supplies and cut out a picture of the Nativity from an old card, glued it on the front of her folded paper and glued pine needles around the cutout. She wrote *A Blessed Christmas* above in her best script. Inside she made a short written holiday message and added at the bottom, *Wish you could be here.* Then she signed it. She hoped he would like what she'd added.

Christmas passed and the icy cold still prevented automobiles from traveling much of the time. Coaxing a stubborn motor to turn over and purr sometimes was mingled with cussing and then either a disgusted slamming of the hood or a loud joyful, "Yes!"

The bitter cold eased into the January 1933 thaw, which brought fewer cold days for just enough time that everyone hoped winter was retreating. It wasn't. The bitter cold winds returned. February didn't bring the usual snow, but blasted through with icy winds. March paraded in with one hopeful snowfall. It did not relieve the mid-west from the bitter cold winds and it did not provide much moisture for the gasping thirsty soil.

Even in the drought in the Black Hills fields bore sprouts attempting to grow and stay green while trees were being dressed in fresh baby green leaves dangling from the branches. Dandelions appeared in the fields before the wildflowers came to adulthood displaying all their yellows, reds, pinks, whites or blues. No rain clouds came to drench the soil, yet a few drops came every so often teasing the ground and the humans who prayed for more.

Grace read the paper while taking a break from ironing after she finished the Sunday shirts and dresses. She would tackle Dad's mended overalls next. Laundry and ironing was a never-ending job. One of these days, Dad was going to have to buy a new pair of overalls. She knew the price of denim pants was up and assumed overalls cost about the same, maybe more. Right now, there wasn't enough money left over for new clothes and she or Mom would continue to patch and mend Dad's old ones.

While reading in the kitchen by the stove Grace told her mother, "The Federal Reserve System will reopen banks under the US Treasury supervision. It's intended to get billions of dollars to flow back into the banks so they can reopen." She stopped and read the next section before continuing. "It says they are going to establish a Federal Deposit Insurance Corporation which is abbreviated FDIC. It insures up to $2,500.00 for everyone who deposits money in the bank. Now that's something, isn't it?"

Mom smiled. "I wish I had even a couple hundred to deposit in a bank."

Grace laughed. "At least that plan will give the rich people a feeling of security knowing that the banks can't take all their money. This will help give some reassurance to those who have some cash to put in a bank and maybe get the economy going again. Wait until Dad reads that. I hope it works." Grace put the paper down and went back to ironing.

Mom began to prepare for her chicken and dumpling supper. She would save some of the chicken for another meal, maybe chicken soup. The necessity to stretch the meals out was always present. With the large family she had to feed, it wasn't easy. She thanked God for last year's garden with an abundance of vegetables, now sitting in jars on the cellar shelves. If only they had $2,500.00, they wouldn't have to worry about stretching the food. Such is life. You take what God gives.

Grace was losing hope of ever teaching again. Maybe in the future a job would come and in the meantime, she helped her mother at home. She could take care of the garden, weed and haul water to the plants since Charlie seemed to disappear when needed. He'd rather go fishing or exploring.

When the ironing was finished, Grace read more news about the newly elected President's plans for the year. "Roosevelt closed all banks and got the legislators to enact a program called the Emergency Banking Act. All one hundred new Democratic members of Congress were determined to address the banking industry."

She was sure they were trying to get something going. Congress couldn't seem to agree often enough in the past. Maybe now they could settle on something and get the economy on an upswing.

"That Emergency Banking Act was passed on March ninth after a single copy was read on the floor to the House of Representatives. Then the Senate received copies and later passed the bill with the legislation to go in effect in January of 1934. Can you imagine that? Things may get done after all."

Grace prayed that whatever the congressional representatives did, it would help the country. They had to do something to give people hope again for a future. She knew the fight to progress through all troubles waned as time piled up. People will survive again somehow, she was sure of that. But what about the drought? Congress couldn't do anything about that. When would God allow the skies to open with the needed moisture?

Finally, a posted announcement at the Post Office stated another dance to come the second Saturday of March and this one in Whitewood. The roads should be clear and no danger in driving, even if the air was still crisp.

Grace felt bold and decided to write Jack one more time. She didn't want to give up. This couldn't be like another Hobart, could it? If she didn't hear back, she'd know he wasn't interested.

February 20, 1933

Dear Jack,

    I hope you do not mind my writing to you. I just thought I would let you know that I plan to be at the Whitewood dance next week. Will you be there?
    Thank you for the beautiful Christmas card. I love it. I hope you have been staying warm.

If you come to the dance, I have a question. I hope to see you there.

Your friend,
Grace

She worried that maybe she shouldn't have written, and then dismissed the thought. He might as well know she was interested. What was it about him? He was different from other men who had been interested in her in the past, even Hobart. Some made her uncomfortable at times, but not Jack. He bothered her in a completely different way and it only made her smile, wanting to be with him. She still needed to know his marital status. She would have to obey her religion and her conscience and let him go if he was or had been married.

When Jack received the note in Grace's beautiful handwriting, his heart thumped and he almost danced around the bunkhouse smiling ear to ear. Before dancing, he stopped and quickly frowned. What question would she ask? He'd sure be at the dance to find out!

He sat down at the table and got out his tablet and pencil. What was he going to say? He had to write carefully and check his spelling. He tore up several pages and threw them into the fire. Finally, he admitted that the one in his hand would have to do. It had to work, or he'd have to accept the fact that he wasn't good enough for her if she read it and dismissed him. He reread his note and checked for spelling. Then he reread it yet again, hoping he hadn't made any big mistakes.

Dear Grace,

Yes, I'll be at the dance and I want to dance every song with you. I'll see you soon.

Your friend,
Jack

He hoped his poor penmanship didn't change anything. He was ashamed of his lack of education. Maybe he'd better prepare himself for another letdown, just like he had before. Grace's dad could be similar to Sarah's dad back in 1918. He just wasn't good enough for a refined woman.

Grace, on the other hand, was thrilled that he wrote. She didn't pay attention to the writing except his signature was beautiful in her eyes. The main thing was that he answered and wanted to dance every song with her. She held the letter to her bosom dancing a few steps with her eyes closed imagining Jack was holding her. Her smile lasted for days.

Mom smiled at seeing her daughter turn into a silly teenager. Maybe this is the one. Jack better not break Grace's heart, or her father would lay into him and he'd never be able to dance again. They needed to know more about this man.

Was this Jack as nice as Grace thought he was? What about his being a cowhand? Could he support Grace if the romance got that far? What is his past history?

Dad told Grace that if she saw this Jack again, to invite him for a Sunday dinner. She was surprised, but happy. That was what she hoped and they would get to know Jack then.

Are happy days here again for me and not just the country?

CHAPTER 19

1933 - LOSS AND MISERY

The Saturday of the dance, Grace assumed Jack probably had a new haircut and his attire clean and neat as he could get it. He appeared to be particular in his appearance. She knew he'd have polished his boots to a shine that would make an army captain proud. She wondered if he reread her letter like she did his.

A new dress was out of the questions and she'd have to remake a used one given to her as payment for tutoring a woman's son a few times. The cotton material was not faded or worn thin and that was encouraging. It had tiny red and yellow flowers on a pale blue background, the colors still bright. Grace made it with a straight A-line skirt flowing outward from her small waist. She added a crisp homemade white collar, starched until it could stand on its own. She was ready to meet Jack again.

The night of the dance, the drive was easy since the remaining snow melted into pools resting along the sides of the road. With the evening hours extended by more light, the travelers could see new growth trying to inaugurate the coming spring.

On the way into Whitewood, the men seemed to keep a running conversation. "You heard that last December . . . fifth . . . I think it was . . . that Congress finally repealed the Prohibition law?" Fred asked while steering the sputtering auto.

"Sure did," Tom answered and smiled. "Everyone is talking about it and it's about time. You can't keep people from having a drink and maybe government finally got the hint."

Fred nodded, "It's the conservatives that kept that law in force for so long. Now we got the liberals who are thinking along the right track. I'm glad that law got changed, even if I'm not a big drinking man." He laughed. The conversation continued on to the economy, friends and whatever else they found interesting.

When they arrived at the hall, Grace searched for Jack. Her shoulders drooped when she didn't see him. Then suddenly the door opened; a gush of cold air whipped through the hall as several men burst in, loudly laughing and ready for some excitement. They removed their cowboy hats and used them to dust their pants by swiping back and forth. Their shirts were blue, red, green or a checkered pattern making them look like spring had entered the room, but without the warmth. The icy air surrounded the hall until the door slammed shut. Everyone turned to look and young girls began to giggle. When Grace saw Jack in the back of the group, she smiled. The night would be good.

She saw Jack talking to a few of the men as his eyes searched the room, for the lady who had captured his attention. When he saw Grace, he smiled and excused himself. Time for him to see where the evening would go and he had a feeling it would go well.

"Hello Miss Lee," he said as he walked up to her. "You sure look nice tonight. How're you doing?"

Grace paused while her mind cleared from dreaming and smiling. "Hello, Mr. Morris. I'm fine. How are you?"

Her head tilted upward at an angle and her lips formed a flirtatious one-sided smile. When had she ever felt this way about a man? Never! She'd thought Hobart was the one for her, yet she hadn't felt like this with him. Jack was indeed different from all the other men she had known. Her quick heartbeat confirmed that.

The two talked about the weather for a bit and how work was for him. She told him she hadn't found a job yet, but was able to help her folks at home and occasionally tutor a child for a few sessions.

The musicians warmed up their instruments, then struck up the music. Jack and Grace joined others on the floor for a couple of waltzes. She liked the slow music because he could hold her close and she could breathe in his manly aroma.

"Hmm. You sure smell nice, Grace. What is it?"

Grace had to laugh. "Well, I just used a vinegar mixture on my hair. Nothing special, but thank you for asking." When there was rain, she used the rainwater to shampoo and then rinse. This time, she'd had to use well water.

"That's special when it's on you," Jack said with a laugh and squeezed her closer.

As a fast dance began, they decided to sit and visit. He picked up a glass of lemonade for each of them and sat in the chair next to her. "Tell me about your life, Grace. What was it like when you were a wee un?"

"I am the oldest of eight. My childhood also included aunts, uncles, cousins, an adorable uncle and grandparents that I loved. My father ran his sawmill down near the Missouri River and we had a big house with lots of acreage to run around in. Well, we had a big house until I burned it down."

Jack jerked his head to look straight at her. "How did that happen?"

"I was about thirteen years old. My mother needed to take the springboard wagon to town and buy supplies. I guess she thought she'd give me some authority. It would save time for her by not having to keep us all in tow or out of trouble. She left me in charge of baby Laura, Nellie, Fred, Bob, and Jeannette. She took Helen, the troublemaker." A little laugh squeezed out.

"That was quite a load, wasn't it?" Jack smiled.

Nodding, Grace continued. "After Mom left, my father built a larger fire in the cook stove. He told me to watch the stove and he'd have one of his workers come about noontime to help when it was time to fix dinner for everyone. He had several hired hands back then. Dad also reminded me to baste the roast that my mother had put in the oven. Then he left with his crew and headed to the woods to saw lumber for his sawmill."

Memories began to flood and she almost shed a tear thinking of the fear that came on that day. "I began to bathe the baby and was having so much fun I forgot about the wood stove. It wasn't long and the fire in the stove got hot enough to almost melt the chimney pipe. The wood ceiling caught fire around the chimney. I hadn't paid attention, but then I smelled smoke, coughed and heard a crackling sound. I looked up to see the flames on the ceiling and wall. The planks were so dry that it spread fast."

She stopped for a deep breath, seeing the fire again. She shivered and then shook her head to rid the memory.

"God, Grace!" Jack grabbed her hand. "You must have been petrified."

She smiled and proceeded. ""I didn't know what to do. There was no one to help, just the children. For a minute, my eyes widened and I watched the flames grow while I listened to the crackling and popping of burning wood. The smoke was getting thicker. Suddenly I grabbed a blanket to wrap the baby up and did the same with Charlie. I yelled for Jeannette, Nellie, Fred and Bob to grab their coats and run outside. Flames were spreading fast, there was no way I could stop it. The bath water would not have done a thing. Once we were outside, I told my brothers to run get our Dad." She smiled while thinking of them on that day. "Off they went yelling, 'The house is on fire! The house is on fire!' They were scared, but their yelling sounded like a song or poem, 'the house is on fire, the house is on fire, put water on the pyre.' I didn't like the sound of it or understand how I could rhyme those words at that time, but it kept repeating in my mind!" She had to laugh and Jack did as well.

"I held Laura and ten-year-old Jeannette held Nellie. We just stared at the flames engulfing our home. The deep red flares shot high into the air with dark black smoke rising above and shifting with the breeze to the east. Thank God, there wasn't a strong wind. When Dad built our house, he cleared all the trees around it and that was a Godsend. My father came on the run, along with the sawmill workers. He didn't know Mom had taken Helen. All he could count was six children. Over and over he pointed to each of us counting, 'Grace, Jeannette, Fred, Bob, Nellie and Laura'."

She paused and remembered that terrible day. "Again he counted and then cried, 'Where's Helen? You didn't get everyone out. You didn't get Helen out!' I kept saying I did.

"I yelled through tears that I *did* get everyone out, but I didn't think to explain. By then the house was engulfed in flames and the whole building soon crumbled into a huge pile of burnt timber and ashes. Dad was beside himself. He kept saying, 'Oh God! Of God! We've lost Helen.' I saw him bend over with his hands resting on his overall knees as he tried to hide his tears, but I knew he was crying."

She almost had to shed a tear as she related that moment. Then she added, "One of the hired hands talked to me and I told him the story between gulps of panic. Finally, he reassured Dad that Helen went to town with Mom and she was not in the fire. Then Dad took a deep breath, straightened, gave a quick swipe with his shirtsleeve over his eyes and looked at we frightened children standing there in

115

tears and shaking. He gathered all of us in his arms telling us that it was alright, we were all safe and that was all that mattered."

Jack could tell her dad loved his family. "God, Grace. You must have been scared!"

"Yes," was all she could utter at the moment.

"What did you do then?"

"We were taken over to a neighbor's and waited for Mom. When she came, the help waited for her and told her the house was gone. She went berserk, sure that her children burned to death. Finally they assured her that we were safe."

"Well, your family sure had a rough go after that didn't you?"

She nodded. "We managed." She wanted to change the subject and hear about Jack. "Now, how about you? What was your childhood like? Did you have any brothers or sisters?"

Jack frowned, jutted out his jaw while pulling his lips tight not sure how much to say. His anger could come out at the life he was dealt. He might as well be truthful with her, though, or he could lose her.

"I didn't have anybody except my Dad. My mum died before I knew her and my Da—dad—raised me." He still thought of his father as "Da" like the child of a Scottish man would. "We had a good life together even though he was gone sometimes. He was a lumberjack and a trapper."

He stopped for a moment trying to picture the face of his father. How could he forget that giant of a man with muscled arms, his ruddy skin, blue eyes and thick curly strawberry blond hair.

"My dad took care of me." His throat caught and he waited a minute while he looked down at the floor remembering all the things that they'd when together. Another man could never match his father as far as Jack was concerned.

"Dad had a woman take care of me until I was about six and then he took me to our cabin in the mountains near Okanogan, Washington. He taught me how to start a fire in the stove and fireplace, to chop kindling wood, how to cook, fish and to use a rifle." He smiled as he recalled his efforts to chop wood, or the mistakes he'd made in cooking and burning food, while he remembered how he'd caught on quickly with the rifle. He'd gotten better with things as he'd grown older.

"Dad always talked about my Mum." He took a sip of his lemonade, turned his glass around several times.

Grace looked at him and saw the memories were vivid in his mind. "Teaching all that when you were so young, preparing you to take care of yourself. You sure loved your father didn't you?"

He nodded, "He was a good Scotsman. Dad told me that Mum was a refined English lady and was disowned by her family when they got married. Then they boarded a ship and sailed to Australia. I don't know how long they were there; probably not too long because they were on a ship to this country when they knew I was coming."

Shoot almighty! I never talked this much before. Grace sure can loosen up my tongue.

Grace interrupted, "That must have been a very hard journey for her. Where did they land in this country?"

"They landed in the state of Washington, probably at the Seattle port. Somehow, they made it to Okanogan where I was born. My Dad told me that I was just about born on the ship. I sure don't know how they made it inland unless I was born on the way and he just said it was in Okanogan." He paused. Should he tell her more?

Grace nodded. "I'm so sorry, Jack, that you never knew your mother. I'm sure she was a fine lady." Her sincerity and interest showed many expressions.

He nodded and didn't know what to say next, knowing he needed to continue. "My childhood was good until I was ten. Then things changed. A man came to the cabin one day and told me that my dad was killed—a fight with another man. I knew that Dad's temper came out sometimes, if someone was cheating or being mean. He always told me to be honest above all else and never to be cruel." He stopped and looked down at his boots for a minute taking some deep breaths.

"I guess the other man pulled a knife and stabbed Dad more than once before friends pulled him off. My dad died right there and the men buried him up on a mountain somewhere." He paused again. After he controlled his feelings, he continued. "I never got to say goodbye and I don't even know where he was buried."

He stopped, breathed deep again, looking up at the ceiling fighting emotions. He wouldn't cry in front of her. Buried deep inside him, his pain stabbed his heart when he thought back to when he was so young. Until now, no one knew his past.

He quickly got control, took a sip of his lemonade and continued, "The man gave me my father's leather belt made in Scotland, his pocket watch, hunting knife and his rifle. There wasn't anything else. I didn't believe the man for a long time and was sure that my Dad would come home."

"Oh Lord! Jack, I'm so sorry you had to go through that horrible pain. It must have been absolutely devastating, especially as a little boy." Her hand reached for his arm while she so wanted to give him a hug. He raised his other hand to cover hers.

In a few minutes, he was able to continue. "After that, things were pretty much no good." He stopped and lowered his eyes to the floor. The pain of his childhood still affected him even though he tried to keep it all in a mind-sealed box.

"I'll get into that another time, but enough about me." He gave a weak smile.

Grace saw the sting in Jack's expression and knew she would find out more at another time. "That's fine." She didn't want to push even though she was curious as to what could bring so much bottled up pain.

"I like hearing about your life better." He gave her a smile just as the music started with a slow tempo and he took her hand. "Let's dance."

The night continued with many dances, a good deal of conversation about current events, hopes for the country's recovery and more about Grace's family. Jack embraced the pleasure of hearing about a normal life, or as normal as life could be. Too soon, the last dance ended and they had to part.

"Before we leave, Jack, I want to ask you something. Will you join my family for a Sunday dinner next week? My folks would like to meet you." She didn't have the nerve to ask if he had ever been married, especially when she looked into his blue eyes holding her breath waiting for an answer on her invitation.

He kept his eyes locked with hers and smiled. So, that's the question she mentioned in her letter. He finally answered, "That'd be right nice."

Grace told him what time to come and directions to her parent's home. She worried that her brothers might not accept him. She didn't care; she liked him, a lot.

They both parted company and almost skipped to their rides. Fred said, "I guess Gracie has found someone she has taken a shine to. Maybe we boys will have to decide if we'll let him court her." The two laughed while Grace's cheeks reddened.

The cowboys teased each other as they returned to the ranch. Each talked about the one they liked, telling about her life, if she was old enough to do what she wanted, if she worked or stayed at home, and on and on. Jack listened, but wouldn't give any details about Grace. He didn't want to share her with his buddies.

He thought about the dinner with her family and wondered if he would pass muster. What if they didn't think he was good enough for Grace?

Damn!

CHAPTER 20

1933 - SUNDAY DINNER

The next Sunday, Jack's old auto rumbled into the driveway at the Lee home and parked next to another, which he assumed belonged to Grace's father. He was a half hour early. The Lees had just returned from church in Sturgis. Grace greeted him at the door and after a minute of smiling and hellos, she introduced him to her parents, Al and Isabella Lee. They smiled and welcomed him, with Al shaking his hand.

"Nice automobile, young man," Grace's father said nodding to the window where he saw the 1929 Ford Tudor Model A shining in the sunlight. His hands crossed his chest resting inside the bib of his blue striped overalls—his comfortable attire after church. The car was a couple years newer than his own. A five-to-eight-year old car wasn't bad with the economy at hand. Not many could afford a new one and some couldn't afford the oldest. He certainly couldn't afford a new one.

Jack nodded back, "I bought it free and clear. I got a good deal and I worked extra time to pay cash for it, Mr. Lee." His chest puffed outward slightly in pride.

Al smiled, "Call me Al. Now sit down and get comfortable," as he waved Jack to the main room. "The ladies are fixing the food, so you're stuck with me for now." He plopped into his large wood chair with the well-worn padded leather back and sear. He rested his arms on the wide wood armrests and nodded for Jack to sit in the other chair. "So you work at the Frawley Ranch? It's quite an operation, isn't it?"

Jack felt comfortable with this man right off and didn't feel intimidated. Grace had told him enough that he knew Al was a good man. There seemed to be a hidden softness to the grey-haired father who looked so stern with his taut mouth and frown lines between the eyebrows.

"Tell me about your ranching work," Al asked and puffed on his pipe.

Jack told him about the Frawley ranches and about the operation. They had a lengthy conversation about cattle, horses, the ranch business and how each loved horses. Familiarity brought acceptance of each other.

Not probing too much, Al tried to ask the right questions of the man who had captured his oldest daughter's eye.

"You got any kin, Jack?"

Surprised, he took a minute to answer. "No sir, I don't." He stopped and stared at the crackling fire remembering the small fireplace in the cabin he shared with his father.

"My mum died after I was born. I never knew her. When I was ten years old my dad was killed, he was, in the state of Washington, our home. Someone wrote a friend of my dad's in Indiana and that man came all the way out west and took me back to his farm. He was my dad's best friend when they lived in Scotland, he was."

"I'm sorry to hear that you lost your father. How was the friend who took care of you?"

"Mac MacGregor treated me fine, but I didn't want to leave my home back in Washington." He could still see the little cabin in the woods where he and his father had lived.

"I remember the long train ride and all the stops before we got to Indiana. I'd never been on a train before." Jack smiled, looked out the window recalling how they wound through the states, stopping at small towns with small depots and a few larger. The plains displayed tall grass, grain, tumbleweeds and thistles. "St. Paul was a surprise. I never saw such a large city and I'd just as soon stay away from all big cities—too much noise and commotion."

Al nodded and smiled. "That must have been quite an experience for a youngster. What did you do when you got to Indiana?"

Jack eased back in his chair and put his cigarette out. "Mac had a farm and I wandered all over the acreage. Sometimes I helped shoo the cattle in or feed the pigs." He paused and remembered how good life was back then. Still at that time, he'd been miserable and silently hid his grief which was replaced with anger at the whole world.

"I was stupid though, made a mistake and ran away from the MacGregors. I was so lonesome for m' dad and thought I had to get back to Washington thinking maybe he wasn't dead." He looked down at his hands and clenched them tight. "A stupid boy, I was."

Al sat and puffed on his pipe. He saw Jack was struggling with memories. "Tell me more."

Jack had never told anyone about his life, but he felt he needed to now. Al reminded him of his own father in some way, but he couldn't pinpoint it. He just felt a connection.

"I got as far as Missouri and got caught by the law. Since I was too young to be on my own, they tried to find a home for me. I was only ten years old, but I would have been better off on my own." He stopped, looked down at his feet and tightly clenched his teeth. When he got control again, he decided to go on.

"A man by the name of Drake showed up and said he'd adopt me. He never did adopt, but sure had other plans for me. He was a vicious son-of-a-b . . . ." He halted his tongue for a second and then said, ". . . a vicious man."

The wood aroma of the fireplace made him think of his dad's cabin, the lost fatherly love, and loneliness crept into his inner soul. Then his thoughts returned to that other world of pain and hate.

Al asked in his deep voice. "What was this Drake's first name? Just wondering if anybody I know from Missouri had heard of a man by that name."

"Funny part is, I don't remember. All I ever called him was Drake or yes sir." Jack knew his mind blocked out as much connection to that man as possible, yet it wouldn't block out the pain and that hateful face etched forever into his memory. He could still see those deep brown narrow eyes, the thin greasy coffee-colored hair falling straight to the collar while his thin lips locked in a sneer of loathing. Jack remembered when the sheriff handed him over to that devil. Drake grabbed him by the collar and dragged him to the wagon full of supplies. He spat out, 'Okay, boy. You belong to me now and you're gonna work for your keep.' Jack still felt how that voice sharpened the terror of his ten-year-old body.

"Drake wasn't a good man, was he?" Al shifted in his chair to resettle in a more comfortable position and rested his feet on the cushioned footstool.

Jack shook his head, "No. I got a beating the first night I was there when I let my temper flare at Drake for telling me I couldn't have a piece of cherry pie because I didn't unpack the wagon fast enough. Drake grabbed me by the collar and bounced my brains back and for'. He growled that I better not sass, argue, or try to run or the next time I wouldn't be able to walk or talk. He scared me good." He still could see how his head had hurt while he held back his tears and watched the others eat pie.

"I understood well what my life was going to be from then on under that bastard." Jack stopped and said he was sorry for swearing.

Al nodded, "Don't worry. What I'd call him would scorch the earth."

Jack's lips curled into a slight grin that strengthened his awareness of this man. He decided to tell more. Grace's father needed to know.

"I woke at dawn the next day with a kick in the side and Drake's yell, 'Get up. Ya can't sleep all day. We got chores to do. Lester here is gonna learn ya how to work for your keep'." Jack imitated the high-pitched voice squawking at him and he remembered how Drake pointed to his son who looked just a little older.

"A right fatherly man, I see," Al said in disgust.

Jack nodded. Drake made sure he knew he was the master. Disobey, and harsh punishment would be the result. "That started my years of doing what the old man said, or else. Often the "or else" came for no reason at all. God, I hated that S.O.B. with a passion!"

Al took a puff on his pipe, looked to Jack and could see the anger. He saw a man who was broken at such an early age and asked, "What did this Drake do for a living?"

"He was a chiropractor and owned a farm not far from town. His business was not a big moneymaker. When he didn't have business, he usually sat on the porch, or in the wagon watching Lester and me to make sure we worked, and worked hard."

The vision came to him of Drake sitting with a jar of liquor always next to him taking swigs to quench his thirst while he yelled at the boys. Then he'd swipe his shirtsleeve across his mouth to catch the dribbles. "When he drank all the liquor in his jug, he'd yell at his wife to bring another. She was prompt 'cause she knew what her punishment would be if she didn't. He was a bastard with her too."

"Good God!" Al shook his head in disgust. "He was an S.O.B. that's for sure."

"You got that right. He made us take care of the small herd of cattle as well as the fields. We also had to keep the barn clean and the fences mended."

He stopped for a minute to stuff tobacco in another cigarette paper, rolled it up, licked the edge to keep it rolled tight, then lit the end, inhaling deeply. After a long exhale, he continued.

"Each spring we had to plow up the fields to plant with corn or wheat, and then harvest it in the fall. When we were young, he had to hire a man, but we still had to help. Lester and I became toughened and knew that complaining would just result in another whipping."

"He whipped you too?" Al's eyes bulged with his eyebrows forming a question mark.

Jack nodded hard and clenched his fists tightly together in between his thighs. He might as well tell the rest even though it brought it all back too vividly.

In a minute he continued, "Often enough. He'd grab me and Lester, make us take off our shirts, then he'd tie our hands up, fling the rope over the barn rafter and hoist our arms up. We couldn't fight or he'd go at us like you'd stomp on a bug.

"Usually after a long swig of whiskey, he'd start to whip us with his god-damned bull whip. The woven leather whip dug into our flesh with each snap." His voice cracked and he stopped and gave a deep gulp trying to compose himself. Even after all these years, Jack felt deeply affected when he remembered those days. The scars on his back burned and the hate scorched his insides.

Al waited. All this pain needed to come out. Willing to listen, he'd wait for Jack to continue.

"Drake stood behind us and cracked the whip on the ground first. Lester and I never knew who would get the first lash. After one got it, the other got it. Back and forth, he went and stopped every so often to take another swig from his jar of whiskey. After a swallow, he'd bellow, 'You boys gonna do what I say now?' All we could do was squeak out a 'yes' each time, not knowing what the hell we had done wrong to begin with."

Al leaned forward and kept shaking his head. "What kind of a person would do that? Yet I know there are men who, in order to feel superior, have to make others feel worthless and powerless."

Jack paused, sat for a minute collecting himself before going on. He had so much hate blistering inside him that he felt he might spit flames soon. He took a deep breath and then another.

Eventually he continued. "Many a time Lester and I passed out." He visualized his head hanging loose on his chest. "Our backs were a mass of bloody gashes."

He pictured Drake standing with his legs parted and shoulders leaning back for balance and his whip in one hand. "Sometimes we heard him saying something like, 'Tha's enough for now. Youztupid boys better remember to do what Izay.'" Jack imitated the voice of Drake again. "Then he'd finally cut down our hands and arms and we'd fall down in a heap."

Al shook his head picturing two young boys hanging from the rafters with their backs cut open. "Didn't the townsfolk know what Drake was doing to you and his own son? They could have stopped it."

"I don't think they knew. He made sure that we acted happy when anyone was around and they never saw our backs or heard him threatening us. Don't suspect they liked him, though, but that didn't help us. I know some of the men sure knew Drake's wife."

Shocked, Al said, "You don't have to go on, if you don't want to."

Jack took a deep breath wanting to get this over with, turned his head to look at Al and saw the compassion. He'd never felt more comfortable with a man since he'd grown up. Maybe it was because Al reminded him of his own father. That gave him encouragement and he was ready to continue. It was time.

"No, I need to tell you about my life so you know me and who I am."

Al nodded and chewed on his pipe and leaned back. His attention never wavered.

"Me and Lester would crumble to the ground when he cut us down from the rafters. Sometimes we were out cold and didn't even know when he cut us down. He left us to take care of ourselves."

He gave a disgusted sound adding, "At least he cut us down." He stopped to take another deep breath and paused for a few minutes.

"Our moans and curses sure came when we tried to ease the pain. We'd get a cool drink from the hydrant and then try to take care of each other's wounds. A whipping could be once a week, once a month, or whenever Drake wanted. My hate grew quickly and I despised that man."

Al kept silent, but attentive and only nodded.

After a long silence, Jack continued while looking out the window and gaining control again. "Lester usually started with 'You can't win with that S.O.B.' and he was right. I could never have hated my father like Lester did."

Two sides of the world gave a shocking contrast back then. While Jack's father had filled him with love, Drake filled him and his own son full of hate and fear. Physical and mental scars remained deeply imbedded. "I sure knew I made a mistake by running away from MacGregor, but too late to escape. I knew I had to face the consequences or I wouldn't live."

Right at that moment Grace came announcing dinner was ready. She was all smiles.

Al started to rise, squirming to get out of his chair after sitting so long. "I'm glad you told me what you went through. Now, I'm ready for some stomach-filling food with a good family. What about you?" and gave Jack a pat on his shoulder as they walked to the kitchen.

Jack couldn't get over the feeling of belonging here. He wanted Al's approval of who he was or he wouldn't get Grace. Did he say too much?

CHAPTER 21

FIRST DINNER

When he walked into the kitchen, Jack was surprised to see a long table with a place setting at every chair. Grace's little brother, Charlie, was already sitting at one of the spots. Her two brothers and the wife of Fred, Frances, entered from the back door.

"Hello all. Frances brought apple pies for dessert," Fred handed the pies over. Seeing the extra person he grinned, "Hello, Jack." Cinnamon and apple fragrance mingled with the pork's garlic, sage and rosemary already in the kitchen.

Jack nodded and said his hellos, shaking both Fred's and Bob's hands. He was nervous with them being there to assess him, as well as Grace's parents.

How the hell am I going to make it through this? Damn brothers anyway!

Mom brought a carved pork roast to the table, ready for the first fork to spear a slice. The aroma caused Al's stomach to growl loudly while Nellie and Laura brought the rest of the food. The family began to sit down at the long wood table, covered with a starched crisp white tablecloth with the edges delicately embroidered in tiny blue and pink flowers connected with green vines.

"Jack, sit here next to Grace," her father said while slapping the back of the empty chair. She was already standing by hers.

All the chairs scraped over the spotless well-used pine flooring as they sat. Grace's father led the before meal grace. Jack had never been to a meal where anyone said a prayer and he didn't know what to do. An uncomfortable feeling enveloped him. A second passed before he decided to lower his head like the rest. His eyes rose to glance around and see each person's eyes closed, hands knitted together. When Al finished, they all responded with a firm, "Amen," and made the sign of the cross.

Jack wondered what that was all about. What had he gotten himself into?

They passed the pork around, then potatoes and green beans along with applesauce for the pork, gravy for the potatoes. Fresh rolls out of the oven accompanied a butter plate sitting at each end of the table ready for snatching and slathering with homemade jam.

Jack was surprised at the order of passing the food around the table. Being used to the ranch hands grabbing as fast as they could, he'd have to watch himself. When he heard Bob ask for the jam to be passed with a "please", Jack worried that he wouldn't do or say the right thing. Then he decided he'd just do his best and try not to embarrass himself. He didn't want to put too much on his plate even though he saw the brothers pile food on theirs and take generous portions. It looked like there was enough food for two families. He'd certainly be filled by the end of the meal.

Conversation was lively while bantering between the siblings brought laughter. The family talked about all sorts of things including who was out of work, who found work, or which family moved away. There was much speculation on the government and farming.

Nellie told the latest about her nursing including about one patient who was very demanding and she got her revenge with a snapping backrub when he demanded his. The group all laughed when they heard she used a large rubber band to snap him every so often.

She added, "Then he said that it was the best backrub he had ever had, which defeated my revenge." More laughter came before the group heard the next sibling.

Laura told about getting some work sorting merchandise for the owner of a store in Whitewood for a few days, and Charlie grunted when asked about school by saying it was okay, a typical answer with no elaboration.

Jack felt astounded by the family's fun while eating and their involvement in each other's lives. He'd never known a family like this. He was overwhelmed while listening and staying quiet to learn more about each member.

Political talk changed the atmosphere as Al said, "This New Deal for Americans that Roosevelt is instigating just might work." He took a sip of water and continued. "Why, there's talk of making it law for a forty-hour week, a minimum wage, unemployment compensation, and something called social security. There's even more programs to get the country back to work. I think he's the man to get the job done. We've got to pull out of this and get the economy going again!"

Fred spoke up. "That's a fact, and I hope he helps the farmers. Look what has happened to the Great Plain States with the economy already. I read that over one million families have lost their farms by foreclosure so far." He stopped to take a bite of meat, and then continued in a low voice, "They thought when the price went up on wheat, it meant they could plant more. So, they plowed up more native grass fields. Those speculators caused the surplus to increase and then the wheat price dropped. The damnable rainless days with nothing but wind came. Can you imagine all the dirt flying around— dust storms like nobody ever saw in the Midwest, plus no relief seen in the near future?"

"I read that three million tons of top soil has been blown clear to kingdom come," Grace interjected. "The drought has ruined winter wheat."

Al shook his head in disbelief. "The New Deal includes the Agricultural Adjustment Act beginning in May of this year. If farmers agree to curtail their crops, by not planting wheat for two years, the government will pay 29 cents a bushel for wheat that they did not harvest. Then it will continue with reductions of 15 and 10% in '34 and '35. They hope this will raise the price since there won't be as much wheat on the market."

He stopped, took a sip of water and then added, "Sounds logical to me and it may work. Wonder how many farmers will agree? I'm sure there will be balking amidst the agreeing."

Fred added, "Yes, and they are doing the adjustment with corn and hogs too. They are going to pay $5.00 per head on the hogs and use them to feed the poor."

Al piped in again with a nod, "Now that sounds reasonable and a good plan to help the starving. I hope that works. It will take a long time to see the results, but something has to begin to change. I read that if they cut corn production by 20%, the farmer will be paid 25 cents a bushel. That should increase the price in the next few years."

Jack sat silent and listened to each person. He had never been at a table with such lively and varied subjects discussed. He didn't want to join in even though he too was aware of the economy and what the government was doing. He just nodded every so often.

Mom raised her head and held up her fork as if it were a sign that it was her time to say something.

"The last letter from Jeannette said they were managing, but desperate for rain. The corn crop in that area had smut this year. That fungus with its black spores won't bring in money. Maybe Steve will agree to that new plan.

"Jeannette said a friend told her that the black wall of dust was higher than any building when it passed and covered them. People are beginning to call the dust storms Black Blizzards. That seems fitting. Jeannette and Steve haven't had it too bad yet because of the trees around their property helping to shield them somewhat, at least around the house. I pray that they can make it through, and us too."

Al smiled at her. "Oh, we'll make it somehow and so will they. You got plenty of goods stored in the cellar. I'll butcher another pig, if we have to cut down their feed. We'll have plenty for bacon slabs. Of course, we have to have you make your pickled pigs feet and can them," he nodded to her with a twinkle in his eye.

"We can slaughter the cow too, if we have to and take some to dry for beef jerky and preserve the rest like usual. Mom, you won't hurt if I can help it. We'll patch the shoes again too and Charlie can have hand-me-downs if he grows more. We'll be fine." His voice sounded assured, yet hinted that his soul wondered if they might hurt a lot worse before times got better.

Jack had a feeling that Al was having a hard time keeping his sawmill running, with business almost nil compared to the old days. If Al didn't get more orders for lumber, he'd have to resort to just selling firewood, and be lucky for that.

Al continued, "Jeannette will be okay, too, because I know they are doing the same. Steve's a good manager and your daughter is like you, canning, making food go farther and all that. She learned from you; so don't worry."

It was evident that Al worried about all his children and hoped they all could make it through this depression. He was that kind of a man. It certainly wasn't easy and yet they all would keep pushing back defeat like Al and Isabella did before, about the turn of the century when tough times hit the nation then.

Fred and Bob said as often as they could they would head to the streambeds to pan for gold. They looked for spots where the flow of water settled creating low beds that may have settled with pockets of gold particles in the bedrock. They dug their pans in the sand and gravel where particles may have landed, hidden from the surface. Filling the pan with water over the grit, they swirled and shook the pan so all lighter debris fell out while the heavier gold particles stayed at the bottom of the pan. If lucky, they might find the miniscule shiny metallic yellow-gold specks. Fred spoke about the men squatting and bending over the stream to work, often having to stop to stretch their back muscles and legs.

Jack was well aware that acquiring even a speck of gold took a lot of work while hope kept each going. Trying to accumulate an ounce was almost impossible and the minuscule fragments of an ounce usually ended up sold because of the necessity for money to buy food, clothing, or pay unexpected medical bills. He'd heard others doing the same thing.

Fred and Bob said they never found any big nuggets, yet acquired enough so they could receive money in exchange to keep them out of the poor man's line another day or week. Gold was around $18.00 an ounce and a speck might weigh far less than one hundredth of an ounce by itself. To get even a few cents in return for several specks was a great deal of work, yet every penny helped.

Discussions continued as the men talked about work and if they could get more or not. Dad said he acquired a small job, but nothing permanent. Someone needed lumber for a small bridge. At least it was some income for now.

Al appeared older than his age and Jack assumed he must have been wearing down with all the physical labor in the past couple of years taking its toll. Mom seemed to be holding up better even after eight children, plus taking in two orphans according to what Grace had told him at the last dance. She also prepared meals for her husband's workers at his sawmill when it had been busy. Grace told him that before the family moved to the Black Hills her grandparents had helped too. It looked like Isabella had the strength of a bull and Jack felt that she could set her jaw tight and tackle whatever came her way with determination to handle it.

While eating and listening, Jack saw a family of hard workers who tried to take care of themselves and each other. He liked that. Thinking the trait made for strong people, he knew Grace came from that stock. It reminded him what he might have had if his mother and father had lived. He liked all the conversation and he learned more about each family member.

After the meal, the women cleared the table and did dishes while the men discussed more topics in the main room. Then Jack began to feel a little out of place. He rose and stated, "I guess I best be getting back to the ranch. I sure enjoyed the day and thank you for having me."

"Hold on there, Jack," Al stated raising a hand to stall him, and yelled for Grace to come. "Jack, here, is about to leave. You want to walk him to his auto?"

She quickly came into the room, her cheeks darkening. "Why yes, I'll be glad to. It was nice to have you join us for the day, Jack," she said as they started to walk to the door. She didn't tell him that she had sneaked peaks at him every so often while helping with the cleanup.

Stopping in midstride, Jack said, "Grace, I ought to thank your mom for the meal."

"Oh, she'll appreciate that," she answered and they walked to the kitchen where Mom was still putting dishes and pans away. He thanked her and then they went back to the door.

Al yelled, "Right nice to meet you, son. Come again anytime. I'd like to hear more about you and I'll tell you some stories about Grace," he chuckled.

"Thank you, sir. I appreciate it. Nice to meet you all," he nodded to Grace's two brothers. Jack turned and quickly opened the door for Grace.

While walking to his auto, he told her how much he'd enjoyed the day. "I've never been around a family like yours. It sure is nice." He tilted his hat a little more to shade his eyes.

"I'm glad. I hope you will come again. We have a family meal every Sunday and you're always welcome. Fred, Frances and little Al have their own home down the hill, but they almost always come for Sunday dinner."

At the auto, she leaned against the door bracing herself with her shoulder. "Someday Bob will get married and if they live close enough, they'll come. We always have plenty of people at the table."

He leaned against the door with the opposite shoulder so they faced each other and he propped one foot up on the running board, then he laughed. "I'll say the table sure filled up!"

After a few more minutes of just looking at each other while smiling broadly, they knew it was time for him to leave. He took her hand as if to shake it, but just held it and enveloped it in both of his. Finally, he smiled and said, "See you soon," and gave her a wink.

His smile lasted all the way back to the ranch while he hummed the miles away with song after song. He felt good.

Damn was not needed this time.

CHAPTER 22

COWBOYING AND WAR

Sure enough, the next Sunday Jack rolled into the drive of the Lee family home about the same time as before. The women were once again preparing the dinner.

Grace greeted him with a big smile and sparkly eyes. She said it would be a bit before the meal was on the table and led him to where her father sat in his easy chair

"Dad, we have a guest."

"I know. I saw the auto pull up out there." He pointed out the window. "Glad to see you again, Jack. Come on in and sit while the women do their work."

Jack did, and with a more at ease feeling then last time. "How are you, sir?"

"I'm doing fine. How about yourself?" Al answered and rose out of his chair to stoke the fire, placing another log on top. The wood aroma added to the warm peaceful setting. He took his time and settled back again asking, "Tell me some more about yourself. Did that good-for-nothing Drake let you go to school? There were no laws back then stating a child had to attend school, no laws to enforce education. Right?"

Jack got comfortable in his chair. "Uh huh, but I got some learning. The townspeople kept after Drake to have us get an education. He at least bowed down to the group on that."

"Did you have any education before that? Drake didn't get you until you were ten years old. You should have had a primary education by then."

Jack sat quiet for a minute and puffed on his cigarette before putting out the remaining stub. What to say? He was telling Grace's dad a lot about himself and wondered what the man thought. He still wanted Al to know what his daughter was getting herself into—if she actually was. Maybe, though, he was saying too much. He decided what the hell and just kept talking. If he wasn't good enough for Grace, he'd probably know soon.

"My dad taught me. I sure did have some education and I loved it. He taught me how to write, read, and do arithmetic and he wanted me to be better than he was when he was a boy. I think my Mum helped him learn some."

Jack was glad his father had taught him and remembered the teacher in Missouri who found him to be a quiet pupil—studious and a quick learner. She didn't give the students homework since most had chores to do after school. Instead, she worked furiously to teach as much as she could in the school hours. Tests were frequent and he remembered receiving good grades. His own father didn't give tests and just expected Jack to remember what he learned.

"How long did you go to school? I don't imagine you were allowed to get to the eighth grade, right?" Al asked.

"Right. When Lester and I finished the sixth grade, our schooling stopped. Drake knew the law couldn't get after him, so he told us we had to work more and make more money for him."

Jack paused and put out his cigarette. "I think he had another reason to halt our learning too. I think he didn't want us to learn too much or we'd know more than he did." He gave a quick laugh.

Al laughed as well. "Sounds about right . . . sounds about right." He nodded and then asked, "How about religion? You get any? Can't imagine that snake of a Drake had any religion in him."

Jack nodded, "That's a fact, but he insisted that Lester and me go to church every Sunday and sing in the choir. He wanted the town folk to think that he raised good boys and he told us we better sing loud."

Al laughed again, "Sounds like he forgot to listen to the sermons."

"You're right. Even at that, making us go to church and sing, gave us a break from work. I liked to sing. I don't have a strong deep voice like Lester's, but I like to sing. I'll tell you, though, I still hated those stupid sermons talking about obedience and forgiveness.

That minister's fire and brimstone did nothing for me. Believing in a good God would take more than just a minister yapping away."

He was still his father's son and that included the temperament; he couldn't push the anger away when he heard those sermons. Understanding a God who said to obey and who took away the only person in the world that he loved, was beyond his comprehension.

Al looked sad at Jack. "Well, I understand when I hear what you went through."

Jack frowned, rolled another cigarette and lit it. "Drake did not follow the word of God any more than the devil did. He had no love in him, not even for his wife and less for Lester and me. He blamed everyone for all his troubles and took it out on us at home. He felt everyone owed him a good life, especially the God that the preacher talked about on Sundays. He forgot that 'ask and you will receive' meant that one must follow God's law first. I did learn that at least."

Tensing up, he took a minute thinking back before he continued. He was spilling everything out to Al and it felt good to tell someone who seemed to understand.

"I often fainted from a whipping and then feel the sting for days. Sometimes Mrs. Drake applied ointment to our wounds. She was not a bad woman and she cared for us. I felt sorry for her. She also received beatings and not only when he drank, but whenever he demanded more from her."

Al sat up, leaned forward and shook his head again. "I can't imagine doing that to my wife. She was beaten?"

"Yup. When Drake didn't have enough money, he forced his wife to go to town and sell herself. He'd tell her, 'Get off your hind end and get out there tonight. You bring back some money.' If she came home with none, or too little, she was beaten. All she could do was get as much money as possible. I felt sorry for her." Jack saw how she hated herself and her husband even more. He heard her cussing him under her breath every so often.

"She told me that she felt she had no choice and no way out. She was trapped and scared. She didn't have any education, less than mine even and she didn't think she could get a job or survive on her own. So she did what her husband demanded. Besides, he'd have beaten her to a pulp if he thought she would run away. I know, because I heard him tell her that. It made me think of his threat to me and she was as scared as I was."

Al interjected, "Power was what he had and he used it like an iron stick. Fear ruled that household, didn't it? I'd sure like to meet that man now. I'd take a branding iron to him and then tie him up to a spirited horse and let him be dragged for a few miles!" Pausing he gave a deep sigh. "Sounds like you have seen a great deal of life and much at its worst. A city would call you a street-wise boy probably."

Jack smiled and thought about when he'd learned what happened to Drake and his wife. "Well, I found out a few years ago that Drake died from alcohol and his wife burned the house down. She left and no one knew where she went."

"Good for her. Now, how about you? Have you moved on from those bad days?" Al asked while looking at the fireplace.

"Yup, guess so. I'm not hardened though, Mr. Lee. I still want a good life. I want to make it like it was when my dad and I lived in the woods in the cabin he built. I remember him telling me about my mum and her being such a lady. Grace reminds me of what my dad told me about my mum."

Al looked at him, smiled and nodded.

Jack could almost see Al's mind saying something like, *Well, now, that's a good thing. If a woman reminds a man of his mother and she was a good person, that man has found his true love.* That's what people seemed to think.

Jack envisioned a picture of his mother. "My mum had to be special, but she died before I ever got to know her. I sure wished I could have. My father did his best and still had to earn a living. When we were together he always taught me things and he never once hit me."

His loneliness for his father ate at his soul while he dreamed that somehow, somewhere he would find love and peace again. He wanted a life the opposite of what he had lived in the Drake house. He wanted a home full of love.

When Jack paused, Al asked, "When did you get away from that Drake?"

"I think it was in 1904, still fifteen years old, but heading close to sixteen. I'd turned into a muscle-hardened youngster and knew I could get work on my own. I told Lester one time that I was going to beat the old man to a pulp one day. Then I'd throw him in the manure pile face first. I could do it with one or two blows when he was drunk. Lester said he'd string his dad up and beat him with a bull whip until there was no flesh left on his back.

"After our next whipping, I sat hunched over trying to ease the pain and decided I wasn't going to take anymore. I decided I was going to get the hell out of there as soon as I could.

"I told Lester that Drake had whipped me for the last time and I was going to leave that hell hole." His fists clenched until his nails almost drew blood in his palms. He couldn't relax. "My last straw had come and broke."

Al gave a probing look at Jack, then stoked his pipe and leaned back before asking, "Then what happened? How'd you get away?"

"Well, Lester agreed and we made plans to get away together. Without notice or warning, we left the next night while Drake was sleeping off one of his drunken stupors. I packed a gunnysack with my clothes and tied a bedroll on, swung the bag over my shoulder and walked out. I never looked back. Lester wanted to go south and I wanted to go west. We walked to town and when we got near the railroad depot, we shook hands and parted."

He paused and pictured every detail of that last time. "I jumped onto a railcar heading west. Later I realized that I forgot to take even the little I had of my father's possessions, which I had tucked away in a corner. I always said I'd go back some day and get them. I never did. I don't know if it was because I couldn't make myself go back or what. Now I regret not doing it."

Al was ready to say something when Grace popped in to announce dinner was ready. The two men stood and followed her to the kitchen. The table was full once again.

This time Jack felt more comfortable with Grace's brothers. He joined in the conversation a little and the group welcomed his comments. The usual passing, bantering and news swirled in the air around the table. In no time, he relaxed and felt at ease, but still found it hard to joke with each one.

Grace served her strawberry/rhubarb pie with a dollop of whipped cream on each slice. "I walked along the stream yesterday and found a good patch of rhubarb and I couldn't resist bringing some home. And the strawberries topped it off."

"Delicious," echoed in the room when each took a bite.

After the meal, as usual, the women cleaned up and the men sat in the big room for more conversation. Fred left to take his little son home for bedtime and Bob sneaked out—who knew where or what he was doing.

Al drew on his pipe and sat for a minute looking out at the garden his wife and Grace had prepared and planted. Various colored plants and new sprouts displayed many vegetables to come for them to eat, either fresh or canned. He was fortunate to have his wife, Isabella, help in nourishing their family.

Settling more into his chair, Al asked, "Jack, you left off telling me about finally getting away from that Drake. Now tell me what you did and where you went. It must have been a good feeling to get away."

Jack nodded. "You bet it was. At first I was scared he'd catch me, but as I got farther away, I began to breathe easier." He talked about hopping trains, landing wherever he wanted. "Sometimes when I'd get off a train, I'd find some hobos and join them for a meal. They usually could find a stray chicken, rabbit or squirrel for a good stew. They were a good bunch. Sometimes I'd find some work for a few days before moving on. "I stopped in Nebraska and worked on a ranch, but left in a month."

He sat quietly for a few minutes and puffed on his cigarette before putting it out. *I wonder what Al thinks. Shoot, maybe I'm saying too much again.*

"Then I headed northwest from Nebraska and ended up on the Pine Ridge Reservation. Black Elk, a Lakota Sioux, found me trying to catch a rabbit. I thought maybe I was a goner for being on reservation land," he laughed.

"Instead, Black Elk invited me to his home for a meal. We seemed to get along fine. He understood me and ended up taking me in. I knew right away that I could trust him. His word was good and he didn't lay a hand on me. He taught me a lot about trust, horses and nature. I always rode a sweet paint while there. That mare was gentle, but fierce when it came to racing. A great friend, Black Elk was, and I sure needed that, I did."

"How long were you on the reservation?" Al asked.

Jack thought Al probably wondered what Indian ways he may have picked up. "Don't remember exactly, quite a while, maybe close to a year," his head tipped with the "maybe" indicating uncertainty of exact time.

"His son, Benjamin Black Elk, became a good friend too. We spent many a day riding or hunting with Black Elk teaching us. Then I finally decided I needed to get out on my own. I might have been sixteen, maybe around seventeen years old. I didn't keep track."

"Hmm. Where did you go then?"

"Well, Al, I hopped the train again and just kept going. Since I knew some ranching, I ended up in Nevada for a while on a big ranch. The cowhands were a good bunch and we were out on the range a lot rounding up the heifers, steers, cows with their calves, branding the calves. At times, I was on a roundup for the livestock sale. That's sure wide-open country down there. I learned about the cattle that broke away from the herd and hid in gullies, in brush by water, or anywhere they could hide." He laughed and remembered the hours searching for lost ones. "We ate a lot of dust and dirt, but I love being out in the open and the freedom."

Al shifted in his chair, grabbed his pipe, lit it and inhaled. After exhaling, he continued. "You have had quite the experiences. I'd like to see the West sometime. Where'd you go besides Nevada?"

"I ended up next in Lander, Wyoming, on another ranch." He didn't elaborate, but remembered telling Grace of his trick riding. He sure wasn't going to mention all the time with the women in saloons. "Then I moved on to Montana and worked on a ranch there."

"Well, you certainly have moved around. Are you the roaming type?" Jack seemed to move after a few years in each place. Maybe Grace was a passing fancy. "You planning to leave South Dakota too?" Was he going to break Grace's heart?

"No sir. I'm not planning to leave. I think I've found a place worth staying on. I'm sure you know that your daughter has something to do with that." Jack smiled, lowered his head and wondered if he had said too much. He didn't want to leave Grace and that was a new feeling for him. Never was he bothered to leave a woman before, but they weren't Grace.

Al nodded. "Well I see a man who'd gone through hell, and may have found his way out. You must have seen quite a bit of country from prairie to mountains and then here. What do you think of this area, the Black Hills?"

Jack smiled, thought for a minute, mentally comparing all the other places. "I like it," and gave a nod. "I like the hills full of the pines, the easy-going people, the open country and everything about it. I feel at home."

Of course, Grace made the big difference in why he liked the Black Hills. And most likely Al had that all figured out.

Damn!

CHAPTER 23

1933 - MORE BEFORE

After Jack said he liked the Hills, Al chuckled, "So you like the Black Hills and everything in it, including my daughter?"

He grinned, a twinkle in his eye, pleased so far with the boy. Actually, Jack wasn't that young. Al cleared his throat. "Changing the subject, just how old are you, Jack?"

"Ah . . . ah, I'm forty-three, sir. I . . . I know I'm older than you'd like, but I'm a hard worker. I . . . ." He didn't know what to say and looked down at his boots. *Damn. He's going to say I'm too old for Grace.*

"Have you been married before, Jack? Or are you married with a wife hidden away somewhere?"

"No sir," shaking his head back and forth, Jack stated emphatically. "I'm not married and never have been. I was getting ready to ask a woman in Iowa to marry me years ago, during the war. It didn't work out." He paused and thought back to that spring years ago while ranching in Montana. Something had nagged again at the back of his mind. He itched for another change, wanting to move on in search of—something—he wasn't sure what.

"Tell me about that woman."

"First let me tell you how it all came about. In 1917, I was in Montana where one of the ranch hands, Tam McNally, had become a good friend. He kept telling me about Iowa and his hometown. One day Tam asked if I wanted to take a trip, he was thinking of heading back to Iowa. I thought about it a long time and then I asked myself why not go?"

Al asked, "How'd you get from Montana to Iowa? Train?"

"We boarded a train at Billings and weaved through the state into North Dakota toward Fargo. There were stops at small town depots, but I'll bet the towns have changed now, after all these years."

In the back of his mind, Jack could still see the mountain range in Montana disappear as they traveled through grassy hills and prairie land. He saw the waves of new grass swaying lazily in the same direction as the breeze and he smelled the musty blue-grey sage bushes swirling through the countryside in a bustling gust of wind.

"We passed through Fargo and eventually entered Minnesota. We were ready to end that trip by then. Our rears felt like they'd never quit the quivering from the rails after day in and day out on the track." His mind still visualized that trip.

"St. Paul was one of the largest cities I'd seen and Tam explained all about the city. I told him it was no wonder he wanted to be on a ranch. The city was too noisy and busy. High-rising buildings kept the noise from filtering to the sky. It just sat there and made our ears buzz."

Jack paused remembering the smoke and dust mingling with odors of garbage in alleys or the aroma of yeast, spices and meats as he and Tam walked around waiting for their next train. The buildings blotted the sun out from narrow streets and the alleys held the odors low. He missed greenery and open space when they walked back to the depot.

Al laughed and nodded. "I prefer these hills and open space," waving his arm toward the window, "I could never live in a city. I don't like 'em."

"We caught the next jump train from St Paul to Waterloo, Tam's hometown. When we got to there, Tam insisted that I stay with his folks."

He remembered how Tam surprised his parents and his mom began to cry while hugging him tight saying after all his years away, he finally came home. His dad smiled, stood proud and shook hands with his son, ending in a bear hug. Jack saw what he had missed all those years without his father or mother. The hurt was deep inside even though he was glad for Tam. He still felt that hurt.

Al interrupted his thoughts. "I hope you two boys found jobs there in Iowa."

Jack laughed and shifted in his chair. "Well it took a while, but we did, finally. Tam got a job with the Rath Packing Company and I found a tanner who needed someone to process the hides for shipping to a manufacturer in Wisconsin. I didn't like that work, but a few years before I helped a rancher tan a few hides and it was enough to get me the job. I needed some money. Still hate that process, though."

Al looked out the window. "I remember in 1917 all the newspapers were full of stories about Europe's war. You know, it began in 1914, if I remember right, when Germany invaded Belgium, Luxembourg and France. That wasn't enough for the German Empire. They wanted to rule all of Europe."

Jack nodded. "There was lots of talk about the United States trying to remain neutral. Plenty of debates took place on whether our country should get involved or remain neutral. Propaganda flourished and no one trusted Germany. President Woodrow Wilson wanted a non-intervention policy. Then news reported the U.S. needed to stand with her allies or see the British Empire, France and Russia defeated. We sure were in the hot seat." Shaking his head, he added, "I hated to see young boys and men going to war."

Al nodded. "Me too. That year also brought a new policy with daylight savings," Al frowned. "Wilson initiated that policy in an effort to conserve fuel needed to produce electric power, but that proved to be unpopular and was repealed later. No good to change the clock as far as I'm concerned."

Jack agreed. "I remember the radio announcing on that April sixth of '17 that we finally declared war against the German Empire and then found ourselves completely unprepared. Our government really had to scramble to get all kinds of machinery, as well as train the men." He recalled how quickly the country begin producing and fast as they could.

"The papers said that President Wilson adopted the policy of conscription because more troops were needed to fight overseas alongside the allies. More enlisted too, but they all needed training, uniforms, guns and ammunition."

Al liked talking about the past even if it was the grim subject of war. "Where I lived, if you told anyone that you were German, you could be harassed or worse. People were afraid to admit their heritage." Shaking his head back and forth, he stopped for a second and then continued, "Our neighbors were the Schumacher family. Now, they were wonderful people and had been here for two generations. Still they were harassed and finally they left our area. What a shame! Thank God, my family didn't have to go through that. You know we got some German blood in us. We didn't tell people back then and hung onto the English side in us."

"I saw it too. When we declared war, that's when I decided to join the Army. I didn't have anything to lose and didn't have to worry about a family back home."

Al leaned forward. "So when did you join? Where did you go?"

"Well, Tam and I finally enlisted together in '18 on July 23. I remember that date well. It took us a while to realize how serious the war was before we knew we had to do our part."

He stopped a minute to separate a cigarette paper, fill it with tobacco, roll it up and lick the edge to keep the paper sealed. Then he put the pouch of tobacco and the papers back in his pocket. He struck a match on the bottom of his boot and lit the cigarette. Inhaling deeply and exhaling with pursed lips, the smoke swirled in the air while he thought about his short military career.

"We ended up at the Guthrie Center in Iowa. After the ten weeks of training, I ended up assigned to another unit, which brought more weeks of training and instruction, but not as physical. I was older than many and the officers knew I was quick to learn so they assigned me to the 163rd Depot Brigade." Jack remembered the feeling of pride and importance. "I advanced from private quick on to corporal. Later, I became a sergeant—shortly before the end of the war."

"Did you get to go to town, on liberty, or a leave, or whatever they called it?" Al had heard about those times from others—not all good—not all bad.

"Oh yeah, we got a few passes and headed to town." He laughed remembering the boys always saying, "Watch out ladies, here we come!" as they walked or rode into town. They looked for the girls, who greeted them warmly. The soldiers met them at the pavilion dances in the park, took them to the soda shop or whatever or wherever else they could—as they could afford. The young girls were thrilled to get attention from a man in uniform and flirted back.

Jack continued, "I met a girl and we got along fine. Her name was Sarah." His cheeks burned when he remembered her hourglass figure and how she felt against him when he held her.

"We met on the days when I got a pass. Things developed from there and we both got serious." He clenched his fists together, still angry at the outcome.

"Is this the one you wanted to marry?" Al asked.

Jack nodded. "I was ready to ask her, but Sarah didn't show up the next weekend. When it happened again, I got worried that maybe she was sick. I thought maybe she got the Spanish flu or maybe she broke a bone. So I walked to her home, knocked on the fancy door and was greeted by her father."

He still could still see the scowl on the father's face and a cigar hanging at the corner of his mustached mouth. He took the cigar and held it in one hand while the other remained on the half-opened door and asked what Jack wanted as he looked him up and down like a distasteful odor. Jack remembered well that feeling of having the father consider him a low-class person.

"I asked if Sarah was there. He shook his head and told me that I was not welcome; Sarah was going to marry a local boy in business and that was that. He said she was in New York and wouldn't be back for months." Jack saw how the father gave him a feeling of worthlessness.

"He said for me not to ever see her again, that I wasn't good enough for her."

Jack remembered Sarah telling him that her father controlled everyone and insisted on things done his way. She didn't want that, yet she didn't seem to have any say in her own life.

"Sarah's dad was a businessman and also knew the politicians and the police. He knew how to work most people and grease their palms, according to Sarah. He told me to get out of there and if I ever came back, he'd call the police and I'd end up in prison." Jack looked down at his boots. "Trash, is what he called me." He could still feel those words stinging, *You're trash. I never want to see you around here again.*

Al's head shook back and forth and he tapped his pipe on the tray. "Well, you're probably better off not having gotten into that family. I'd bet my last penny on that. Did you just turn around and walk away, or did you hit him?" Laughing, he added, "If it had been me, I might have hauled off and hit the man, probably ending up in jail."

"Well, sir, I didn't hit him, but my words might have scorched him a little. I called him some pretty nasty names and told him that I knew Sarah loved me and that he just lost his daughter because she'd hate him for what he was doing."

"Good for you. I'd bet you were right. Did you ever see her again?"

"No sir. She never came to any dances, to any of our hangouts, and I never saw her around town after that. I watched her house a couple of times to see if she would come out. The ol' man apparently didn't see me or knew I was out of luck." He still remembered leaning against the tree wishing she would come out. "I sent her a couple of cards, but they came back to me unopened. I never saw her again. Since then I never found anyone until . . . ." his voice trailed off, but his mind continued, *until I met Grace.*

Al smiled, sure what the probable ending was when Jack stopped abruptly. "Why did that man call you trash and think you weren't good enough for his daughter?"

"Well, sir, he must have checked up on me. I don't have much education. My vocabulary isn't great. Reading and listening are two things that helped me to learn more. And I like to keep up on the news and I can learn, sir. I just do it my own way." Jack wanted him to know that he wasn't ignorant just because he hadn't gone to school longer.

"Now that's an honest answer and you don't sound stupid at all. I'd say you're a pretty smart fellow. Don't let anyone ever tell you different. I'll tell you something, I never got to finish school either. So we're in the same boat and I sure don't want anyone to tell me I'm stupid. He'd never say it again." Al's body shook with laughter knowing the culprit would have landed on his backside.

Jack's eyes widened and his eyebrows rose, then quickly a smile crossed his lips. He knew now that he and Al had more in common. "Grace went through school to become a teacher, didn't she?"

"Oh yes. Mama and I made sure our children had a good education. Grace went to the Springfield Normal School that trained women to be teachers. Normal School is like a high school-college combined. She decided to be a teacher and she loves children. She was a good one too and taught until . . . ."

147

He stopped as Grace entered saying, "Cleanup is done." That ended the conversation between the two men.

Jack wondered what the end of Al's sentence could be. As soon as they'd seen Grace in the doorway, Al stopped mid-sentence. What was Al going to say? She taught until what? Until she married? Then what? She isn't married now. So what happened? Did she get a divorce? Is she a widow? What else could it be?

What else could he have meant? How to find out?

Damn!

CHAPTER 24

TRUTH

After the meal, Dad suggested that Grace show Jack around the property. They both nodded, smiling at each other and walked to the door. Outside the slight breeze gave some relief from the heat of that 1933 summer. As they walked, Grace showed him the few animals they kept, the barn and the work area of Dad's sawmill. Then she led him around to the root cellar that sloped into the side of the hill just below the house.

"We keep our produce down here. It stays cool and fresh longer. The canned goods are here too and it's also available if there's a tornado," Grace added as she pulled the handle to open the heavy wood door. "That's one reason the cellar is dug into the hillside."

Opening the door and stepping down with him behind, she waved her arms around to show the provisions stored. An aroma greeted them of mustiness, dust, potatoes and a hint of ripe apples from a large barrel. The sun quickly gave light to the steps leading into the cellar and then the surroundings turned to dim shadows all around the large space.

"We have been fortunate to have plenty of produce to store because we have a huge garden and our water supply is still good. We can help our neighbors, if needed, with the extra jars on our shelves. We are truly blessed."

She saw that Jack was surprised. Possibly, he thought too many people never would have helped anyone else, especially during this depression. Did Jack find Grace's parents the kind of people he wished he had?

"You have a good family, Grace," his voice low as if in reverence of the silence surrounding him. "Good people."

She nodded, smiling while they walked around the little open space in the dugout cellar pretending to be inspecting jars of various colors from deep purple to orange and yellow, to red or green and other color variations. The jars created a picture of mixing all the variations of hues.

They emerged back into the bright sunlight again, squinting until their eyes adjusted. Jack closed the heavy door and asked, "Have you ever had to use this for a tornado?"

She shook her head. "No, thank God. I hope we never do. Some parts of the state have had tornadoes, but not near our home so far." She looked at the large wood-sided two-story house that was her parent's home. The solid foundation possibly would stand if a tornado hit. The walls, their belongings and the roof would all go— the same as the sheds and the large sawmill building. She hated the thought of all the whipping and ripping of wood, furniture, clothing along with everything else being spun into oblivion.

After stepping back up into the full sun, they walked around some more. Jack leaned against the chicken coop wanting to learn as much as he could about her then asked, "Tell me more about yourself, Grace, after you grew up."

She knew it was time to tell him. Lowering her head, she began. "I need to tell you the main reason I'm here. First, though, I have to go back into my history. In nineteen-eighteen the Spanish Flu weakened my lungs and then in 'twenty-five, I contracted tuberculosis."

She paused to see his reaction. Would he just walk away?

He just stood with a sympathetic look as if waiting to hear more. There did not seem to be any sign of rejection or revulsion.

A sigh of relief escaped Grace's lips before she continued. "I was at the sanitarium for three years and now I'm cured. I couldn't go back to my home in the southeastern part of South Dakota and so my parents left their home and business and moved here just for me." She stopped and wondered what he thought of her now. Her throat constricted and she tried to gulp air. "I've lived with them ever since."

He placed his hand on her shoulder, and then tipped her head up with the one gentle touch of his other hand to have her look into his eyes.

"You sure got the wrong end of life's deal and too young to boot. I'm sorry, Grace, I wish I could have helped you back then somehow." Now he understood what Al had been about to say before—until . . . Grace got TB. It didn't change his feeling toward her. "You must have been scared too."

Grace could see that his feelings seemed even more caring. She was surprised because she had expected him to back away from her. "Well, yes I was scared, but I didn't give in. I'd say you suffered more so. You didn't give up either."

Neither one had told the other their full story, but enough. They understood one other, though, and seemed to feel the bond tightening. They stood on the hillside and watched the sky slowly turn pink, then shades of purple and finally to a dark grey-blue dusk. The air gave no hint of possible rain just thirsty dryness. Jack looked toward the house and decided he didn't care if anyone was watching.

"Grace, I like you and your family. I feel good here, especially with you. I want to kiss you. Please?"

He'd surprised her and reminded her of a little boy pleading for another piece of chocolate. "Yes, you may," she smiled immediately looking again into his shiny blue eyes.

He stepped closer, put his arms around her and bent down to meet her lips. Ah! The sweetness each felt. He held her tight, only he wanted more. She did too.

Finally breaking away, Grace said, "I know my family likes you." Giving a flirtatious smile, she added, "I do too. Will you keep coming?"

"I'll come every chance I get. I wish I worked closer and could see you all the time." He reluctantly broke the tight embrace and stood back just a little holding both her hands while continuing to look into her deep brown eyes.

He moved close again and the next kiss lasted longer and was more intense. Jack had a hard time keeping control of himself. She sure got under his skin!

Just then, thirteen-year-old Charlie interrupted, "Dessert is ready. If you want some, you better get up to the house now." He laughed as he started to run back ready to tattle.

Quickly the lovebirds separated and tried to act natural. Grace answered, "We're on our way." Then both of them laughed as they walked hand in hand to the house.

The day ended with Jack, Grace and her parents smiling. Al invited him back, "Come anytime, whenever you can get away from work. You're welcome for dinner or just a visit. I don't think Grace would mind," he added with a smirk.

"Thank you sir, I will," Jack replied and shook his hand smiling. "Thank you, Mrs. Lee for the great meal."

Then Grace walked him to his car. They shook hands while their eyes met until they finally had to let go and say goodbye. When the car rambled down the hill and to the main road, Grace finally turned and walked back to her home with light steps.

Dad was waiting with a smile. "Grace, I don't know what you know about Jack. He told me quite a bit and he is a fine fella who has had a tough life. Did he tell you about that man in Missouri?" He didn't speak Drake's name, or the name he'd give him, instead he held his tongue.

Nodding, Grace said she knew a little. She suspected her father had probably learned more because he had a way of getting information out of a person and the two men had talked quite a bit.

"What kind of a man would tie a boy to the barn rafters and use a bullwhip on him for no good reason? Did it to his own son too! I'd sure like to get my hands on that demon and whip him until there'd be only bones left. He broke a good boy. The pain in Jack's eyes almost made me cry

She was shocked. "He was whipped? I didn't know that. When?" There were so many questions racing through her mind. No wonder Jack didn't want to tell her about his life.

"He was whipped whenever that drunken bastard. . . pardon me. . . that man . . . wanted." The word slipped out this time.

"It started when Jack was only ten years old when that man took him and it continued until he finally ran away before he turned sixteen. That man doesn't belong in the human race," his contempt echoed in his voice. "No one deserves that, especially a young boy. Can you imagine?"

Eyes wide, Grace replied, "I knew he'd lost his father and had been in some kind of dysfunctional home, but not that he was whipped."

He continued, "I think he was overwhelmed by our family. He hasn't seen many good homes from what I can tell. We need to welcome him and show him our love. What do you think, Gracie?" He gave her an impish smile.

She beamed. "Oh yes, Dad. I saw that you really seemed to get along with him. I think you respected him and he respected you too, didn't he?"

He nodded. Mom, seated in her rocker, stopped crocheting. "Well, I think that you have found your sweetheart, Gracie." She smiled at her husband, "He looked at you the same way your Dad looked at me when we first fell in love. I like Jack too."

"Your brothers told me that he seemed like an upright man and he was good for you. They hadn't heard anything bad about him from any ranch hands or townsfolks. He's a hard worker and an honest man who stays out of trouble, according to their inquiries."

Dad exhaled from his pipe and added, "He hasn't been married either. Almost did once, but that didn't work out and it's best for him it didn't." Dad didn't go into details, but that was enough for Grace.

She couldn't have been happier. Now she had to find out if Jack was serious enough about her. She was convinced that he was, yet they needed to let the relationship take its course.

While driving back to the ranch, Jack couldn't stop beaming. He bellowed out songs as he drove. He noticed that the world seemed to become brighter with nature's hues all around and the hills full of life. The air was crisp and fresh as he opened his window to inhale the aroma of the crops in the fields. He really liked Grace's family. Of course, he already knew that he loved her. Had he finally found a place where he could be at home and could belong? Would the Lees accept him as a husband for Grace? He worried they might say he wasn't good enough for her or was too old. Only the car was witness to his talking and singing to himself.

"Well, it's about time that the gods let me meet a wonderful woman and a family that is as good as this one. Maybe, just maybe I can be a part of it. Or will this be taken away from me too? I've waited long enough for someone. Please don't take her away. I need her.

153

He offered these thoughts to whom—God? Not aware if he was praying, he needed someone or something to hear him and give him assurance that he and Grace would always be together. One moment he felt at peace and sure they would. The next moment uneasiness settled in and he wasn't completely convinced they would be together. Could Grace and her family accept him as he was?

Damn!

CHAPTER 25

1933 – MASS, MARRIAGE?

The next time Jack arrived at the Lee home, he began to further relax and felt comfortable with the family. The fear of saying or doing the wrong thing seemed to ease. The brothers and sisters teased each other and joked often. All knew it was in fun. No one lost his or her temper, only pretended that they had. Jack liked them all, even the brothers. He wanted to belong. This was the family he'd never had.

He made as many trips to Whitewood as he could. Calving on the ranch was now finished. The branding and separating the bulls, cows or heifers to sell would begin soon. He bribed some of the fellow ranch hands to trade their free time, agreeing to do their work as well as his own on other days. Usually he worked it out and he was free on most Sundays.

The prairieland did not receive enough moisture for normal lofty grass. The cattle chewed it down all too quickly and caused the owner to sell more cattle this year. Those chosen for sale benefitted in richer pastures to fatten before the sale date.

Every so often, instead of driving to Whitewood, he met Grace at a Saturday dance and they spent the entire evening together either dancing or sitting engrossed in each other's company.

On one such night, Grace asked him if he would come early the next Sunday morning and go to Mass with her. She'd told him weeks before that she was Catholic and he hadn't said anything about his religious beliefs. In fact, he didn't have a religion; didn't believe in all that nonsense.

Jack frowned, turned up one side of his mouth and thought for a minute. He was not the church-going type. But then with a nod he agreed, not telling her that he would do it only to please her.

Religion hadn't done anything for him in the past. Why did he need it? He'd only got the backhand of God before; nothing that helped him. He thought maybe he could sit in church and just go along with her. When he was under the hand of Drake, he'd done it and decided he could do it again. A slight smile crossed his lips when he thought that this time it would be one hell of a lot easier since he'd be with Grace. Anything to make her happy!

The next Sunday he arrived early and the family left for Mass in Sturgis. Grace rode with Jack in his auto pleased to be riding with him, just the two of them. In church, they sat together with her family in a pew and she shared her missal with him, pointing to where they were. The missal was in Latin and at each part of the Mass as he leaned his head down, she whispered to him what the meaning was, or why they were saying something. She'd point to the right place in the missal. Her Latin seemed perfect. Jack sat, knelt and stood when everyone else did, although he felt out of place. He tried to follow along; nevertheless, he had a hard time.

He was not impressed by what he considered all the hoopla and everything in Latin. How could anyone understand it? The best part was leaning close to Grace to hear her say those words so easily and to listen to her sing so soft and sweet. He wanted to ask why all that pomp and ceremony? He'd only go to church for Grace and no one else. She sure got to him and it wasn't God's doing!

On the way back home after Mass, Jack gave a sigh of relief while breathing in the fresh warm air blowing through the open car window. The fragrance of maturing crops in the fields along with Grace's light touch of vanilla invaded his senses. The day's cool beginning quickly turned to hot and there were no clouds to ease the burning heat. He thought if a person stayed out under this sun too long, a wolf or coyote might consider him just right for eating.

"Well, what did you think of the Mass?" Grace paused for a minute looking over at his handsome profile while he drove. "I'm sure it was strange, but you get used to it. Mass is all in worship of Jesus."

"I don't know how you even know what's going on. It's all in that Latin. I was glad you whispered some of it to me." He frowned while his eyes remained on the road. "Grace, do you really believe in all that hogwash—in Jesus and God?"

The question surprised her and her head jerked around to view his profile again. "Why yes, I surely do. My family and I are so blessed. We have had some setbacks, but the Lord always provides for us." She looked over at him and gave her purse an extra tight squeeze as she turned to look at the road. "Jack, didn't you feel anything when you went to church as a child?"

"I went because Drake demanded." A bitter taste settled in his mouth and he felt like spitting out his anger.

"I sure didn't get anything out of it. I guess it turned me off religion. I never stepped foot in a church again until today. Everyone seemed to like today's service, though. Are they always like that?"

"Yes. God eventually does bring peace and hope. He never gives up on a single soul and he is always there in the background. Look where He has brought you and me." She turned to see what his expression would be. "Here we are. If God had not given us His love, we wouldn't have met."

"Well, I guess that makes sense, but why did God put me through so much hell first?" He slipped even though he tried so hard not to swear in front of her. "Sorry for the language."

"That's alright. Would you be here if you hadn't gone through that? You might still be in Indiana or you might have turned out like that Drake."

His jaw jutted out as he clenched his teeth tightly, then he spoke. "I would never be like him, but you've got a point. I probably wouldn't be here if I hadn't run. Guess I better thank God for that, right?" he turned and grinned at her.

"I think so." She smiled and they held the silence briefly while the auto chugged slowly up the hill. She decided to change the subject. "I'd love to hear you sing. When we get back home, maybe I'll suggest we all gather around the piano and sing some of the familiar songs. Will you sing along, Jack?"

He laughed. "Sure, as long as you pick some of the popular songs of nowadays." He'd not tell her about singing along in saloons with a piano player when he was a young cowboy out for fun. That brought another smile as he parked by the Lee home.

After dinner, Grace gathered everyone to the piano for a sing-along while Laura did the finger work playing the keyboard. Jack's voice was rich and velvety as he stood beside Grace and swayed with the music. She kept her voice low so she could enjoy his. The rest of the siblings joined in. None were songs he sang in saloons in the past years

They sang several songs before they stopped for dessert. Grace said, "Your voice is beautiful, Jack. You have to sing more. Maybe I can teach you some of the Latin songs and responses."

He liked the idea of her teaching him and that would mean more time together. "Sure, why not?"

When he was able to manage a Sunday off from work, he went to Mass with the family. In a short time, he picked up some Latin and prayers. He was a quick learner and had a good memory. Many times after dinners, they gathered at the piano to sing. His voice rose with emotion and clarity.

While at the Lee home, he felt like a part of the family. He enjoyed hearing about their life along the Missouri and other stories of antics by one or another. One day after dinner, he and Grace walked to town, which was approximately two miles from her home. She showed him the various businesses and explained who lived in which houses.

On their way back home, they took a lane through a wooded area. Not far into the trees, he stopped and turned to face Grace. He bit his lip and then clamped his mouth tight.

She wondered what was wrong. "What?"

He took both her hands. "I need to kiss you, Grace," he said in a husky voice.

She stepped close, looked up into his soft blue eyes and smiled. "Oh Jack, yes. Kiss me and hold me." Her body tingled.

Jack pulled her close and gave her a soft kiss. She wrapped her arms around his neck and he pulled her tighter. Their kisses became more passionate and full of desire. He felt the heat and firm yearning for more; she did as well.

Like an invisible thump on the head, Jack stopped, not daring to go further and took a deep breath, exhaling slowly and long. They finally eased away from each other to control their passion.

Jack cleared his throat and whispered, "We better get back before I do something I shouldn't," and gave her a sly grin.

"Umm hmm," she replied softly.

They began to walk hand in hand until they arrived home. The day was settling into a pink dusk and he knew he had to leave. He wished he could stay and share Grace's bed with her.

Enough of that! Grace is a true lady. Respect her always or you'll lose her.

During the following weeks, Jack thought long and hard about how he could afford to rent a house and marry Grace. He wondered if the money he already saved would be enough. In the past, he'd spent his money as soon as he'd earned it. Lately though he saved and no longer spent on other women. Now he had to think of a future.

Before this, he never worried about anyone but himself. Now he had to think about Grace and maybe a family. God! How was he going to do that? Reality was hitting him in the stomach.

Damn!

CHAPTER 26

PROPOSAL DEMANDS

The next time they met at the Lee home, Jack and Grace took another walk. The sunny, hot day of August 1933 saw fields gradually turning the color of straw. The day was as scorching as July; still it seemed perfect—perfect for what he wanted to do.

Every turn brought them to an array of nature's beauty. Spruce trees were abundant displaying their amid the birch greenery while fields contained reddish-orange and patches of early fall flowers here and there mixed with fading green. Even though the plants yearned for rain, the colors were still quite abundant. The heat did not bother the two lovers. They only wanted to be together regardless of weather or anything else. They strolled down the path slowly, holding hands.

Finally, he spoke. "Grace, I'm planning to rent a little house near here," wondering if she would get the hint.

"That's nice, Jack, I'm glad for you." She thought she knew what that might mean. "Is that going to cost you a great deal?"

He smiled and nodded. "Yeah, I can. I get a good enough pay and I'll still have some left over. I've also got some service bonds I can cash in if we need to."

She caught the "we" and smiled.

He continued, "The man I'll rent from is moving into Spearfish to work at the Homestake Sawmill and he wants a good tenant. He said if the economy starts to improve, he may be able to come back. So it isn't permanent, but he'll rent it to me cheap. I'll make payments each week to him."

"That's a big step for you, Jack. Then what?" She wanted to know what he was thinking. She began to fidget in anticipation.

"Then what? Well, Miss Lee," he said as formally as he knew how, "I want to marry you. I want you to come live with me in our own home. Will you?" He looked down to meet her eyes fearful that her answer would not be what he wanted.

"Marry you? Oh Jack, I've longed for you to ask. Yes, yes, yes. I'll marry you." She almost leaped into his arms. Their celebration kiss left them longing for more. Her arms wrapped around his neck as he held her as tightly as he dared. Both began to formulate plans in their minds.

Suddenly, Jack pulled away. "God Almighty! We're going to get married and have our own home, Love." His hands clasped her shoulders and he looked into her eyes with the delight of a child who just opened the perfect unexpected Christmas gift.

She felt this is what he'd wanted for years—a real home with someone to love and someone to love him back.

"Yes, and you'll have my whole family as your family too. We all love you. Of course, I love you the most!" They kissed again to reseal their commitment to each other.

"I want to get married as soon as we can, Grace. I need you."

"I feel the same way. There is one thing, Jack, I want to get married in my church and for you to become a Catholic so we don't have any problems with religion. I know that it takes time and preparation, but I really want that. Will you?"

She wasn't sure she could go ahead with plans if he said no. She'd always dreamed of marrying someone of the same faith. "Please, for me?"

Jack stammered, "Ah . . . ah . . . join your church? What are you talking about?" He frowned, looking serious and asked her, "Why do I have to join your church? I don't need that and I don't believe in all that hogwash. I'm willing to go to church with you, but that's it."

Grace felt an imaginary punch to her stomach. "My faith is my life," she answered softly after a pause lowering her head. "I want my husband and family to believe in my religion. God is there when we need Him."

He stepped back releasing her. "God sure as hell wasn't there for me!" His voice rose while he fought back memories of his youth. "I went through hell because no God ever answered my prayers." His voice was stronger and he no longer had a smile.

"Religion doesn't work for me. Sure, I've gone to your church on Sunday, but I don't get anything from it. I just go to be with you. I can't join a church just because you want it." The hurt of his youth roiled in his stomach and took over his mind.

Grace's jaw dropped. She couldn't believe that she had misjudged this man so badly. "Tell me why you hate God so much." Her voice was almost a whisper.

"My dad was killed and I never knew my mum. Then God slapped me into hell when He put me with that goddamned Drake. That took any last thread of God out of me. Don't tell me there's a God who cares about me." He didn't even apologize for his language and anger transformed his appearance to one Grace found shocking.

The silence following his outburst brought Grace almost to tears. She knew Jack remembered all the beatings he had taken in that house where there was no love or mercy. His eyes showed the bitterness sealed in his soul. He'd forgotten their talks about how God had brought them together. She was devastated.

"But it wasn't God that did that to you. That Drake made his own choice to be the way he was, not God. You can't blame God."

"Well, God sure as hell didn't let me have a choice. I was stuck with that S.O.B. and God never did a damned thing for me." His jaw was tight and his eyes squinted in rage while his whole body stiffened. His face turned red while hers remained pale.

Grace closed her eyes and thought for a moment. Then added, "If there is no benevolent God, how come we met? Don't you think there is a reason that we met? I think God had a hand in it."

"Sure there's a reason. We both were at that dance. Grace, I don't want to join your church or any church. It won't work for me."

She fell silent for a couple of minutes just staring down at the ground. When she spoke, her voice was low and sad, "I think we had better stop and go back." The hurt she felt caused her eyes to glisten, ready to spill tears.

Jack nodded and they walked back to the house in silence, not holding hands. All the beauty of nature seemed to have turned to grey. When they arrived, Jack's shoulders slumped. He looked down at the ground. "I guess I better leave."

She just nodded, afraid to speak. He walked to his car and left. Grace stood staring at the dust as he drove down the hill. Then she slowly turned and walked into her home heading straight for her bedroom.

Her parents knew something was amiss. "They must have had a fight," Mom said as she watched Grace climb the stairs. She continued her crocheting even though she wanted to go to her daughter, but knew it was not the time. Grace needed to let some of her tears flow first. They'd talk later.

"That fella better not have done anything to her," Dad sputtered. "I thought he was going to ask her to marry him. Wonder what went wrong."

Mom didn't look up. "We'll find out in due time.

When Grace didn't come down for supper, Mom later went up and knocked on her door. "Gracie, I have some soup for you. Dad said it was perfect with the chopped pork sausage added. Can I come in and leave it for you?"

The reply was a weak, "Okay," and she sat up in her bed and wiped her puffy red eyes. "Mama, can I talk to you?" She only called her mother *Mama* when she was desperate for some loving advice or just love

"I'm always here for you. Let me sit down on the bed next to you." Mom quickly put her arms around her daughter. "Remember that there is always a tomorrow and it will be brighter."

"Oh Mama, tomorrow won't be better. He won't join the church. I so wanted a family all in one faith, but he won't do it. I can't live without God as my lifeline which will extend to any family I have—if I ever have a family." She slumped as sobbing began once again. "What can I do? I love him, Mama."

"Let's think about it and he will think about it too. You know that your Dad was against the church when we got married too. In fact, the priest disliked your Dad so much that he wouldn't marry us. So we went to a Justice of the Peace and got married anyway. Later we were married in the church when your dad reconciled his mind. So you never know what will happen. If you love Jack and he loves you, I think it will work out."

She gave her daughter a tender squeeze and listened to the full scenario of the afternoon between the two lovers. "Do you remember what Dad told you about Jack's terrible childhood? How would you feel if you thought God had deserted you? That's how Jack feels. Think about it."

Grace didn't answer, yet her mother's words filled her with guilt. She had forgotten. That night she didn't sleep well, thinking about Jack rejecting God. She didn't understand his side completely because God had always been there for her. Why did Jack's life have to be the way it was?

At the Frawley Ranch, Jack couldn't get the argument with Grace off his mind either. Sleep would not come as he tossed and turned. He turned on his back with his arms above, head resting on his hands. His eyes were wide open staring at the ceiling, not able to close.

Life wasn't fair. Why did he have to join her church? He didn't want to join. He didn't want to be told that he had to do this or that, and do it the way another wanted, unless it was work related. He didn't want to go to church every Sunday just because the church said so. Yet stopping for a moment he thought of what Grace had said about there being a benevolent God and that there was a reason for everything.

Okay, okay. Maybe some of what Grace said was right, but why did he have to go through so much hell first? Where was his justice or someone who cared about him? Finally he'd found love and now he could not understand why Grace had the right to tell him he had to become a Catholic! Why?

Like a calf trying to get away from the rope holding it for branding, his restlessness caused him to turn every couple of minutes until his bedding pulled out, bunching here and there. Finally, he got up, tiptoed out the bunkhouse door and walked the grounds. After an hour of arguing with himself, he went back inside, but sleep still wouldn't come, his mind unsettled. Too soon, the early morning light crept through the window and settled on his face. The other ranch hands were beginning to stir, swinging their legs over their beds ready to begin the day. He did too even though he felt like dragging his covers over his head to hide from the world.

Here Jack was 43 years old and acting like a child. He blurted out, "Damn anyway!"

Two of the ranch hands jerked their heads up from pulling on their boots. One asked, "What's wrong, Jack? You look like you had a rough night." He and the others laughed.

"Yup I did," he muttered and jerked his boot too hard with a twist causing his little toe about to be severed. "Damn!" That was the way that day went, and the next.

Days passed with Jack cussing the world. He didn't know what to do and wondered about just saying yes and going along with it even though he didn't believe the way Grace did. There was no one he would talk to about this. He was alone in a decision once again. Run away and move on? Could he stand to walk away from Grace?

He continued to beat up his bed each night. Dark bags began to appear under his eyes while his mouth pinched together with his chin jutting out. When out on the range with a herd, he had plenty of time to think and he wasn't sure he liked his thoughts. Still, he kept trying to come to some decision. He talked to his horse arguing even though there was no reply. Could he accept Grace's religion?

Damn!

CHAPTER 27

BEN

After many nights of staring at the ceiling in his bunk, Jack suddenly bolted upright. *I know what I need to do. I have to talk to Ben!*

On his next day off, he would find Ben and have a good talk. Benjamin Black Elk was the closest person to a brother he ever had. When he first ran to get away from Drake, he ended up on the Pine Ridge Indian Reservation and Ben's father took him in those long years ago. Ben and Jack became good comrades. There was no one else Jack trusted to discuss his problem, especially since he couldn't talk to Grace's father. He felt the loss of the closeness he had developed since knowing her dad. Wondering if he would ever have that friendship again with Al, Jack could only seek Benjamin Black Elk.

Steering the auto down the dry dusty reservation road on his next free day, he rolled the window down to let the breeze blow in. The air was as welcome as a gentle wind while out on the range—as long as another car didn't pass and push the dust through his open window slapping him in the face. In a short time, he found Ben's home and parked close by.

All of a sudden, the door burst open and Ben laughed loudly. "Where the hell did you come from? I haven't seen you in years. How the hell are you, Jack?"

Jack smiled and grabbed Ben's outstretched hand and in a minute the clasp fell into a bear hug as if they were back to the old days when the two were just teens.

"It's good to see you again. How the hell are you doing, Ben?" Jack replied.

Ben had aged and there were more wrinkles around his bronzed skin, but his muscles were still firm from work and his eyes still sparkled with friendship. The years that had passed didn't seem to matter. The two, as teenagers, formed a close bond while traipsing the hills and learning each other's moods, deep feelings of anger and dreams to be free. Each had their own vision of freedom back those long years ago when they were so young.

"As good as can be expected for this old man." Ben smiled, noticing Jack's body was tight as a bowstring.

"How are you doing these days?"

Jack shrugged. "Well, I needed to see an old buddy. But before I get into my life, I want to catch up and know what is going on here." Jack didn't want to discuss his problem just yet.

Sitting at the well-worn kitchen table talking with mugs of hot coffee in their hands, the two felt like old friends once again. Ben told him what was happening on the reservation and how the depression was affecting them.

"My people have gone through bad times before. We are managing, substituting for what we don't have. We'll survive. We aren't going to get fat or get rich, I'll tell you that!" He laughed and then added, "The government has the special work relief project now called the Civilian Conservation Corp. Some of my people can work on those projects. At least they are getting paid. Someday the government will come up with something."

They reminisced about their days of carefree wandering around the hills, hunting, fishing or racing their horses. They hadn't forgotten Jack's stay on the reservation as a young boy. The length of his time there wasn't long, but the bond a was brotherhood.

Jack knew that Ben refrained from asking what was bothering him even though he saw how unsettled his White friend was while talking. "My wife is fixing the meal. You stay and eat with us. She's making her fry bread too."

The aroma of grease and fried dough invaded Jack and his stomach growled. He laughed and agreed to stay.

After the midday meal, Ben stretched his legs. "I think we need to take a ride and see some country."

Jack agreed. He never got tired of being on a horse. They rose and walked out the door heading to the corral.

Ben took the roan gelding eager to step to a usual gait. Jack's mount was a young paint mare in brown and white eager to step to the same gait. Once in the saddle, Jack began to relax and conversation came easier. They continued discussing current life while the sun gradually crept lower. A feeling of peace surrounded the hilly, dry toasted grassland. A stillness settled over them.

Jack eventually began the conversation he needed. "Ben, I found a woman I want to marry. She's a great woman, but she wants me to join her church—the Catholic Church. I don't want to. Your father did more for me than God ever did." He repositioned himself in the saddle and let his mount settle beside Ben's horse. "I don't know what to do."

"So, God didn't treat you right. What do you think he did for my people, treat us right? It wasn't God and we don't hate Him for it. We've looked up to God, or our gods, to help us. Remember what Dad said about letting the past go and learn to have peace?"

Ben stopped for a minute to let that sink in. "Dad knew what was important."

Jack thought about that. "Even though you made peace, don't you still have some resentment or anger at the Whites?"

"Oh, there's still some resentment. We've learned to live with it and keep our peace. We sure can't go back and change things. Neither can you."

"You're right there." Jack gave a deep breath and told him about Grace, how they met, about her family and how much he wanted to marry her.

"I just can't see becoming a Catholic. Would you join a woman's religion just because it was the only way you could marry her?"

Ben laughed softly still sitting tall on his horse bareback style. "Don't get me into that. I married because I loved my wife. We sure didn't agree on everything, yet we worked things out. She gave into me more than I expected, and still does. She's my woman and that's all that's important. I'd have gone with anything she demanded to marry her. We're happy even though life isn't perfect."

Jack remembered that Ben's family was religious and went to church on Sundays. "You still go to church?"

Ben nodded. "Uh huh, most the time. My wife and I grew up with it and your woman probably did too. She's probably not going to change and so it is up to you to decide what to do. I don't know how you feel, but I'd say that she would be one I wouldn't want to lose." He paused and looked at the horizon. It was about time Jack settled down with a good woman and gave up the wandering.

"Hell, you sure put me on the spot. I've got to think on it. I want Grace more than anything." Jack still didn't know what to do even though Ben had certainly given him some good thoughts to ponder. Maybe he'd join the Catholic Church just to please her. Would that be wrong, would that work? Probably not. He still wasn't sure what to do and would have to think on it long and hard.

After a pleasant afternoon of conversation and remembering, Jack finally climbed into his auto and headed back to the ranch with a muddled mind. The starless night brought darkness over the land, the same as his mind—cluttered with a foggy mind.

When he arrived at the ranch, he still didn't know what to do. Should he become a Catholic or not? He'd have to do a lot more thinking.

Damn!

CHAPTER 28

HOPE DWINDLES

The Lee household seemed dreary. Grace moped, cried and kept trying to resolve in her mind the problem with the man she loved. Was she unreasonable in asking him to join her church? She knew that Jack thought God gave him far too much heartache and misery when he was little—but it wasn't God. She just wanted her family to all go to Mass and have a strong faith. Life seemed so much easier when there was unity in faith. What was she going to do? Could she accept him as he is? She so wanted him to join her church. Her religion was all that she knew and it gave her peace and comfort.

As the days drug on, Grace couldn't laugh at any joke her dad told and she couldn't work beside her mom with any enthusiasm. One evening her dad sat in his chair with his pipe and yelled, "Gracie, come in here and sit by the fire. I want to tell you something."

Grace came and slouched on the sofa, her head drawn and body slumped downward.

"Young lady, you aren't rolling with the punches. You think this is the end of the world? Well, you're wrong. You and Jack love each other. You'll figure this problem out. He's a good man and you need to think hard before you throw him away." He stopped and took a puff from his pipe, raised his head and closed his eyes for a second.

"You know your Mom had quite a time with me at first because I was so against the church. But I'd of done anything for her because I loved her. Eventually we worked it out. You and Jack will too." He shifted to reach his pipe.

"Now, you think about your demands and think how you can resolve all this mess. Jack will come around. He loves you. You know that he asked me for permission to marry you." He lit the tobacco and puffed. "He's a good man."

Grace was surprised and had no idea Jack had talked to her father about marriage. Then it dawned on her why her parents were grinning every time they saw the two together just before her world collapsed.

"Papa, I love him so much. What am I going to do?" Tears flowed and she sniffled.

He liked her calling him "Papa" and remembered the times when she was little and came to him in tears wanting his love and advice.

"Give it time, it'll work out and you will be happy again." He hoped he was right.

Grace nodded, while wishing it would all work out right away. She so wanted the uncertainty to end. Then she worried. What if Jack didn't come around to join the church, or what if he didn't even come to see her again?

Lord, help me, please. I don't want to lose him.

Three weeks crawled by with each day bringing less hope for Grace. What was she going to do if things didn't change? Maybe she'd go back to the southeastern part of the state even though the doctor had warned her against it. She could stay with her sister and look for work.

She whispered in her pillow, "I can't stay here with Jack so close by. I have to get away. Maybe I'll find a way to afford a train ride to Yankton. I need to do something. If I can't have Jack, I can't stay. I will never love anyone else. I guess I'll just be one of those old spinster teachers—if I can teach again—and that's even doubtful."

Another day passed with Grace trying to come to terms with telling her parents that she wanted to leave, maybe ask for some money. She had no idea if Dad had extra money, especially with the hard times now, but he was always there when someone needed help. She'd have to find the courage to tell them her plans.

One evening after supper, Grace looked from Mom to Dad. "I need to tell you what I want to do." She stopped, smoothed her skirt while trying to get the nerve to tell them and then she swiftly continued.

"I've made up my mind, but I don't know how I can manage it." Her frame showed the loss of weight, and the darkness under her eyes revealed the sleepless nights.

Her parents looked at each other questioningly. Each gave a slight shrug with their shoulders indicating neither knew what she was thinking. Then they quickly looked back to Grace.

Dad spoke. "Well, nothing is impossible. What are you thinking? Are you going to resolve the problem and become Jack's wife in a different way than you had hoped? I know you will remain a Catholic even if Jack doesn't join the church. So what do you want to do?" He leaned forward in eagerness.

She gave a weak smile and answered, "I want to go back to the southeastern part of the state again." She told them her plan, finishing with "I just can't stay here." A lump sat in her throat, trying not to break loose and she dropped her eyes to her lap.

Her parents stole another look at each other and were silent for a minute. Dad searched her face and softly spoke, "Gracie, when are you thinking of doing this? Not too soon, I hope."

She knew that he wanted her to wait longer and probably thought Jack would eventually come around. She wasn't sure it would be soon and maybe not even in two or three years.

"Yes, soon. I have to get away and find a new life," she muttered again.

Mom leaned over and took her daughter's hand. "Now child, you hold on for a little longer. You can't leave yet. In another month, the world may completely change for you and bring a new light. This isn't the end of the world."

After more discussion, Grace agreed that she would wait a while longer even though she was determined to get away soon. "I'm still going to leave."

On the Sunday after her announcement, Grace dressed without any enthusiasm for Mass. She didn't care what she looked like because her spirit was gone and she just wanted to wilt away. God would have to get her through this. So far, He hadn't seemed to listen. Maybe Jack was right about God's not caring.

She continued to dress and suddenly jerked her head up to look at the crucifix in her room. "Oh Lord, I'm sorry. I didn't mean it. I believe in you, you always hear me, and I thank you for the blessings you have given me. I just want to know what to do now. I need your help." A tear fell before she would wipe her eyes with her handkerchief.

The Lees sat in their usual pew at church and waited for Mass to begin. Suddenly Jack appeared and squeezed in the pew to sit next to Grace. He saw her astonished expression and with his eyes silently pleaded for her to let him stay. Mom and Dad just nudged each other and smiled. Grace worried about her appearance. She had never let herself go so badly even when she was sick. Ashamed that she hadn't even put on powder to cover her shiny nose, she looked down at her hands as her cheeks turned pink.

The fragrance of Jack's shaving cream along with the polish on his leather boots and his own manly scent unsettled her. She wanted to put her head on his shoulder and breathe in with contentment. The desire between the two increased. She wondered if she could make it through Mass without touching him.

Jack didn't wait. He leaned closer to her and took her hand while the priest gave the sermon. She looked up with a smile and his blue eyes twinkled back with satisfaction.

After the service, Jack asked, "Grace, can I drive you back to your home?" He looked down at his boots afraid she might say no.

"Yes, Jack you may. I'd like that." Her acceptance was quick, though she was apprehensive about what he might say on the way home. Should she remain firm in her request? Oh! What was she going to do? She said a silent prayer for God to help her decide for the best.

Mom waved them off with, "I'll have the food on the table in about an hour. You're welcome to join us Jack."

He smiled back and nodded. "Thank you. I hope to." Or would Grace tell him to leave?

The two walked to his car and he held the passenger door open for her. After sitting, Grace adjusted her skirt. Then she folded her hands over her purse sitting on her lap and stared straight ahead, as Jack climbed in and started the auto. She fidgeted and wondered what he would say.

Jack made light conversation as he started the auto and kept pace with others leaving the churchyard and turning onto the road. Then Jack slowed and crept along the dirt road.

"Grace, can we take a side road through the country? I need to talk to you."

She nodded and worried. Was he going to join the church or not? If not, what would she say? How would she react? She wasn't certain—not certain about anything.

He pulled onto a tree-lined path leading to a patch of woods. He parked and after a deep breath, he glanced at Grace and paused before speaking. "Grace, I love you and I'll do anything you want, even join the church. Please, Grace, love me back." He kept his hands on the steering wheel with his head bent low.

She sat up straight and looked out the window. "I love you too," she replied softly. "But I don't want you to join my religion just because of me." She faced him and added, "You need to forgive too, Jack, not just join my church."

"I'll work on it, but I can't seem to get rid of all my hate." He slumped in his seat lowering his hands to his lap. Now she also wanted him to forgive too? Was this another hit from above—telling him that he was still not going to have her?

They discussed forgiveness briefly, then fell silent on the subject. Soon they stopped talking altogether.

Arriving at the Lee home, Grace's mother looked up as the two entered and smiled. Grace's face revealed the struggling just like she and Al had all those years so long ago. "Dinner is about ready. Grace, you have time to freshen up," she hinted assuming that her daughter might want to at least comb her hair and powder her nose. "Jack, you go ahead and join Al in the meantime." He did.

In about ten minutes, Grace appeared wearing a freshly starched deep blue dress revealing her trim figure. A powdered nose accentuated her smile and her dark sparkling eyes.

In no time, the table was full once again with conversations that were never ending. There was always something to discuss with the country in such a state. At least the family thought they had hope now with Roosevelt and his plans.

When the women finished the cleanup, Jack and Grace took their usual walk holding hands. Often conversation hadn't been necessary, just being close was all they wanted. Now, though, they needed to resolve the obstacle stopping them from moving forward.

"Grace, I know I'm supposed to let go, but every time I think of what I went through as a kid, my anger takes hold. I want to beat up someone or even worse."

"Yes, you will when your mind wanders back to those days, or you see something similar. Still, you can change. Remember that God never gave up on you. Don't give up on Him, Jack."

He paused before speaking. "Sounds easy; doesn't work, though, for me. I'm trying, Love, but I can't seem to let loose of it. Give me time. How am I supposed to forgive Drake, let alone God?"

She nodded. "Maybe you can picture this—close your eyes for a second."

Jack did and leaned against the tree trunk where they stood.

"Do you see the anger that is on fire? See the hot red and blue flames burning a hole in your soul?" She paused for mental effect. "Now grab hold of that angry flame and throw it in the dirt, or garbage, or pigpen. Just throw it away. You can do it. Grab it and let it go." She waited a second, and then saw a grin form on his lips. She wondered if he'd thrown his rage out of his soul that quick.

"Okay, do you feel the relief? Don't you feel lighter, more alive, with a good feeling?"

Jack opened his eyes and grinned. "Well, I can see it when I close my eyes, but I don't feel any better. I'll tell you one thing, if it ever does work I'm throwing that flame to a cornered rattler and let him finish the job."

Laughing, she answered, "I never thought about a rattler. That certainly would take care of the fury. Keep trying. Someday you'll find that you can do just that. You'll let go of all that frustration and be able to forgive. Now, it doesn't mean forget because you never will. Forgiveness is completely different and it frees your mind. You also have to forgive yourself."

Jack never thought he'd be trying to forgive. Maybe Grace was right and he just needed to keep working at it. He wondered if he could fake it and tell her he had forgiven so they could speed up the wedding. He didn't want to wait just because of something that had been inside him for years. He was getting tired of waiting.

His life was like sitting on a wild bucking mustang with him strapped to the horse's back and suffering the pains of hell in his rear end. What could he do?

While Jack worked on forgiveness, he and Grace went ahead and met with the priest after Sunday Masses for marriage counselling. At the same time, Jack began studying to become a Catholic. He wasn't sure he could go along with all that was in the catechism. Nevertheless, he tried to memorize the prayers and study to be prepared for the next meeting. Gradually, he was beginning to understand the significance of the Mass now.

After the second meeting at the church, Grace rode back to her home with Jack. Fall's burnt orange, red and yellow foliage blanketed the ground or littered the road. The car's tires sent leaves flying in all directions. There was a promising chill in the air. Everyone wondered if it would bring snow or just bitter cold.

Grace watched the swirl of leaves. "This is like the death of one season and waiting for the birth of a new. That's sort of like you, Jack. You will have new life." She could see some change in him already. "Don't you feel you are changing?"

Frowning as he kept his eyes on the road, his mind seemed to be swirling. Was she right? "Well, Love, I don't know; maybe. The sessions helped me understand how Jesus suffered, but never gave up on his determination to finish his mission."

His remark made her hopeful that maybe the priest was getting through to Jack. She knew it would take time and, yet felt he was not as resistant as he had been with the first session. Was he sincerely listening and understanding? She hoped so.

"Will you help me learn these prayers? I kind of remember the *Our Father*, but not the others." His mind flashed back to when he was a slave to that demon and each Sunday they said the *Our Father* in church. Drake made sure he had that prayer memorized.

Suddenly he thought of a Negro cowboy he worked with and heard his words, *My grandma said that her master could never take away her faith and love for God, her true master. She refused to let one man do that to her.*

"Jack, Jack. Did you hear me?" Grace looked at him and wondered where his mind had travelled. It certainly wasn't with the present.

"Huh? Oh, I'm sorry, Grace. What?"

"I said yes that I will help you with your prayers and anything else. What were you thinking about?"

He bit his lip and shook his head. "Oh, I recollected a man I worked with and what his mother told him. Sorry." He kept his eyes forward. Telling that story to Grace wasn't necessary right now; he needed to think about it. He'd do that when he was back on the range. Sitting on his horse always gave him time to study life, to think about what he'd learned through the years. It was his time to think and concentrate.

His arguments against God were weakening even though the wall had not been broken down completely. Jack still hated the life dealt to him when he desperately needed love.

Damn!

CHAPTER 29

LIGHT COMES

Heading back to the ranch late afternoon, Jack's mind whirled in thoughts. Was he actually beginning to believe in God? He guessed in the back of his mind that he always knew there was a God, only not one who seemed to help him. The question of why he had to go through all that hell when he was a youngster didn't seem to be answered.

He still missed his dad and all the years of not having a fatherly love. Could he talk to Al who seemed a good substitute for a father figure?

His mind kept turning back to Drake. Why did he have to be so vicious and why did he hate everyone? Jack never did anything to him. He could not accept all that hate he received as a normal way of life. It sure wasn't when his father was alive.

His anger built, yet his foot on the pedal eased without him realizing it. All of a sudden, he stopped the car. A path led down to a creek through a multi-green meadow fed by the water nearby. He parked, got out, walked to the stream and sat on a log near the water's edge. Trees overhead shaded the stream in flickering sections of aqua, light brown and grey as the ripples gently moved onward across the pebbles. He hunched down swirled his hands in the water and cupped them to take a sip.

Wiping his mouth on his shirtsleeve, he searched his soul and rage took over while he stared at the flowing creek. He began to scream in pain at all the agony he had bottled up inside.

"I hate you Drake and I hope you are down in hell burning up!" His fingers rubbed his eyes and he sniffled. The inner pain was intense and brought him to his knees.

"All those whippings—why? Now I hope you are getting that torture."

On and on he went screaming as he remembered all the times he was hurt physically and mentally from ten years old on. He echoed all the anguish and fear that he had as a young boy.

"You scared the hell out of me when you'd get that whip out or hit me on the head. There wasn't anything that pleased you except when you took the whip to Lester and me." The lashes on his back were a stinging agony that he felt repeatedly as he remembered hanging from the rafter.

"God, I never knew what I did wrong. Why Drake? Why God? What did I do to deserve that?"

Jack couldn't control the tears that flowed steadily. He bent over in mental pain while he remembered all he received at the hands of that vicious man. His screams were similar to a wild animal in agony. He had never cried before over those years of brutality, the loss of his father, and all his lonely years up to now. His body began to shake with his sobbing and continued even as the sun was settling on the horizon.

An hour or more passed while releasing all that bottled up agony, then he began to calm. Wiping his eyes with the back of his hands again, Jack opened his eyes to the most beautiful glow of ever-changing deep aqua and purple settling on the ripples of the stream that quickly deepened as the day was retiring.

When Jack stood, he felt a tremendous relief and gave a deep sigh.

"My God, I feel good! How the hell did that happen? All my hate doesn't control me now. I hate what Drake did, but I don't hate him now. He was vicious and I fell into his hands." Remembering how he got there, he shook his head from side to side. "I don't hate God either."

"It was my fault for running from MacGreagor, not God's doing. I made the choice to run away."

He suddenly realized that he placed himself in that position. Shaking his head again, he smiled and raised his eyes to the dark sky and blinking stars and laughed. He felt years younger.

179

"Yeah, I guess I can't blame you, God, can I? If I'd stayed with the MacGreagors, I would have had a good life. I'd still have that little pack of my dad's belongings." He remembered all in that pack of his father's—the leather belt, pocket watch, hunting knife, rifle and a few things that belonged to his mother. Still seeing that pocket watch in his mind, he regretted never going back for that parcel he left at Drakes. "I guess I've thrown blame everywhere except to me and I didn't stop to think."

The God he had been rejecting all those years seemed ridiculous now. Without his past, he wouldn't be in South Dakota this day, ready to marry his love. Standing and staring at the creek for a long time as darkness settled in, he thought of all the blessings he received such as finding Black Elk and Ben, traveling through many states, always finding work, seeing mountains or plains and learning about all kinds of people. He thanked God for all that and especially for finding Grace.

Another big sigh came and a smile appeared from ear to ear. "Man, I feel good! I can breathe without feeling weighed down. Wait until I tell Grace. Finally, he strode back to his car with new energy and light steps. He rid himself of all the hate he carried for years that night.

Damn, life is good!

CHAPTER 30

TELLING ALL

"What happened to you, Jack?" The Foreman, sitting on the porch for a last cigarette, asked when Jack parked and jumped out of his car late that night.

"Oh, I was just doing a lot of thinking and found a good quiet spot. I got to ask you though, if I can switch a few shifts so I can take off for another day soon. I really need to take care of some things with the woman I'm going to marry."

His boss saw romance had been in the air and had even met Grace at a dance. "Jack, if you can work it out with the other men, go ahead. I was young once."

"Thank you sir," he said, before heading off to the bunkhouse. By then the cowhands were asleep, sprawled on their bunks after a full meal and talk of work for the next day, or of women. Jack tried not to wake anyone crawling into his bunk. He sat down on his bunk, leaned back and before he even got his boots off, he was in a deep contented sleep.

After taking extra shifts the next few days, Jack became tired, yet he stayed happy. When he finished double duty, he jumped in his old auto and headed to Whitewood. He whistled as the car bounced along the road and noticed all the changes while he breathed in the aroma of wheat fields recently harvested. Trees becoming a dormant green seemed to be anticipating the change from fall to winter. Some of the brush was beginning to turn a grey-white-straw color while wildflowers by the roadside still showed off their colors even as their stems began to wither. As far as Jack was concerned, it was a glorious day.

When he arrived at the Lee home, Grace heard her mother greet him at the door, opened wide for entry. He spied Grace at the kitchen table. She was peeling, coring and slicing apples. He walked in saying, "Grace, you look great today."

She smiled back and told him that she was surprised to see him. "I'll be finished with this in just a couple of minutes." Giving a sly smile, she took the next apple and began to peel with new vigor

"We can take a walk if you'd like." Her crisply starched apron, tied behind her back accented of her tiny shape. Her hair glistened while her brown eyes sparkled.

"I'll wait. I'd like to take that walk." Sliding into a chair next to her, he gave her a quick kiss while her mother was turned away, busy at the stove. A smile crossed his face when he released her.

"Mm, I'll take more of that," she teased in a whisper.

Just then, Al popped in. "Hello there, Jack. What brings you here?" He took a cup of coffee Mom had just poured for him. He sat on the opposite side of the table from his daughter and Mom joined him in the chair next to his. Al snitched a few slices of apple and chewed before raising his cup for a sip. The aroma of the fresh cut apples overpowered the coffee scent.

Jack said, "I haven't felt this good in years, in fact most of my life." The Lees were the kind of family he'd wanted from ten years old, and here he was, with the most wonderful woman in the world and her parents accepted him.

They all visited awhile discussing the economy and local news.

Al said, "Just heard that our neighbors down the hill are losing their home. We sure hate to hear things like that."

While he nodded, Jack looked down at his cup and then spoke. "Everywhere you look and any newspaper you read, it's that or someone desperate for work and looking like they will pass out any moment. The other day I was in Spearfish to get some equipment for the boss and I saw a man on the street holding his hat out praying someone would give him a dime. I couldn't just walk pass him as if he weren't there. So I gave him a couple of coins."

"Good for you!" Al said quickly and finished his coffee.

Jack was fidgeting, wanting to be alone with his daughter. He kept glancing at Grace in hopes she was done with the last apple.

Al smirked. "Why don't you two go take a little walk? I'll help Mom finish up."

"Yes sir. That sounds good," Jack answered and quickly stood waiting for Grace to do the same.

Holding her hand, he helped Grace off the porch and they slowly walked toward the tree line not far away. Then he took her in his arms and gave her a longing kiss.

"I got to tell you what happened to me since the last time I was here."

Grace wondered what could make him smile so wide and be so happy. "Tell me."

He gave the complete account of how he somehow ended up at that creek and poured his soul out to the gentle moving water. He didn't leave out anything, even his sobbing and screaming.

"When I finally stood, Love, you can't imagine the relief I felt. It was like a ton of weight had been lifted off me. I could even breathe easier. I guess I forgave, because I don't hate Drake or God for my life anymore. I finally got enough courage to face it. I did it, Grace. I listened to God and I accept Him and no longer have that hate eating away at me. You've helped me to see that God never left me. He was always there."

"Oh Jack. How wonderful!" Her tears broke spilling down her face.

He wiped them with his fingers while tracing his thumbs over her smooth cheeks. "I know that God gave me the strength to live through that and He gave you to me. What a gift! I never want to let you go."

Their kisses became more urgent. Neither wanted to let go, but finally Jack released her with, "Whew! I got to stop, but I sure don't want to. Got to keep you an honest woman." He leaned over and took a deep breath, clenching his fists, and then straightened. "God, what you do to me, Love."

"It's both ways. I have to have some self-control too. We'll just have to have patience." She was so tempted to forget control. Still, her conscience reminded her of her strict religious training almost uttering, *No, no.*

When they got back from their walk, Grace and Jack told her parents that they would be married as soon as possible and he

183

definitely was joining the church. He told them about his experience by the stream and forgiving.

"We knew it would happen!" Al roared while clasping Jack's hand and slapping his shoulder. "Good for you."

Mom gave her daughter a tight embrace and turned to him. "Jack, welcome to our family. We will love you like you were our own son." Then she gave him a hug. Al nodded in agreement beaming his approval.

Overwhelmed by the statement that they would love him like a son, Jack's eyes became misty.

"God almighty, I'll have a family that I belong to!" He almost choked up, and then quickly clearing his throat, he gave Grace's hand a tight squeeze.

She squeezed back. "I knew you would, Mom and Dad. I give Jack my heart and you two are making us very happy."

Dad clapped his hands and rose. "Let's bring out a bottle of my wine from the cellar and have a toast to you two." He laughed while heading to his private homemade selection.

"This is a special occasion. Sorry I can't go to town and buy a bottle of champagne now that there's no more Prohibition, but we'll toast with a sweet intoxicating drink anyway." His step seemed lighter than usual as he almost bounced down to the cellar.

Jack left that evening filled with contentment, while humming all the way back to the ranch, he saw more and more beauty in the landscape. Had that splendor always been there?

The fading green in the patchy fields, were turning to pale gold, even in this drought, the grass rolled rhythmically with the breeze as if keeping time to music. Exquisite royal pines were preparing their winter coat while the orange leaves on the birch branches swayed as if to shake the gold and orange free. The deepening blue-black sky of the evening seemed like a promise of night peace. Where was it before? It was there all along, but only the love in the heart showed the beauty of nature, let alone the goodness of people.

Jack said "Thank you God for this beauty."

Winter came with the continuing dry air, not producing much snow, only icy cold wind that tore through the state. Yet the weather didn't affect the two lovebirds. Christmas came with the usual festivities, but not many gifts. Jack celebrated his first Christmas with the Lee family. Actually, it was the first Christmas he'd ever really celebrated. It was a meager holiday and all agreed that there would be no gifts given, except love. Their economic situation mirrored that of many Americans, at least those who still had some form of livelihood. A wild turkey dinner with dressing, potatoes and canned peas was the best Mom could provide, yet enough to fill each family member's stomach. Dessert was a spice cake topped with an applesauce mixture. The family gave thanks for the blessings they received. They prayed for those less fortunate and asked God to provide for them.

Less sugar, flour and coffee became the normal. Meals were adequate but none of them was patting his stomach in over-full misery. Sugar was used sparingly, the same as flour. Mom reused coffee grounds at least twice and usually three times. At least they still had plenty of cream for their coffee to cover up the weakness. Ol' Bessy still was a good milker.

New Year's Eve brought in 1934 with little change, just bitter cold, windy days and nights accompanied by little moisture. The New Deal was making progress, nonetheless ever so slowly. Hope was more prominent in the country; more smiles appeared on faces that had previously only shown the ravages of worry with too many struggles.

Grace and Jack were together as much as possible. When there was a bitter, biting wind, they often ended up in either the kitchen or the main room alone. Sometimes they played cards or other board games and sometimes they just whispered to each other with plans for their future.

Time seemed to pass too slowly.

Damn!

CHAPTER 31

GROWING IN FAITH AND LOVE

Grace and Jack set plans to be married in St. Martin's Church in Sturgis. It would take a few months of preparation and then the wedding banns had to be announced in church. Of course, they had to get the marriage license. Both were impatient and wanted time to move more quickly. Every time Jack visited, he asked how much longer before they could be together in their own home.

She declared. "It never fails, when the pot is watched, it won't boil. We have to forget time and just concentrate on getting our home ready."

Jack laughed. "It isn't at all easy for forget time, Love. I'm tired of waiting. Can't we just go to the Justice of Peace now and get married in the church later, like your parents did?"

She laughed. "Not since we have come this far. Besides, it won't be that much longer."

Their home-to-be sat in Crook City, not far from the Lee home. At least the bedroom and the main room contained the basic furniture. The kitchen area was at one side of the main room and it had a small gas refrigerator and stove, but no pots or pans. They needed all the utensils, linens, bedding and personal items. Grace was making curtains to add her personal touch to their home.

Sundays continued to pass with Jack accompanying the Lees to Mass as often as he could. He told Grace that he began to like the religion more and more, not just because of the mystery, but because he saw such faith in her. He saw how she relied on God to guide her and strengthen her, especially when he heard about her keeping her trust in the Almighty while fighting tuberculosis. He wondered if he would ever have that much faith.

She wanted him to talk and open up more, and she seemed to be doing a good job of doing that. He felt his tongue was as loose as a dangling thread in a windstorm.

Their conversations were private and they talked a great deal when they were alone. He told her of his guilt over walking away from the MacGreagors who treated him as their own. Sneaking away had been a terrible thing to do to them and he regretted it too many times to count.

One day he took a deep breath and blew it out forcefully. "Grace, you have shown me how to accept myself the way I am. I feel I can finally breathe fully. From now on, I'll only look to our future and the blessings I have now. God, I love you!"

Jack completed his studies to become a Catholic and both completed the marriage preparation counseling. Now they were ready for the wedding. The church announced the upcoming nuptials four Sundays ahead of the wedding date and asked anyone who might have reason that the two should not marry to notify the church at once. Nobody did and the date was on.

One thing hampered the wedding—the Great Depression was not over and money was too tight for Grace to buy a bridal gown or even a special dress. She sewed a simple cream-colored cotton and rayon dress with long sleeves buttoned at the wrist. The dress fell straight from the waist down to where it flared slightly at the hem, between her knees and her ankles. The bodice had silver colored buttons down the front and a delicate lace highlighted the collar.

Her mother purchased the material with money she had hidden away wanting Grace's special time to be the best they could afford. Wishing for expensive material was pointless. The depression had taken its toll on the Lee family only not as ruthless as it did for millions in the rest of the country. Mom could not complain. Well, maybe just a little since she could not give her daughter a brand new wedding outfit. Yet they still had a home, food, clothes even if worn, and shoes even if patched. They were not desperate. She gave thanksgiving to God for what they had.

Grace took her old dancing heels from her teaching days and polished them until they looked close to new. She knew that she could not afford to have a photograph taken of her and Jack on their special day. Even without one she'd always remember it exactly as it had been.

Jack had his dress suit cleaned and pressed. He bought a new deep blue tie for the occasion. He polished his boots until they were shiny enough to see his face. Two days before the wedding he told Grace, "I'm so nervous I could drink a bottle of whiskey."

She laughed and said, "Don't you dare."

"Yes Ma'am," he gave her a bow and a grin. There was no way he would do that. Jack never had more than one drink and never drank to excess. Too many memories of his youth surfaced when he smelled liquor.

He told himself, "I've found love and will always take care of Grace. When we are old and grey, I'll still tell her I love her."

On their wedding day, April 7, 1934, the sky was clear. Apple blossoms and dandelions were out in force. The early morning air was crisp and then turned warm with the sun shining bright. The trees still wore their drought-dull green and the young plants in the fields pointed their stalks straight to heaven as if praying for moisture to keep them alive.

Grace was aflutter. She hadn't slept much the night before and she kept smoothing her dress and pacing back and forth in the kitchen.

"Young Lady, you're going to make dust out of the wood floor if you don't settle down. Eat some breakfast," Dad said and shook his head. "How can a woman be so nervous over a wedding."

"Now Al, you didn't see me on the morning of our wedding. A woman wants that day to be perfect in every detail. I was just as bad or maybe even worse, even though we just went to the Justice of Peace to begin with," Mom answered.

"Well, I'll be a ...," he couldn't think what to say that was proper in female company, then finally added, "a cooked goose. I never! I hope she gets over it like you did, Mama." His belly jiggled as he laughed and Mom gave him a frown.

Their daughter just kept walking around and finally forced herself to take a few bites of toast while still standing and pacing. At ten o'clock that morning, her marriage would begin in St. Martin's Church in Sturgis with Father Columban officiating. Bob and Laura were proud to be their witnesses.

"I wish my sisters could come," Grace said, but knew it was impossible. They were fighting to survive the continuing drought and poor economy like everyone else. Jeannette and Steve were in a fierce battle to keep their farm. Helen now had twin baby girls along with her two year old, so she could not travel with three babies even if they had the money. At least Ralph was teaching again.

Nellie, Laura and Frances had helped Mom the day before and that morning to prepare food for family and a few close friends who would be coming to the Lee home after the wedding. Potatoes sat on the top of the stove to keep warm while the rabbits remained in the oven slowly baking—timed to be ready when everyone arrived. The women had baked many loaves of bread as well as rolls. Their homemade jams and the churned butter sat in little dishes covered with cheesecloth to keep insects away until the mealtime.

"Well, when the food is gone, the people can visit over coffee, Dad's wine or else over water. We just can't add any more food," Mom said when they finally decided they'd had enough. A couple friends were bringing a dish as well. The table would be full and everyone could thank God that even during the depression they were allowed to have this feast.

Jack told Grace, "What a family! I never knew people could be like this. I'm glad I'm becoming a part of it. After all the times at dinner here, I've come to like Fred and Bob—even after what they put me through at the dance." He laughed. "I can see that they watch out for your parents too. Some men wouldn't do that. And the humor you all have is really something, especially when you josh over the gizzards. I am so glad to be a part of your family, Love."

Finally, it was time. Both parties arrived at the church.

Before the wedding, Jack received baptism into the Catholic Church. After that, the wedding Mass began and he received his first communion during the service. Grace smiled when he received the host so reverently. In between, he kept looking down at his new bride and smiling—he thought she looked more beautiful than ever. His chest puffed when he thought, "She's mine!"

Several Lee friends attended and even a couple of Jack's ranch hands along with his two old friends families, Lehmanns and Ramsers, whom he lived and worked with in past years.

189

When the wedding was over, Grace hung onto Jack while they acknowledged all the well-wishers outside. The crisp air did not affect the couple at all. Soon the newlyweds got into Jack's car and headed up the hill. Other cars followed with horns honking. Laughter and honking could be heard throughout the drive. While riding back with Jack, she sat as close as she could and beamed with happiness. "I'm glad that's over!"

"Me too. Now, Mrs. Jackson Allen Morris, you are mine." They both laughed and he gave her hand a tight squeeze while smiling broadly.

By noon, everyone was back at the Lee household. Nellie and Laura raced home before the others left the church parking area. They had arranged the dishes on the table with the prepared delicious foods. The aromas surrounded everyone when they walked inside. Fresh rolls, butter and jelly seemed to disappear as fast as replenished. Mid-afternoon Mom brought out a simple sheet cake with the frosting decorated in fresh yellow wild roses from the grounds. All commented on how beautiful the cake looked.

The two lovebirds couldn't seem to part and held onto each other tight. Neither could eat much, and only sipped on Dad's chokecherry wine while looking into each other's eyes with longing. When evening came, the couple finally left for their new home. The ride was short and Jack carried her into their home, not letting her down until after several kisses. Later he brought their belongings into the house while she surveyed her new surroundings in pleasure.

When they crossed the threshold and closed the door, he embraced her with a deep longing kiss. The sky was turning a dark blue with the moon rising and the pale gray-blue light filling the room. That was all they needed.

Jack and Grace became one in the hopes and dreams of all lovers. After all those years, he'd finally found someone who truly and deeply loved him. He loved her more than she knew. She was what he had been searching for all those years. Finally, his search was at an end.

Grace thanked God for Jack's love. She was grateful to have found her soulmate.

Their future was beginning.

CHAPTER 32

THEIR HOME - FAMILY

Grace's family and friends had helped accumulate needed items months before her wedding. There were mismatched dishes, mismatched silverware, pot, pans, linens and everything else a home needed. She had purchased some bowls and knives when she was teaching and packed them away. Her family and friends completed the rest.

She and Jack had worked hard to scrub and arrange everything the way they wanted it. Spotless was her aim, and it was, before they moved in. Grace organized the kitchen area. Jack decided how to arrange the living area, which also worked for her. They were proud of their tiny home constructed of leftover or used siding and the tatty shingled roof. It wasn't much, yet they felt fortunate. She saw he delighted in coming home after a day's work and announcing, "I'm home, Love," when he walked through the door.

There were few disagreements between the two. The only annoyance for Grace was when Jack traipsed in with muddy boots across the wood floor heading for his chair to sit and relax. She got tired of cleaning up after him even though she knew ranch hands, farmers or day workers didn't always care if there was mud or dirt on the floor after a hard day. They were tired. Only she knew Jack would have to change!

The next evening he came home, opened the door ready to announce he was home when his mouth dropped open. Grace greeted him at the entry, her hands raised to stop him right there.

"What's this for?" he asked frowning. "What'd I do?"

Her answer was stern, "From now on, my love, you wipe your feet on that rug before you come any further, or take your boots off." Her tone meant business. "I don't appreciate cleaning the floor after you traipse in all dusty or muddy every day. If you take your boots off or wipe your feet at the door, I will only need to wash the rag rug every so often. Please wipe your feet."

Jack did as he was told, kicked off his boots, then entered. He caught her, swooped her off her feet while carrying her to a chair and held her on his lap. "As you say, Love." They kissed and enjoyed the next moments together.

Returning home from work one night months later, Grace with an added twinkle in her eye. She bounced over where he was standing in the door ready to remove his boots and gave him a long, tantalizing kiss.

"Well, aren't you in a good mood?" He smiled and responded to her warmth. His eyebrows rose in a question mark. "What?"

"Yes, I am in a good mood. Come, have supper and then relax. I think we need to do some more planning for our household. Eat and then we'll talk. Excitement affected her eating and she kept fidgeting with her fork while looking at him with a smile. "Eat as much as you want. I made enough stew for at least two more meals." She was stretching the food the best she could. It contained a lot of broth, but still was nourishing.

He still had the question mark on his face. "What do you have up your shirtsleeves now? I hope it won't cost too much. We're just managing to scrape by as it is." He couldn't help but smile at her even though he wondered what was coming.

"We 're going to stay home tonight and not go see Mom and Dad," Grace said with another twinkle in her eyes.

Sometimes they visited her parents in the evening. The two men still got along well. Al seemed to be a substitute father while accepting Jack as if he were his own son even though there wasn't that much difference in age, only about ten years.

After eating, doing dishes meant that Grace washed while Jack dried. They teased back and forth. When done, they snuggled on the couch before going to bed.

Finally, Grace told him about her excitement tingling in her body. She had confirmed with her mother what she suspected. "My sweet husband, what would you say if we had a baby? I think you would be the perfect father."

"Love, you'd be a perfect mother. The trouble is that we can't plan that. If it happens, it happens and I'd be so excited I'd probably whoop and yell for an hour. A baby would make us a complete family wouldn't it?"

Grace smiled and raised her head from his chest and looked into his blue eyes. "Well, my love, we are going to be a family in about six months I think. I talked to Mom and she agreed that I am expecting your baby. What do you think?"

All of a sudden, she was sitting upright as he held her at arm's length with eyes becoming moist. "We've made a baby? My God! Oh, Love, we're going to have a complete family. God, I love you so much. Our own family with a baby!"

After leaning back and pulling her close again, they just enjoyed the moment; each remained in their own thoughts. In a few minutes, Jack broke the silence, "Grace, do you have any idea if it will be a boy or a girl? Some women seem to know."

"I can't tell. We won't know until it is born. I can't wait to find out. Do you want a boy or a girl?" She was afraid he would be disappointed if it wasn't a boy.

"I don't care which one. I just want my baby!" he replied with a larger smile not knowing how he was going to wait all those months? He'd have to have patience.

Grace wondered what this pregnancy would do to her. How would she change—not only in looks since she always saw women with a full belly leaning back to keep their balance. She already had expanded and her dresses were ready to pop buttons. Would she become irritable and weepy? Was her husband wondering what she would be like? She'd just be happy when the morning sickness subsided. She also wondered what the sanitarian doctor would say. Would TB affect her baby?

During the following months, Grace saw that Jack began to find ranch work taking more and more of a toll on him. Why was he getting so tired? He'd lived on a horse for years and always felt great. Now he couldn't seem to keep his energy up. Was he getting old? He was only 45 and that didn't seem that old to her. A baby was coming and it was no time for him to feel sorry for himself over a few aches and pains. He had to earn more money, yet she worried about him.

Grace went through the usual progress of pregnancy. Jack was very attentive when he was home doing all he could to help. He even cooked a few meals and did dishes while she rested in the ninth month. When he felt the baby kicking, she knew he had so much love for his unborn baby. He'd be a very good father.

She lamented, "Lord! When will this baby come? I can't even bend over to put my shoes on! He or she can stop growing now. I feel like a whale."

Laughing, Jack gave his wife a big hug and reminded her that she was always telling him to be patient. "Now it is my turn to tell you to relax and let nature take its course."

When he got a break from work, Jack panned for gold in the creek along with Fred or Bob. He needed to earn more. Each man found just enough eventually to buy, if lucky, a little gasoline or flour. Every speck was a help in keeping them from destitution. They never considered themselves in the category of poverty, nevertheless the government probably did.

Eventually, the days passed from winter to spring. Trees became green again and the wildflowers in the field displayed a variety of colors. As it always does, spring brought renewed hope for a better future.

Very early on Tuesday, May 7, Jack got a jolt. Grace nudged him hard to wake him up. "Jack, we have to get to the hospital now. I'm ready to have our baby!"

Bolting out of bed, he let out a loud "damn" as his toes hit the bedpost. Quickly he put on his clothing, boots, grabbed the prepared bag and started the car. Grace did the best she could to remain calm—it didn't work. He helped her to the car, jammed the gas pedal down and tore out of their drive spitting gravel high.

The road was quiet since it was still the middle of the night and no other cars were in sight. In between moans from Grace and swearing from Jack for the vehicle to go faster, they bounced along. Somehow, they arrived at the Deadwood hospital before Grace squeezed his leg into a black and blue pulp.

Once they arrived at the hospital, the doctors and nurses took over. One pried Jack's hand loose from Grace's and told him to go to the waiting room. Husbands, not wanted in the delivery room, ended up pacing the floor in that room.

In a short time, Jack felt he'd waited far too long. Had something gone wrong? He went from one end of the small room to the other end praying that God wouldn't take Grace or the baby from him. He begged God, the first time he'd ever begged in earnest. Prayers came fast and earnest.

Time seemed to pass in slow motion. Finally, the doctor came out to announce Grace was fine and they had a healthy baby girl. Jack was so relieved and happy he pumped the doctor's hand until finally the doctor put his other hand on Jack's to release the grip.

Yes! He believed that God had heard his prayers. He realized that God knew how much he needed Grace. This time God had not let him down. He had heard stories of women dying in childbirth and he had been so scared while waiting.

They finally allowed Jack to see his wife. He gave her a big kiss before the nurse brought in the baby. She handed him the tiny bundle. Jack looked scared and felt helpless. He passed the bundle to Grace. When she opened the tightly bound blanket from around the baby, Jack could see more than just the face of his new daughter. He fell to pieces.

"So tiny!" In tears, he whispered, "She's beautiful and so are you, Love." He gave Grace another tender kiss. In no time he was rocking the infant—until there was a wail. Looking up at Grace with a question on his brow, he said, "I didn't do anything to her. Honest."

She laughed and responded, "I know you didn't, my love. She's hungry. I'll feed her. "You go and call my parents. They will want to know."

He'd forgotten about her parents. Off he went to find a nurse to lead him to a telephone. When Al heard the news, he whooped and yelled with joy. "When she gets home we'll come to visit, unless we can come sooner. Now you enjoy that baby. Give your wife and new daughter our love."

After much discussion, the new parents decided to name the baby Gail Isabel. Grace decided "Gail" because a friend she knew had that name. They both agreed with "Isabel" as the middle name, similar to her mother.

After visiting for a while, Jack left for home. His joy was evident by the smile on his face. "We've got a baby! God, it's great," he told himself while driving. When he got home, he suddenly felt very tired and collapsed on the bed. Instantly he was asleep.

By the next week, their household had changed drastically. Gail, the new baby, changed the routine completely. Night did not bring sound sleep. Instead, wailing every few hours for food woke the parents. Jack's comments were not as nice as his wife's. Eventually he learned to turn over and go back to sleep. Grace did not have that privilege, getting up each time to take care of Gail's feeding and changing her diaper.

Al and Isabella visited often. Grace told her mother, "Lord, I never knew a baby could go through so many diapers! That's all I do anymore—change and wash." Mom smiled took over the folding that day. Baby outfits were starched and ironed along with Jack's shirts and Grace's dresses. Al rocked the baby and visited with Jack while playing with Gail and the women worked or Grace received advice from the pro—her mother who had given birth to eight children.

Days, then months passed with Jack coming home from work and playing with the baby. He sang to her some songs he remembered his father singing to him. He also sang some from his days in saloons.

"Good Lord, don't sing those to her! She doesn't need to hear them and get a warped mind."

Laughing and singing a little louder, he reminded his wife that Gail was still too young to understand any words. "I want her to hear me sing and she seems to love it. When she gets older, I'll stop those songs. Right now I love to see her wiggle and kick with delight when she hears me sing."

"Well, just remember that she can't hear those when she gets to talking. I can just see her belting out a tune that you sang while someone is visiting or we are in church. I'd be mortified. Promise me you won't."

"I promise."

Major changes happened to the Lee family when 1936 swooped in. Grace got a frantic call one afternoon. When she answered, she heard a weak voice—her mother's.

"Grace, Dad is gravely ill. He had a stroke and he has lung problems too. We took him to St. Joseph's Hospital in Rapid City since Nellie is nursing there. She will be a big help and he'll feel like family is there. Fred brought me home just a bit ago. Dad will stay in St. Joe's for several days and then we will bring him home. He has to quit working so hard and he absolutely must quit smoking. That is going to be a battle. You know him."

Grace was stunned. She had never pictured her father sick, never being in a hospital. "Mom, when Jack returns, we'll come right over. I can bring the baby and stay with you for a while." She worried the baby would be too much for her mother, but she had to be with there. Maybe the baby would help her forget for a moment. Tears came easily.

"At least we will come and see what to do from there. You take care of yourself, Mom, and get some rest."   "I will, Grace. Now, don't worry about me. I'm fine and I will manage."

When Jack came home, he took his family to Whitewood where Grace found her mother out hanging clean sheets on the clothesline; she went to help. Jack found Fred and Bob in the kitchen, talking at the table, each holding a beer. "What are the plans, boys?" he asked.

Handing him a beer, Fred began, "Well, I'll bring Dad home in a couple of days. We have to convince him to sell his sawmill. Bob and I are thinking that maybe we can build Dad and Mom a home closer to Whitewood. We have the lumber and time since a job is hard to come by for us. The sale of this place will give us money to buy a small piece of land for the folks. Or maybe we can buy on a credit plan so we can get started on building before the sale here." He stopped and frowned. "Maybe I can try Dad's method of horse-trading and get the seller of some land to allow us to start building before this place is sold. Our Lee reputation is solid with the folks around here that know us."

Bob slammed his empty beer can down on the table exclaiming, "Sounds like it should work, as far as I can tell."

"I think that may be the answer. Al has worked too hard and that's probably why this happened," Jack answered and took a sip of his beer, then looked up at the ceiling. "I'll try to help build." He didn't know how he could spare the time or energy, yet his two brothers-in-law were in the same situation. Jack was older, though, and tired after a day's work. Somehow, he would manage.

Fred took another sip. "Thanks. First, we'll let things sit for a while and try to do Dad's work telling him to just supervise. It'll be a tough sell, but we've got to convince him no more hard labor."

"We hope we can get Dad to agree to a sale pretty quick. He's as stubborn as they come, though, and we may have to give him a push," Bob added. They all nodded laughing.

After a long visit with her mother, Grace and Jack left for home. At least little Gail gave Grace's mother a break from worry along with some peace while rocking the child. They returned on the day after her father came home from the hospital.

Bob's wife, Clarice, came during the week for a day or two to help as often as she could. She and Bob had married shortly after Grace and Jack and they now had their son, Billy. Bob would bring her when he helped run the sawmill.

Some days Fred's wife came, but she had her hands full with their two children, little Al and baby Jeannette.

Grace also stayed a few days to help her mother. A lump stuck in her throat stuck and she tried hard to push it down when she gave her father a firm hug and kiss on the cheek. He seemed so weary and small; not the big strong man they used to know.

After days of helping to keep Gail out of trouble, Jack told Grace it was time for her to go back to their home. At least it wasn't too far away and she could come every so often to help Mom. Jack always brought her over any time she wanted since she didn't drive.

The struggle of accepting her father's fate wore on Grace. She never swore, but Jack heard a few words under her breath. He felt helpless in consoling her.

CHAPTER 33

1937 - ANOTHER

Time passed quickly with Grace managing baby Gail, doing all the usual work including visiting her parents and helping there. Jack tried hard to help Fred and Bob build while looking for work and managing their finances. He kept a record of their meager income and all the expenses. Figures including rent, heating fuel, gasoline for the auto, food, clothing, medical needs, telephone, or everything else that came up, appeared on the tablet opposite the income. The difference cost Jack extra worry lines. He and Grace worked hard to find some way they could cut back and save. Often their credit at the dry goods store added up more than anticipated.

"At least we have this worry instead of being homeless and hungry. We have much to be thankful for," Grace said and Jack agreed.

They attended Mass every Sunday, sitting in the same pew with the Lee family. Jack had become a part of that family as if he had been with them for years. His faith was solid now that he had Grace and their baby. He realized the blessings he had received.

Jack began to feel the weight of more years adding on and he came home every day from work more tired than the day before. He decided to leave Frawley's Ranch and began to work with the WPA on various manual labor jobs. However, he found digging ditches or building roads considerably harder than riding a horse. Building a structure wasn't quite as difficult, but he wondered if he made a mistake in quitting the ranch. No sense crying over spilled milk—he'd just have to keep going.

One evening he greeted his wife as he opened the door and sat in his easy chair completely worn out. Gail wanted to climb up on his lap, but Grace grabbed her. She saw how tired Jack was.

"You rest. Gail and I will take a short walk so you can have some peace and maybe get a nap before supper is ready." She stalled the meal on purpose so he would rest and have a better appetite.

"Come along Gail. We're going to see if we can play in the snow while walking to the mail box."

"Coat on, Mommy," Gail answered with glee wanting her mother to help her with her coat. She always liked to be outside and her name suited her. Even if not spelled "Gale," the name fit, always on the go and investigating.

Off they went, enjoying the fresh crisp winter air that February afternoon of 1937. Gail was now one and half years old, full of energy and talking constantly.

Grace suspected that she might have another baby, but wouldn't mention that to her husband until she knew for sure. As time moved forward, she was positive they were going to expand their family. She worried about how they would manage since Jack's pay wasn't much from the WPA or any odd job he could get here and there from a couple of businesses in town. Gold panning only produced minimal amounts of cash, yet every penny gained increased their income. He was doing the best he could and they always seemed to survive. Sometimes she wondered how.

Thank God, Jack was a good shot and could bring home a deer every season along with wild turkeys, grouse and rabbits. They had chickens for eggs and could butcher a hen for a meal when needed, and her mother had taught her how to stretch meals well. She became an expert at making a stew or soup with little meat, canned vegetables and a broth. It always gave them several meals. Sometimes she made casseroles with lots of noodles, macaroni with cheese, or biscuits and sausage gravy. Each meal was filling. In the spring, summer and fall she gathered plenty of dandelions to go with bacon slabs to make dandelion potatoes. She hoped her garden would flourish again, in the spring, so she could have plenty of produce to can for the next lean winter. She was certain she could keep her family from starving and thanked God for all their blessings. Rent and utilities were more of a worry.

March came and she sat down on the couch close to Jack one evening asking, "Jack, would you want more than one child. I know that you love Gail, but would you love another as much?" She was sure of his answer, but it was a way to lead into her news.

"Well, sure. I'd love all my children. Maybe we should have as many as your mother," he teased.

Grace cringed at the thought. "Well, we'll see about that. It's God's call on that. Right now, I think you could love two children equally. So, my sweetheart, we are going to have another baby."

Sitting up straight, Jack's mouth opened and no sound came at first. Finally, he found his voice, "Oh God! Grace, you sure?"

"Yes," nodding her head up and down with a wide smile.

He grabbed her, pulled her onto his lap and gave her a kiss that showed his joy.

"When?"

"I estimate it will be in October. So we have plenty of time to prepare for another one."

He embraced her again keeping a grin on his face, and then suddenly he frowned. "I'm going to have to find more work. We'll have to save for the hospital and doctor. Tomorrow I'll go to town to get my name on every list for work again. They already have me down, but I'll tell them it's urgent."

With the depression, jobs were still scarce around the Hills. Farmers couldn't get back to farming without moisture, so they looked for other work. A few jobs came Jack's way, but they were only temporary and he kept looking for more work. He was so tired when he came home each evening, yet knew he needed to earn more money. Sometimes he worked for a man just for the trade of gasoline, sugar or flour. Grace heard his swearing at his aching body and the damnable depression.

She hated to see Jack cash in a portion of his Veterans Adjusted Service Credit, but they needed it for the hospital. Even though he hadn't fought in World War I, he was a veteran who had been ready to fight. The war just ended too soon for him to go overseas. The benefit provided $1.00 awarded for each day served in the United States and $1.25 for those who served overseas. The American Legion helped push this through Congress for the World War I veterans. Jack took advantage of the credit for his about-to-be expanded family.

Besides making clothes for the fast growing Gail, Grace sewed shirts for the new baby from material received as a gift and a pair of little overalls from clothes handed down. When she could, she sewed a new top or dress for her ever-expanding body.

Then a call came that she did not want to hear.

"Grace, it's Fred. Dad had another stroke and he's paralyzed now on the left side and can't speak clearly," He tried to clear his throat from the lump sitting there.

"Oh, my Lord! What's going to happen? How is Mom? What are we going to do?" she asked as her mind swirled with questions.

"Mom is okay, you know her. Bob and I sold his sawmill right off yesterday, closed everything up, and we've begun building hard on the house closer to Whitewood. We'll be close and can help Mom." Bob, now married to Clarice, lived in Whitewood and they would help too. That eased some worry for Grace.

"I'll let Jack know and we can come over soon." She patted her stomach as if to tell her baby it was okay. When she got off the phone, she broke down, sobbing. Her memories of her father flooded her mind—how strong he had been both mentally and physically. She knew he would have a hard time accepting his new situation. Mom would have her hands full trying to take care of him.

That evening she and Jack drove to the Lee home. Grace saw that it was hard for Jack to keep control when he saw Al who had become like a father to him.

"Well, Al, I see you decided to take it easy and let someone wait on you for a change. It's about time. You deserve the break. Take advantage of the pampering." He didn't know what else to say, but squeezed Al's hand tight, holding it for a long time.

Al gave a one-sided smile and nodded. He probably wanted to say that he knew he had no choice and at least had his wife beside him. Words wouldn't come out right and no one understood what he said.

The weeks passed quickly and between her brothers and Jack, Grace saw her parent's new home rise. It looked solid. A couple of friends helped when they could. The men decided to stucco the outside walls of the two-story house with cement, sand and lime. The power company brought a line to the site for electricity and later a telephone line came. Frances, Laura and Clarice set off a plot for a garden and hoed the area until it was ready for next year. Fall was upon them now and Mom and Dad moved to the new home. The men had transferred their paralyzed father into the automobile, carried him into the new home and sat him in a chair, making sure he wouldn't slip off. Showing him how they laid the floor plan out and what materials went into the process, Dad nodded his approval. Mom was pleased with her new residence.

Dad seemed to accept his present life and tried so hard to communicate with his wife. She began to understand some words. No one else could.

By September, Grace bemoaned, "I'm like a barrel! How much bigger can I get without exploding? You must be wondering why you ever married a woman who has turned into a blimp."

"Ah, Love, I'd marry you ten times over. Pretty soon we'll have a baby to show for it."

She snuggled in his arms, the best she could, more than ready to get that baby into the world. There was no cooperation from nature and another month passed while she waddled, holding her back or stood with her hands supporting the huge bulge to ease the pressure. She thanked God that summer had passed and she was not suffering from the intense summer heat. At least a cool breeze sailed through every so often and the nights began to feel quite nippy. She thought she might have a boy since she was so large.

Rich yellow and burnt orange appeared on the hillsides amid the pine, which changed to dull deep green or grey-blue in preparation for winter. Leaves soon settled on the ground beneath the baring branches. October meant time to finish the canning. Grace already had canned the peas, green beans, tomatoes, cabbage and beets harvested from her garden. Laura helped her. She had gathered berries from the surrounding hills in the spring and summer to make jams. At least that was out of the way early. Would she finish the rest of her canning before the baby arrived? After all, it was now October 25 and she was ready to have this child.

She had just finished with the last jar of carrots that morning when she decided to rest while Gail napped. "I'm exhausted!" She leaned back on the couch and her eyes closed, then suddenly opened wide.

"Oh, that was quite a jab! Are you ready to come," she asked patting her tummy and then leaned back on the couch again. In a few minutes, she had her answer. She rolled off the couch to get to the telephone. Jack was helping her parents. Their phone rang and rang. "Please answer," she begged.

Finally, her mother picked up. When she heard Grace's pleading, she said they would be right there. Hanging up quickly, she found Jack telling Al some of little Gail's antics.

She burst into the room. "Jack, Jack, get home. Grace needs to go to the hospital. I'll come and take care of Gail. Run down and get Frances to come up here to stay until Fred gets home and he can bring Gail and me back here." She didn't want to leave Al alone.

Jack raced to France's home, just down the slope, and quickly explained the emergency. She, her little Al and baby Jeannette, came quickly.

"God, I would be gone! Let's go." He muttered as he quick-stepped to the car while Mom threw off her apron and ran to climb in before Jack spun out of the drive. The tires spit pebbles and squealed as they raced out. Mom held on, knowing not to tell him to slow down. Thank God, Grace wasn't that far away, just at Crook City, a couple of miles from them.

When they arrived, Jack hopped out of the vehicle and raced indoors, his eyes searching until he found her. "Grace, Love, let's go. Mom is here to take care of Gail." He looked around and worried the child had run outside. "Where is she?"

"She's still napping. Help me up and get me to the hospital. I don't think it will be long." She hung onto Jack as he helped her out the door.

Mom gave her daughter a quick hug as Grace climbed into the car. "Don't worry. It will be fine. I'll take care of Gail. My love and prayers," she said as she closed the car door.

Jack had already climbed in and ground the gears into place. As Grace gave a groan and held her tummy, he said, "Hang on, Love. We'll be there in just a bit." He whispered a few swear words, knowing the hospital was not that close. He drove well over the speed limit to cover the fifteen miles to Deadwood Hospital as fast as he could.

"Don't have this baby before we get there," he told Grace when he saw her struggling with the pain. If he was stopped by a patrolman, he'd get an escort—he hoped.

As soon as they arrived at the hospital, the nurses swept Grace away. They pointed where he was to wait. Jack knew the way and went to the waiting room, lit one cigarette, then another. The room filled with hospital smells that he apparently tried to overpower with smoke.

After what seemed like hours, yet actually less than 30 minutes, he began to worry if all was okay. Silently he prayed with all his heart for his wife and baby.

Grace too felt that hours of pain had continued, but then she heard the wail of a newborn. The doctor held up the baby and announced, "Mrs. Morris, you have a baby girl and she looks perfect." He handed the infant to the nurse with, "You can finish up now."

As he was about to walk out the door, Grace heard the nurse stop him. "Doctor, you better come back. There's another one. Mrs. Morris is still in labor and another baby is coming."

He replied in disgust, "Nurse, you should know that is just nature finishing the process. Now you take care of it."

"No, Doctor. At least check this woman," she spit back. "There is another one; I can feel it." Grace could see that the nurse wanted to pull him over.

He reluctantly came back. Then after checking, he frowned, "Well, there is another. Now we'll get this one out." He would not apologize.

About fifteen minutes after the first baby, another arrived. "Well, now we have a male and you have twins, Mrs. Morris." He held up the baby and firmly stated, "There is no indication of another one." He checked just to make sure, soon giving the nurse a condescending glare, telling her to finish up.

Grace smiled and relaxed in her exhaustion. Two babies—and one is a boy. She was happy that she had given Jack a boy too.

When the doctor came to the waiting room, he spoke with a smile, "Mr. Morris, you are quite fortunate. Your wife delivered twins, a girl and a boy."

Jack was stunned; he sat back down. "Two? A boy and a girl? My God." He paused before continuing. "How is my wife?" He was afraid that two babies were more than she could survive.

"Oh, she's fine. In just a bit the nurse will come and get you. Then you can see your wife and your twins." He put his hand out and Jack shook it with a forceful motion until the doctor broke free and retreated down the hall.

When the nurse led Jack into the ward where Grace was, he began to feel tears sliding down his cheek. He gave her a soft kiss and just kept looking at her brown eyes so full of joy. The nurse arrived with the two infants, one in the crook of each of her elbows, held close to her body. She placed them in Grace's arms and left with a smile. In a quick movement, Grace held out the two bundles wrapped tightly for Jack to accept.

He carefully took each and placed them close to him, one in each arm. He couldn't take his eyes off the babies and began a gentle rocking. "Love, you have given me everything I could ask for; not only you, but two babies to join their big sister."

She smiled. "We really got more than expected this time and I'm glad that you got your son. No wonder I was so big. Now we are going to have to find names for these two sweethearts."

Jack kept his eyes on the babies and wondered how could he provide for five now—to feed and clothe them? Panning for gold on his free days, odd jobs, and working for the WPA might not be enough. Jack would have to see if he couldn't get more work even though he knew his lower back hurt like hell. He wouldn't give up and let his family suffer.

Why wasn't the economy improving? People were still trying to climb out of the pit of despair, starvation and all the rest of the agony of the Great Depression such as a permanent job, or a job, at least. Rainless days still ate at the fields and pushing the topsoil somewhere else. Jack worried about his family dropping into that pit of starvation.

Damn!

CHAPTER 34

DOUBLE THE TROUBLE

The hospital recorded the names given to the twins. The proper name on the one birth certificate was James Alfred for Jack's father and Grace's father. The other birth certificate was Joanne Margaret for the saint, and in honor of Jack's mother, Margaret. Grace and Jack wanted two names that fit like gloves when said together, so Jimmy and Joanie they became.

The week flew by and Jack brought Grace home. Upon arrival home, she held one baby and he the other as they walked through the door. Gail stood behind her grandma, not certain she wanted to get too close to those things. They looked bigger than a doll, cried too loud and squirmed too much. "Mama, we don't want those," she pointed to each twin. "I want you and Daddy to take them back. We don't need them."

The adults expected something like that and had discussed it beforehand. Jack stepped in trying not to laugh, "Mama, give me the babies and you give Gail a big, huge hug to show how much you've missed her."

She did just that, and sat beside Gail hugging and whispering how much she loved her and wanted her to know about her role as a big sister. "I love you, sweetheart. You can play with the babies after they get a little older. In the meantime you are going to be my big helper and I really need you." She continued to let Gail know she still loved her just as much as before. "You'll be like their earthly guardian angel. How would that be?"

Gail beamed, "Okay, Mama. I'll keep 'em out of trouble for you." Her chest puffed up and her chin jutted out proudly accepting her new responsibility. Grace almost laughed.

The days passed with Grace barely able to keep up with the chores along with feeding two babies and fixing meals for the rest of them. A problem arose immediately with Joanie and she didn't know how to remedy it. Her body would not accept her mother's milk and Joanie could not keep it down. Day after day, Grace tried, but the milk always came up and Joanie seemed to gain no weight. They took her to the doctor and his only suggestion was to try goat's milk informing them that often goat's milk worked for fussy-stomached babies.

"Alright, I'm going to find us someone with a goat and buy the milk," Jack stated when they all left the doctor. After he drove Grace and the children home, he took off on his search. Soon he returned with some goat's milk in a jar.

"Let's see if this will work. If it does, the owner said we could buy the goat. I don't know where we'll get the money, but we'll do it somehow."

"Alright, I'll put some in a bottle and then we'll see," Grace answered. She had sterilized some bottles in a pot of boiling water while Jack was out searching. When he returned with the jar of goat's milk, she was ready. "I'll warm up a bottle and put the rest in our refrigerator." They had acquired the little coil-topped GE refrigerator months ago when a friend decided to get a newer one. Jack had rigged up a line from the ceiling light over to the wall to plug in the machine.

As soon as a drop of the goat's milk hit Joanie's tongue, she began to pump hard on the nipple. There was no letting up until the bottle was empty. Grace propped Joanie on her shoulder and began patting her back. She didn't throw up and in no time, a huge burp erupted which made Grace and Jack laugh while Gail giggled. Jimmy was asleep and missed the excitement. His twin was going to live after all.

Jack clapped his hands and said, "That's it—we're buying that goat. I'll fence off part of the back for a pen." This got Gail excited, thinking it would be a pet. They strongly warned her never to get inside the fenced area.

How the children grew! Grace was bedraggled with chasing Gail or keeping her occupied in between changes and feedings of the twins. Somewhere in each day, she had to do the laundry that grew with continual diaper changes and she still had all the rest of the duties. When Jack was home, he tried to help, but almost every day he was out looking for work.

"Don't let anyone say to me that twins are as easy as one," Grace said. "I'll give them a piece of my mind."

Days and months passed slowly while the country still crept through the Great Depression. Jack read the newspaper and related a section to Grace while she fed the babies. "The average precipitation in South Dakota was only twelve percent last year and it's falling." They knew that the grasshoppers had hit once more, devouring any green that the drought hadn't already destroyed.

Grace added, "I read that the Soil Conservation and Domestic Allotment replaced the Agricultural Adjustment Act. This new plan gives farmers and ranchers some needed help."

Jack nodded and pointed to another section in the paper, "South Dakota has about eighty-eight percent of farmer's cropland on benefit payments now. It is the main resource of income for most farmers who were able to keep their land."

The Works Project Administration provided a means of earning money. The workers were mostly unskilled men, like Jack, and worked on the proposed projects. These WPA works included new schools or other public buildings, bridges, roads, public parks, dams and other massive undertakings. Jack was a part of that when he could acquire a job. Sometimes he had to stay away from home a day or two at a time sleeping in his night sack, which he hated now that he was no longer a young man. The need for income was worse since there were three babies to feed so he had to keep pushing. He would take any assignment the WPA gave him—just like millions of others did.

It seemed like only weeks, yet it was months, before the twins were crawling and trying to play with Gail. Joanie walked first at nine months and then Jimmy decided to join her. Chaos soon reigned in the household. A constant, "No, no," could be heard from Grace.

"I'm going to go insane pretty soon with these children!" Grace sputtered on an evening when Jack came home from his job. She didn't notice how tired he was. "Can you read to them or play with them while I get supper?"

He nodded and sunk into his easy chair. "Bring them to me. I'm too tired to pick them up." All he wanted to do was lie down. Instead, he sat Gail on one leg, the twins on the other and began to read from "Winnie the Pooh." The children's baby language and wiggling quickly settled down, as they listened to their daddy read. In a short time, the twins were asleep while Gail stayed wide-awake, leaning forward as she turned the pages to see the pictures.

The year 1938 seemed to be a repeat of all the trials of the country and Grace's family. She was frugal and never wasted a thing. Her mother taught her all the tricks of stretching and saving that her own mother had developed over two depressions before. The first was in 1893 when her mother was just a young teen. It was an economic depression, but at least did not include drought. The failure of banks along with the price of silver falling caused railroad companies to declare bankruptcy. By the peak of that depression, about 25% of the workers were unemployed. It took time to climb out of the depression, but by the early 1900's the country did. Now here they were once again—fighting depression.

Often Grace had carefully unthreaded the seams of a dress or shirt and saved the thread to use again. She remade the material into an outfit for one of the children. Sometimes a worn out pair of Jack's pants made overalls for the little ones. Grace stretched food and made their coffee weaker and weaker by reusing the old coffee grounds and adding a few new grains. Picking dandelion greens for dandelion potatoes saved money as did picking rhubarb and berries for jams or pies. Wild onions helped as well. The meat market gave out soup bones free to the first who came and she was quick to get there early for her package. The boiled bones were a good source of protein for nutrition and a little speck of meat helped in soups or stews.

She listened to the radio for all the latest news. On November 11, Armistice Day, she heard a new song composed by Irving Berlin. He hoped it would become a patriotic song and on that day in 1938, a singer named Kate Smith sang "God Bless America." Moved by the voice and words, Grace shed some tears. In no time, the song spread across the country and everyone began singing the words, especially alongside Kate Smith's beautiful recorded voice.

New Year's Day 1939 did not bring much relief to people desperate for jobs. At least there was rain more frequently and even a few cloudbursts. Each rainfall brought celebrations and increased hope. The rain helped Grace's garden grow well.

The year seemed to pass in a flurry of children, chores, or worry. Each season took more of a toll on Jack's health. Drought still plagued the country, but the government programs kept many people from dying of hunger. The wheat prices seemed to rise slightly. Maybe the country was going to beat the depression after all.

That year when the twins were just toddlers, they were out back playing in the dirt. All of a sudden, Jimmy came running to the house yelling, "Mama, Mama, Joanie has something in her pants."

Grace thought it meant a change of clothes. She opened the back door screen, stepped out, and heard Joanie screaming in pain while bending over and her rear sticking upward. She rushed up to her and immediately saw the problem—Joanie had sat on a spikey cactus. Little needles protruded out of her bottom. Grace gently picked her up and took her to the house.

"Joanie, we have to get those needles out. It will hurt, but when we get them all, you will be fine again." She propped her over the arm of the sofa. How was she going to get her overalls off? She decided she was just going to have to get as many needles out as she could first.

Screams, feet flaying up and down and back and forth didn't help. Jimmy sat on the sofa holding Joanie's hands and they both continued to shed tears. Grace held her down with one hand and used the other to manipulate the pliers around each needle. After about an hour, Grace wiped her forehead and took a long breath.

Just then Jack walked in. He thought Grace was spanking his daughter. But with pliers? "What the hell are you doing to her?" he yelled.

She glared at him and said, "I'm getting these needles out of her bottom. You can take over and see how you do." Her endurance had evaporated.

He saw then what the problem was and immediately felt shame. "I'm sorry, Love. Let me see if I can help."

He didn't have any easier of a time. If any neighbors heard the screams, they probably wondered who was beating up whom. Jack couldn't calm Joanie any more than Grace did. Finally, finally all the needles were out. Grace removed the overalls and panties. They saw the welts and redness. Grace cleansed all and then applied an ointment and Jack took Joanie carefully in his arms and rocked her. Tears and screams stopped.

That day's experience brought laughs later when the Lee family heard about the "cactus bottom" story.

Grace's father remained the same, paralyzed and with jumbled speech. Her mother never complained. She took care of him by herself with love, depending on her sons to move him when she put new sheets on the bed or have him sit in a chair for a while. Sometimes they carried him outside to sit and enjoy the sun and fresh air. The family helped as much as they could while Mom stayed by Al's side except when doing her chores.

She told Grace that in the afternoons, she usually read to him, a great deal from the newspaper. The old westerns, though, gave him the most pleasure. In the evenings, they listened to programs on the radio that sat next to his bed. At night, Mom put on her nightgown and crawled in bed with him, letting him know that her love for him never wavered. Days and nights passed with sameness, thinking only of the moment and not of the future.

When 1940 came, the Midwest began to recover and moisture returned. Farms were beginning to slowly blossom, partly because of new irrigation methods; the rivers and lakes began to fill. Many ranchers dug out their stock ponds, which had filled with topsoil blown in with the dust storms of the past years. Now the precious rain once again filled the ponds.

Grace and Jack made the decision to move closer to downtown Spearfish and not live so far out. Joanie no longer needed goat's milk so they sold the animal. They found a little house sitting on a hill overlooking the town. It was quiet, yet near enough for the family to walk to town if needed. Their new home gave them more room along with lilac and raspberry bushes on the back of the property. Tall trees shaded them from a couple of neighboring homes. Grace spaded the large garden and began to plan the seed arrangement.

After supper one evening, she looked at her family. Jack was sound asleep. Gail was reading to the twins, turning pages after pointing to the pictures. She had memorized the story including almost all the words. Then Grace frowned, wondering why Jack was so tired and hurting so much anymore? He used to come home after work full of energy and help her or he played with the children. Now he came home exhausted and in pain. She would see if her mother had any answers the next time they visited. Maybe Jack needed to see a doctor.

Time passed before anyone was aware of the speed. The seasons brought the country closer to conquering the depression. The government programs to help the economy and the farmers worked, yet it would take more time to recover fully. Years of decline meant now it would be years of climbing out. Grace knew that Jeannette and Steve probably benefited from the farm programs. Helen and Ralph benefited from the educational programs and Ralph had finally obtained a teaching-superintendent position again. Fred and Bob were still struggling yet managing while Nellie was doing very well in nursing. Charlie was a grown man now and many a young woman had tried to capture his heart, without success.

Suddenly, Grace and Jack realized that it was time for Gail to begin school. Grace had taught her so much that she might be ahead of the other students. Jimmy and Joanie would be celebrating their fourth birthday in October, with a celebration at the Lee home in Whitewood.

After that, the autumn sunshine lingered with its yellows and golds until the air turned crisp, then bitter cold. Winds blew until stark branches shivered and quaked in the icy gusts. The bright sky occasionally changed to stormy clouds bringing needed moisture. Every little bit of moisture helped and they hoped the drought was finally over.

Jack found work hard in the icy cold, which certainly didn't help his lower back pain. When he came home one evening, he asked, "Love, can you fill a hot water bottle so I can put it on my back?" She was finishing the dishwashing.

"Arthritis must be setting in to give me trouble," he added and shifted trying to find a comfortable spot.

Grace heated the water and filled the little flat red rubber container. She screwed on the top, wrapped a towel around it and tested it before placing it in behind her husband. "There, maybe that will help."

Winter crept through the months with its icy gusts and little snow. Then spring came again, trying to push away the drabness and bringing hope that life was changing for the better. The hills became alive with wild grass shoots scattered amid wild flowers. The murmuring and whispering of life among the birds, young field mice, bees and all sorts of insects brought hope. People hoped there would be no whirring of the dreaded grasshoppers this year. Swollen clouds soon let rain escape, bringing joy to many who stood out with raised arms, laughing and welcoming the shower. The smell of fresh wetness was exhilarating, along with the pleasure of the noisy pelting rain.

During the day, Grace began to turn the soil in her garden and fill the rows with seed she saved from last year's harvest. She decided to expand her garden and worked on another five feet of hard soil.

"I pray the rain keeps coming so my vegetables will thrive. We sure need a good harvest this fall to keep us going through next winter," she said to the twins, knowing they did not care. Yet she needed someone to talk to in hopes of keeping her mind off her husband.

Jack seemed to fade more and became so weary while his lower pain continually pestered him. Not wanting to worry Grace, he kept trying to work for the WPA even though he could only do so much. He began to look like an old man with added grey peeking through his blond hair and his shoulders sagging lower. He walked much slower than he used to.

When the children played in the yard, Grace quickly watered her garden, washed clothes in her wringer washer, or ironed. The children's clothes, all in cotton, needed ironing as well as the adult clothes. She would not allow her children to be out in public with wrinkled clothes.

She played games with the children, teaching them while they had fun. Gail's voice showed that she had acquired her father's musical talent. Jimmy also sang and followed with the same ability. Joanie's talent was not singing, but she loved to color or draw. Grace made sure their father did not bellow out with one of his old saloon songs.

Even though Jack came home worn out each day, he still read to the children—when and if he had the energy. The sessions were

214

shorter than in the past so that he could lie down to take a nap before the evening meal. Grace did her best to keep the children quiet while he napped, although noise didn't seem to bother him.

The summer's hard work of fighting weeds and watering rewarded her with a garden producing an abundance of vegetables. When it came time to can the produce, Laura arrived to help. What a relief for Grace. In turn, they both helped their mother with her canning.

Fall lingered and finally winter brought the usual icy winds and some snow. When the moisture did come, it was quickly absorbed by the thirsty ground.

The Lee family, and all Americans, heard about the war in Europe, but the U.S. was trying to stay out of it. Germany's Hitler was invading more countries. He attacked Poland, Denmark, Norway, Belgium, Luxembourg, the Netherlands, France, Yugoslavia and Greece. More pressure had been put on the United States by England, desperate for help in fighting the enemy. They didn't want to fall under the German rule.

December began bitter cold. Then an unimaginable blow hit the hearts of all Americans. December 7, 1941 brought the country to tears, fear and rage. As Grace and Jack listened to the radio, they heard the reports of the Japanese attack early that morning on Pearl Harbor by 360 Japanese bombers. The first wave hit at 7:55 a.m. on one side of the island and the second bombing came on the other side. The U.S. military shipyards and docks along with airfields were under a surprise attack, completely unexpected. By the end of the assault, eighteen ships had sunk or been destroyed and one hundred seventy aircraft were destroyed. The final death toll stood at 3,700 souls. Radio announcers gasped or gulped to control their feelings as they told the country of the catastrophe.

"My God, what a tragedy," Jack's voice cracked. Even though he hadn't been in the service for over twenty years, he felt a brotherhood with those who were injured, who had lost their lives, or those who witnessed the horrible, meaningless killing. He lowered his head and shook it back and forth as if to rid himself of visions too gruesome to contemplate.

Grace shushed him. "Listen. There's more."

215

They then heard that the United States had declared war on Japan and troops immediately dispatched to various locations. The shock in their home reverberated across the country. War!

When they read the newspaper later, they saw pictures of many young men signing up for the service. They wanted revenge on the Japanese.

In no time, the U.S. joined England and other allies. President Roosevelt declared war on Germany. Now there were two wars to fight and in two directions. Mothers cried, as they feared the loss of their sons. Dads hid their fear. The young men rushed to join, sure that they could win quickly and come home as heroes. The wives and young girls rallied round their men. War brought fear along with determination for victory.

"Where will this end? How can we fight on so many fronts?" Jack asked.

Grace nodded. "May God help us and all those young men going to war?" She prayed that her brothers would not have to go to war. The most likely would be Charlie. She didn't want to lose her baby brother.

They soon got word that Charlie enlisted in the Air Force. He trained as a gunner fighting the Nazi. Gunners became great targets for the enemy while they sat in their little bubble for all to see and for the Germans to shoot to kill. Grace worried about her baby brother almost as much as Mom and they prayed continually for his safety.

Would God ever give the earth peace? Everyone prayed that 1942 would bring the end of the war. The young servicemen chanted their resolve to end it in a year.

But would it?

CHAPTER 35

RUNNING DOWN - 1942

One winter evening Grace looked at her husband while they sat reading after supper. "Jack, you're losing more weight and you have too much pain." She was worried and knew that his energy level had dropped considerably and he was far too thin. "You need to see a doctor."

"Oh, I'll get over this and be fine soon," he tried to convince her.

His energy was gone after just a few hours of work and his lower backache never let up. He didn't want to tell her that his urine was getting darker and he even had some problems breathing. "I don't know why I get so damned tired. I'm sorry, Love. I'll be better soon."

A week passed and Grace insisted that Jack go see the doctor. "Now, along with everything else, you're often nauseated and you're having more headaches while your backache never stops. Jack, you can't keep this up. Please, please go see the doctor. Promise me you will." A tear trickled down her cheek showing her worry.

"Alright, Love, I'll go. Don't worry. I just have some bug. I'll be okay soon." He'd tried for months to tell her not to worry but hadn't succeeded. "You'll see after I talk to the doctor. He'll give me some instructions to get me over this."

Grace felt he was ready to see the doctor anyway, not sure that the physician was going to be able to help him, but he'd go—for her.

"I probably just spent too much time on a horse and now I'm paying for it," he laughed.

She didn't laugh and knew that wasn't it. She worried. She also was scrapping the bottom of her mind on ways to make meals with almost nothing except either potatoes or onions. Maybe she could get enough meat off the bones she got at the butcher's shop for a meal. At least they had saved enough for a month's rent.

In a few days, Jack was at the doctor's office waiting for the nurse to call his name. After the examination by the doctor, he took a far too long way home, stalling as long as he could. He drove through Spearfish Canyon, then up and down the farm roads. He needed to clear his mind. He stopped at a quiet spot by a stream, sat staring and wondering why this had to happen.

Grace worried while constantly looking out the window for Jack to drive up. *I never took that long with a doctor's appointment. What is happening? Why doesn't he come home?*

Another hour went by before she finally heard the car rumble and sputter to a stop. Jack climbed out slowly looking like a weathered old man.

Grace fretted when she saw him park. She wondered what the doctor had said. Quickly opening the door, she greeted him with a reassuring smile and hug. "I'm glad you're back. I was getting worried. Do you want some coffee? What did the doctor say? Do you have some medicine?"

Jack had to smile. "Love, I'll answer all your questions as soon as I sit with a cup of coffee. Please?"

He sat in his easy chair, slumped down and stared out the window. His defeated expression reflected back from the window glass.

Grace quickly came with two coffees, handing one to Jack. She sat on the couch and leaned forward. "I put just a teeny bit of sugar in so you could overlook the bitterness since I made the pot some time ago and kept it on the burner. I'm sorry. What took so long?"

He nodded and gave a weak smile. Sipping slowly he kept his eyes on the floor not looking into her questioning eyes. Finally, he leaned his head back before righting it again.

"Grace, the doctor thinks I have Bright's disease which he said they also call Acute Nephritis—whatever the hell that means." He paused, sighed and tried to figure out how to explain the rest. "It's a

218

kidney disease. He took a urine sample and sent it in. I'll get the results in about a week and he'll know for sure then."

"All right. So what do we do? What medicine will help you get better?" Grace tried to hide her fear. She knew there was more to learn and wondered about the name "nephritis" which sounded something like "arthritis" which was manageable. "Did you get some pills, or what do we need to do?"

He looked at her with a sorrowful expression. "No, Love, I don't have any medicines. He said we'll wait and see what the results are." Telling her how serious the doctor's prognosis was could wait for another time. "The doctor said it appears to be in the advanced stages. He said to just wait and see what the test showed."

She didn't like to wait, but had no choice. "All right, that's what we will do." She reached over and took his hand. "I'll do whatever you say. I love you, Jack." She saw how tired he was. "Go take a nap. The children are all over at the neighbor's right now. The house is quiet."

"I just might do that." He rose slowly and shuffled into the bedroom, shoulder slumped low. Within two minutes, he was sound asleep, moving every so often to try to find a comfortable spot.

Waiting for the test results made the days pass ever so slowly. Grace's patience ran low. She wanted to know the results of Jack's test and find out what to do to get her husband well again. She wrote her sister explaining what the doctor had said. Since Nellie was a nurse, she could help Grace learn more about Acute Nephritis or Bright's disease.

The telephone rang one afternoon. Grace rushed to pick up the receiver and answered, "Hello?" She could maneuver the cord just far enough to reach a pencil and paper if needed.

"Hi Grace. Can you hear me alright?" Nellie's voice sounded far away but clear.

"Yes. Hi Nellie." She hoped her sister could help her understand this disease. "Did you get my letter?"

The answer came with a soft expression of seriousness. "Yes, I did. Are Jack or the children around?"

Grace's stomach constricted, knowing the question meant this couldn't be good. "No. Jack's downtown getting some supplies, Gail is in school and the twins are out playing with the neighbor children.

Why?" She didn't like the sound of her sister's voice and slumped down in her chair.

Nellie cleared her throat and began slowly, "I asked a couple of the doctors here at the hospital, and I also found a huge medical book, which is a complete family guide and gives a lot of information even though it was published in 1904.

"I read up on Bright's Disease and Acute Nephritis in the *MEDICOLOGY, Home Encyclopedia of Health, a complete Family Guide.* What a treasure of information!" She took a deep breath. "The two names of the disease are actually the same thing, just different titles. Nephritis is the more common name anymore." She stopped for a moment, stalling.

Grace didn't care about the book and interrupted. "What did you find out? It's serious, isn't it?"

"Well yes, Sis, it is very serious if that is actually what the test proves. Nephritis is a disease that plugs the filters in the kidney and upper urinary tract. It is often an inherited condition." She stalled for a moment. "I think you should wait and go with Jack to his next doctor's appointment. You need to hear what the doctor says. When is Jack's next appointment?"

"In a couple of days. What aren't you telling me?" Grace didn't like her sister's evasiveness.

There was a pause before Nellie continued, "Grace, there are too many medical terms, and I think you need to find out first what the tests show. After you hear from the doctor, I'll call you again. I'll be praying the tests show some silly, simple thing. Okay?"

A lump in Grace's throat kept her from asking more. "I'll let you know. Thanks for calling."

She knew that their lives were going to change for the worse. She felt a headache suddenly develop and tried to convince herself to calm down.

Grace couldn't concentrate on household chores over the next two days. Jack was too exhausted to find more work and slept often. She could see the pain, physically and mentally, that he was going through. At least the children were quiet when their daddy was asleep. When he woke and sat in his chair, he would play a game with the children, read to them, and hug or kiss them on the top of their heads. Always his pain was evident.

220

When Grace went to bed, she curled up next to her husband and soothed his lower back with soft massaging. Her fingers gently caressed the whiplash scars on his back and kissed them trying to erase what Drake had done to her love. Sometimes he would turn and give her a smile and a kiss. Oh, how she longed for his love! When he turned away and faced the wall, her pillow became damp with her tears. Her prayers were silent pleas to God. She prayed continually for a miracle and that Jack would be healthy again.

Finally, the day came to learn the test results. Grace insisted that she go with Jack to the doctor's office. He didn't fight it. She was going to have to know what this meant. They were silent from the time they climbed into his car until they parked by the office. She knew that he now had blood in his urine and pain in his groin also. When he opened the car door for Grace, she stepped down and immediately grabbed his hand as they walked in.

The doctor entered the patient room and kept his eyes down on Jack's file. When he closed the door, he sat on his little stool, adjusted his glasses, fingered his mustache, and then gave a nod to Jack. "I see you brought your wife. That's good." Then he opened the file and began.

"Mr. Morris. Your test confirms that you have Acute Nephritis. This disease destroys the kidney and urinary tract due to the toxins. You can possibly slow this disease down by doing some treatments." He paused to check the file notes and readjusted his stool before forcing himself to continue in a somber voice.

"Stay in bed and keep the room warm and humidified. You can purge your body with laxatives, but only do so with small doses." He paused again and then turned to Grace.

"Mrs. Morris, something else that may help is to put the patient in a tub of water at 106 degrees for twenty minutes. Then thoroughly rub him dry and put him in bed with hot water bottles to make him sweat. He needs to perspire for one to one-and-a-half hours. This will help purge the toxins from his system and may help to get rid of waste materials. It's not a cure, but again may slow the disease down a bit."

Grace nodded. She bit lips, afraid to utter even one word.

Then the doctor looked from one to the other with concerned eyes and a lower voice. "I'm sorry to say, but uremia caused by Acute Nephritis is usually fatal. Since you are quite advanced, there isn't much of a chance that you, Mr. Morris, will survive." He pulled out a sheet of notes that he read aloud before handing them over.

"Only drink pure water or mineral water, have a diet of foods with little nitrogen and sodium. I know that is hard, but try to stay away from protein such as in meat, fish, beans, leafy greens and dairy products. Butter and oil are acceptable. The ones I mentioned to stay away from all have nitrogen and you need as non-nitrogenous a diet as possible."

Grace accepted the list even though she was mulling over in her mind what on earth Jack could eat. "We'll do our best." He couldn't eat most of what she cooked!

Jack interrupted in a low voice, "Doc, I want to know how much time I have with my family."

Grace sucked her lips further inward, placed her hand over her mouth and closed her eyes wishing she could shut her hearing off. She didn't want to hear the doctor and yet she had to know.

The doctor frowned, looked from Jack to Grace again, looked down to the floor and then back to them. "I have to be honest. I don't think you can be cured, Mr. Morris. You are in the advanced stages. You need to prepare for hospital care and make all your final arrangements. As far as how long you have, well there is nothing to say if it is six months or a year. We don't know." He paused to gain control of his own feelings, muttering how he always hated this part of the practice of medicine. "Think about what you will do later, Mrs. Morris. Your husband is terminal."

Grace slumped and moaned feeling as if a sledgehammer had hit her in the stomach. She felt Jack squeeze her hand tight and was sure that he had a lump in his throat.

Looking at both, the doctor added, "Make the most of the time you have. It is precious." He rose and shook Jack's hand and then turned to Grace, shook her hand and looked soulfully into her eyes. "I wish I had a pill that would cure her husband."

Jack nodded goodbye and took his wife's elbow leading her out of the office. She was devastated.

He was crushed by the weight of the prognosis. If this was an inherited disease, could his children get it too? How could he protect them? He wanted to lash out and scream. How could this be happening, when he'd finally found his love and a family? His expression revealed that he could cry, but had to be strong for Grace. Anger hid under the surface of his skin and fear hid deep in his mind.

Grace couldn't lift her head and tried to hold her tears in. Once they were in the car, she couldn't hold back any longer and shook violently with sobs. Jack scooted over to her and took her in his arms. His tears dampened her head. They held each other for a long time, not knowing what to say and not wanting to let go of each other. Once the sobs ceased, Grace looked at Jack and said, "We will work this through. I will be by your side and I will always love you, my sweetheart."

That created another large lump in his throat and all he could do was nod. They held each other for a long time not talking and trying to get control so they could face the children.

Jack's first words were full of anger at God. "Why the hell did God have to do this? It isn't fair. Here I believed God was finally giving me a good life. He gave you to me and now He's going to make you suffer. Damn, damn." On and on he yelled.

"How can I provide for my family if I'm not here? Why God? Why do this to Grace and my children? Hadn't I paid enough for my past sins and for the hell I went through as a child? Why take it out on my family?"

Grace sat quietly while he kept talking. She wanted those answers as well.

Jack finally settled down and lowered his head against the steering wheel. Then he started the engine and they headed home. He wanted to be with his children as much as he could and to keep Grace by his side every day.

CHAPTER 36

1942 - LOVE ALWAYS

After the doctor visit, the months brought grief and anxiety for both Grace and Jack. Spring did not bring hope and then summer felt grey and hopeless.

Jack was getting weaker and Grace continued to massage his back to ease the increasing pain. Caregiving involved so much, but somehow she had to keep going.

Laura, her sister, moved in with them so she could work in town and be a help to Grace. She played with the children, helped with chores and listened to Grace when Jack slept.

He shuffled from bed to the living area and sat in his big chair to watch the children play. Looking out the window, he said that he wished he could be riding on a horse again out on the prairie while the wind blew through the grasses and against his sun-weathered sunken-in face. The freedom of being on a horse and racing in a wide-open prairie was now just a dream that would never come true again. His complexion became a pale greyish while more darkness appeared below his eyes making him look even more a skeleton than he had a couple of months ago.

The hours slipping away did not pass slowly enough for Grace. She wanted to keep her husband with her as long as she could, even if he was so sick. Her anticipatory grief continued as she prepared for the end. She wasn't sure what she would do, but knew she had to find work somehow to support her family. All she could do for right then was to take in a little seamstress work. A couple of women gave her a little work. Her family now existed on that, his Veterans benefits and help from her family. They would not let Grace and her family drop into poverty, yet the stress of her siblings' pocket books and their own life was not easy. They struggled to feed, clothe and shelter their own families and Grace.

Jack's service in the Great War provided him with the VA benefits he'd never thought he would need, especially not for something like this. It wasn't much, but every penny helped.

Grace's family decided that she needed a family portrait with Jack. The children would want to remember their daddy, as they'd known him. So the family saved their money, gave up something here and there, until they had enough for the photograph. More sacrifice by them!

Grace dressed the children in their best outfits, which she'd made. She pressed Jack's suit and shirt. She wore her dark blue dress with the white collar her mother had given her. The picture was a treasure that she would hang on to all her years. She didn't know when she'd be able to display the picture for all to see. She didn't want to share him. Questions about him were something she could not answer without crying and she would not cry in front of others, especially her children, and steeled herself to answer.

As late summer arrived, Jack's condition had deteriorated enough that the doctor, when he came for his weekly visit, told Grace to transfer her husband to the Battle Mountain Veterans Administration Hospital in Hot Springs. Time was running out for Jack.

On the day the ambulance came, Grace had the children all kiss their daddy and say goodbye. "Now, you be good for Aunt Laura while I'm taking care of Daddy." She swallowed hard and couldn't say more. Then Fred led her to his car to follow the ambulance.

Her brother drove while she slumped in the car seat next to her Mother and let all her tears flow. When she finally could speak, she asked, "What am I going to do? I don't know how to go on without him."

Mom couldn't do much except give sympathy. "You know that we all will help you. You will be all right. Give yourself time. Right now, you have to be strong for your husband and children. Praying will help you get through this." Mom could well be going through similar circumstances one of these days.

More than an hour later, they arrived at the VA Hospital. While the doctor checked Jack and the nurses assigned a room for him, an elderly woman approached the family.

"Hello. Are you Mrs. Morris? I am Freda, a volunteer here, and I will help you any way I can." Freda asked as she looked into Grace's drawn face. "I've been through something like this myself and I know that you must be barely holding life together right now. I will do whatever I can to help you."

"Thank you," Grace whispered. She surmised that this woman with the kind face and grey hair must have lost her husband.

"Well, I want you to know that if you decide to stay, we have a room available for you just a short walking distance from the hospital here. Your meals will be provided and we will help you anyway that we can." An organization of veteran's wives that Freda belonged to tried to help veterans and their families as much as they could. "There will be no charge. You may stay as long as you need. When you are ready to let your husband rest this evening, we will take you to your room."

Surprised, but pleased, Mom answered because all Grace could do was nod. "Thank you. Grace will let you know. We so appreciate you doing this."

Settled in his room, Jack leaned back on the pillow exhausted. Mom gave him a kiss on the cheek and whispered, "Son, don't worry about Grace or your children. We will take care of them. They will be fine. We love you."

Fred nodded his goodbye, biting his lips, and took Mom's arm as they left the room and headed back home. "I'll come back next weekend. Grace and Jack, you discuss what you want to do and if you want to come home, Grace, in between, I'll take you both ways, or Bob will."

Nodding, Grace remained at Jack's bedside. She didn't want to leave the room and asked if she could stay the night. The doctor approved. She told Freda that she would not be going to her home that night. The woman understood and left telling them she would be praying for them.

Grace and Jack talked about the cleanliness of the hospital while all the medical smells invaded their nostrils and the sounds of bells, shuffling feet, rushing nurses and talking filled their ears. They prayed together. He told Grace how his faith had increased with the knowledge that God was in control and would guide him as well as Grace later. God would take care of them, he said to reassure her.

She was happy that his faith was so strong, yet not sure if hers had increased. She didn't understand why God was taking her love away from her. The *why* kept interrupting her thoughts and prayers.

She saw that Jack was too tired to talk and needed sleep. "You rest, my sweet husband, and I'll be right here when you wake." She softly ran her hand over his tired, thin face.

He gave her a weak squeeze on her hand and nodded with a smile. "I love you, Grace," and a tear trickled down the side of his face moistening his pillow.

She bent over the bed, gave him a kiss and whispered, "I love you too. Goodnight my love." She kept her hand on his all night while she tried to sleep on the cot the hospital furnished and sat next to his bed. She stayed with him through the week.

The next weekend Grace reluctantly returned home because the doctor said Jack still had some time before the end. Immediately the children, jumping and bouncing, ran to her as she got out of the car, yelling how much they missed her. That week she felt like a robot taking care of the household duties, playing with the children and praying for Daddy with them. Laura stayed and became her anchor along with her mother.

The next couple of weeks continued to roll by in this same routine of living in a trance and praying—one week at the VA Hospital and the next at home. Then late fall arrived killing the summer and bringing the golden season. When October blew in on crisp winds, Jack worsened enough that Grace did not want to leave him. Grief and sorrow engulfed her. She tried to hide her feelings from her husband, yet didn't always succeed.

She had agreed to take the room that Freda offered the first day. They walked there that afternoon for Grace to see where she could spend some private time. Looking around, she saw a clean, light, airy room with a patchwork quilt over the starched sheets. Her window looked out to the bustle of the town. Freda gave her a key so that she could come and go as she wished. By now, the room was too familiar and the view had turned to a dried-up, dreary, deadly fall. She could see no color or liveliness, nothing to give any hope.

Grace spent her days and evenings at the hospital. While Jack slept or writhed in pain, she wrote her parents or prayed. She knew

Mom read her letters to Dad, and she wrote Laura including three pictures she had drawn for the children to color.

Laura wrote back about any gossip she could come up with and about how well the children were doing. The war didn't bring much good news and rationing was driving her insane. She traded with friends who needed gas so she received extra sugar for the children. She walked Gail to school each day, with Jimmy and Joanie in tow. Then the remaining little group either stopped at the grocery store or went on home so she could do the cleaning, cooking, washing and ironing. Complaining about her responsibility would do no good, but sometimes the burden was difficult for her to handle both mentally and physically. She vowed not to let her sister know and cause more worry. She wrote Grace that on weekends, Bob or Fred came and took her and the children to the Lee home in Whitewood. Seeing the children flourishing brought a crooked smile to Dad. Mom gave much attention to the children including many hugs.

Some days the sun gave warmth while other days dreariness seemed colder than the actual temperature. Grace fought through each day while watching the slow deterioration of Jack. They tried to pray. His pain was so intense that painkillers only slightly softened his agony and he couldn't always pray with her. She tried not to let him see her tears and he not to let her see his. All of Jack's agony mounted as his suffering lingered on. His torture seemed to last far too long as if a repeat of his childhood with Drake year after year.

At one point, he looked at Grace and asked, "Love, will you get me a tablet and a pencil? I want to write a letter to each of our babies. Maybe the letters will let them help to remember me and how much I loved them."

She was surprised and her sorrow deepened, knowing he would soon leave her. A nurse quickly gave her the paper and pencil and she rushed back trying to hold back her tears.

He struggled to write even though the pain was eating at him like a hungry wolf. The letter to each child was short and said how much he loved them and added something personal for each one. Gail was to help take care of the twins. Jimmy was to be the man of the house and watch over his mother and sisters. Joanie was to be a good girl for Mama. He folded the little letters one by one and gave them to Grace to give to the children when she thought they should have them.

His final words made her sob. "I love you, Grace. I'm so sorry," was all he could utter.

She leaned over and gave him a gentle kiss on his forehead as her tears flowed down on his bony face. "I love you too, my sweet husband, and I always will."

Jack's battle ended. Life left him on October 27, 1942, two days after the twin's fifth birthday, which both parents missed. Grace held his hand as he passed away with a smile on his face. She sat there for more than an hour not wanting to give him up. She would never forget the way he looked when younger, compared to this final hour.

Her brothers were with her and witnessed the end, blowing their noses every so often. Finally, they held her tight as she left Jack's side and they led her to the car. They took her to Whitewood so her mother could help her first in her deepest sorrow. She needed to calm down before facing her children.

She fell into the arms of her mother sobbing. Mom sat with her, holding her close and told her, "Dad cried when he heard. He can't talk, but he feels and he wishes he could hold you and comfort you." She rocked back and forth, holding Grace tight, talking and trying to ease the pain.

When she went to her father, Grace leaned over the bed to give him a hug. He put his good arm around her and held her tight while they both cried. He tried so hard to say that he loved her, but the words were jumbled. She still understood him.

Later when Grace calmed down, Fred and Bob drove her home. The car pulled up in front of the small home as the children flew out of the door to greet their mother. Their questions assailed her and she did her best to answer calmly, "When we get inside, I'll tell you about Daddy."

Seating each child on the couch, she knelt in front of them and tried to smile. "God's angels came, lifted your Daddy out of bed, and took him up to heaven," she paused and took a deep ragged breath trying to compose herself. A forced smile, shaky voice and glistening eyes revealed how difficult she struggled not to cry in front of them.

"Why?" Each child asked and frowned. "We want Daddy to come home," they said in unison. Picturing the angels flying down and lifting their daddy up to heaven, they thought the angels could bring him back the same way.

Grace shook her head. "God needed him to help straighten out heaven, take care of His horses and fix His throne."

Jimmy asked, "When he does all that, can Daddy come back?"

"No, he has to stay and continue to help, but he is having God watch over and take care of you. Now, why don't you all go outside and pick some flowers in honor of Daddy? We'll find a pretty jar to put them in." She couldn't handle much more or she'd fall apart, not wanting to do that in front of the children. Laura stood by helplessly, but when Grace nodded to her, Laura herded the children out to the back yard.

The next few days were indescribable for Grace. The children's questions, their anger and need for attention wore her down. She could only put one foot in front of the other and keep going. The children and the funeral arrangements drained her. Somehow, she made it through each day, but sleep did not come quickly. She still didn't know how she and her children were going to live. Her thoughts went to what she had known. Go back to teaching was her hope. But could she do that with three small children?

The Veterans Administration helped with the funeral and burial. They ordered the gravestone at their expense. She arranged for the funeral Mass at St Joseph's Catholic Church in Spearfish. Most of the people who had come to their wedding came to give final honor to Jack and his family. The Ramsers and Lehmanns, old friends of Jack's, wiped their eyes, as did many others at the funeral. Veterans from the Spearfish area escorted his casket down the aisle covered with the American flag, which they later folded ceremoniously and handed to Grace at the burial site.

Fred gave the eulogy including, "Jack was the proud and loving father of his three children. He dearly loved his wife." He paused to clear his throat and take a deep breath. "He was a gentle man, never laying a hand on anyone." He told how Grace met him, his courting and how his devotion to his family never wavered. "Jack did not have a good childhood and searched for peace and love. When he found Grace, he knew his search was over and love filled him." He related more about Jack as a member of the Lee family, ending with, "He will always remain in our hearts and he can be assured that we will do everything we can to help his wife and their children."

Grief dominated Grace's life, yet she would not and could not talk about her loss. She followed the custom of the time that people should not talk about the deceased, or grief would linger. She understood that she needed to move on with life and she must not talk to her children about their father—they were resilient and would forget—so they said.

Grace tried to refocus her life even though her heart was broken and she was lonely, so lonely. Oh, how she missed her husband! Her tears flowed in private. She was a devastated woman who was too proud to let anyone know of her inner pain, telling herself that she needed to be strong and get over her loss. To look to the future was difficult since she could not imagine a future without Jack. She prayed every day and night that God would heal her heart and guide her.

Only eight and a half years with Jack would have to sustain Grace through years of the heartache she hid from others. She knew that many others also suffered inner pain.

She remembered her husband's joy when he'd found her and had a real home to belong to after so many years of searching. His happiness had shown through in his actions as a husband and father. At last, he had found love and peace.

Why this had to happen, Grace did not understand. It would take years or maybe never. All she had now were memories.

"I'll be with you sometime, my love. Wait for me," she whispered every so often.

Give sorrow words; the grief that does not speak
whispers in the overwrought heart and bids it break

Macbeth, William Shakespeare

EPILOGUE

Death leaves a heartache no one can heal.
Love leaves a memory no one can steal.
From a headstone in Ireland

After Jack Morris died in 1942, Grace and her parents moved into a home on Main Street in Spearfish, South Dakota. The two women took up mending and sewing for those who could still afford a seamstress with World War II affecting every household. Grace also worked for the Works Projects Administration (WPA) and later for the J. C. Penny Store. Her mother, Isabella, took care of Grace's children while she worked.

Al's speech never improved and his heart kept deteriorating while the paralysis forced him to lie in bed all day. Grace's father, Al Lee, died at age 68, on January 14, 1945.

Eventually Grace went back to school at the Black Hills Teachers College in Spearfish to renew her teaching certificate and obtained a position in Rapid City, South Dakota. She took the public bus to and from work every day until she retired. Grace was a dedicated teacher and many students thanked her years later for being their teacher and for her dedication.

As the years passed, Grace watched her children grow to adulthood. She saw her grandchildren enter the world and she became a part of their lives. She inspired each one.

Gail married Vincent Baumgartner and they had seven children. Grace was always a part of their daily lives; later residing in a mother-in-law apartment attached to their country home. Gail died September 9, 1997, and her husband died in 2009, both in Rapid City, South Dakota.

Joanne moved to Denver, Colorado where she met and married Larry Brand, and they became the parents of three children. They co-owned a guest ranch in Aspen, Colorado and later owned a real estate and property management company. Joanne's husband died in 2000. She is now retired in Colorado and writes, paints and volunteers.

Jim graduated from college, joined the Naval Officer Candidate School in Newport, Rhode Island, and assigned to three tours in the

Mediterranean Sea. He attended graduate school at the University of Colorado and worked in several states. He now resides and volunteers in Rapid City, SD.

Grace had many worries throughout her life as she nurtured her children and grandchildren. Her faith was her anchor. She thanked God that her mother and siblings were always there to help her. However, no one could take Jack's place.

Her mother, Isabella Lee, died on March 14, 1968, at the age of 89, and buried next to her husband, Al Lee, in Spearfish.

Tuberculosis did not kill Grace, but grief killed part of her soul; it remained with her all her life. She had only eight and one-half years with her only love, Jack Morris. She could not share that short time with others, especially her children. No one will know how many tears she shed over her loss.

Grace Morris lived to be 92 years old. She died on December 11, 1992, and buried next to her husband, Jack, in Spearfish, South Dakota. They finally reunited after half a century of separation with Grace waiting all those years.

The words of Ring Lardner, *They gave each other a smile with a future on it,* was a very different future then the one they had envisioned. Yet love always remained.

Late in her life, Grace wrote:

> *"What a consolation it is to have memories. My memories have left lovely pictures in my mind. I shall try to accept what the tomorrow brings. This is today so I live it as it comes."*

Jack Morris – 1918   Grace Lee – 1920

Jack Morris   Jack Morris in Lead, SD.
Est. 1930   Est. late 1920s or early '30s

Grace and a friend
1923-24

Jack and a friend
1920-25

Grace Lee – est. 1923

Jack Morris – 1938

Al Lee and Gail
Est. 1937

Isabella Lee
Est. 1940

Jimmy & Joanie—4 months old

Joanie, Gail, Jimmy-3, 5, 3 yr.

Isabella Lee, Bob Lee, Laura Lee Good,
Fred Lee & Grace   Est. 1945

Chuck & Isabella
1943

Grace holding Joanne, Gail, Jack with Jim propped on his knee,
1942, before Jack was gone.

Joanne's letter from her father

ABOUT THE AUTHOR

Joanne Brand wrote from the heart of her characters. She researched facts to present truth, as well as pertinent historical information to keep the reader in the era of her novel. A snippet of fact as well as history is the basis that she then wove into a believable story.

The author grew up in South Dakota, and then moved to Colorado as a young woman. She now resides in the Denver area and is an accomplished author, painter and she volunteers in various projects. She feels her life's experiences and her love of reading have given her valuable education and understanding.

See the author's website: joannebrand-author.com

Made in the USA
Lexington, KY
18 June 2015